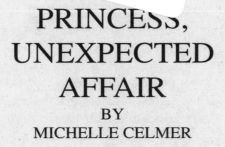

PRINCESS,
UNEXPECTED
AFFAIR
BY
MICHELLE CELMER

AND

FROM BOARDROOM
TO WEDDING BED?
BY
JULES BENNETT

MILLS
BOON

"I think you should marry me."

He said it so calmly, so matter-of-factly, that the meaning of his words took several seconds to sink in. Then she was sure that she must have heard him wrong, or he was playing some cruel joke. That any second he was going to laugh and say, "Gotcha!"

"I know it's fast," he said instead. "I mean, we barely know each other. But for the baby's sake I really think it's the logical next move."

My God, he was *serious*. He wanted to marry her. How was that even possible when only a few days ago it supposedly hadn't been an option?

"But…you want to be prime minister."

"Yes, but that isn't what's best for the baby. I'm going to be a father. From now on, I have to put his or her best interests first."

Dear Reader,

Welcome to book eight of my ROYAL SEDUCTIONS series, the story of Princess Anne Charlotte Amalia Alexander and the heir to the political throne of Thomas Isle, Samuel Baldwin.

I can hardly believe that this is my last book in the ROYAL SEDUCTIONS series. <sniff> It seems as though only yesterday I introduced you to the royal families of Morgan and Thomas Isle. Since then we've been through a lot together. Marriages of convenience, illegitimate heirs and secret babies…just to name a few. And now an unexpected pregnancy has the royal family reeling.

There is a consensus on Thomas Isle that royalty and politics do not mix well. Leave it to Anne and Sam to put that theory to the test. And though you may think you know these two, what's going on in their heads, things are not always what they seem. There are family tragedies, boundaries pushed to the limit and mysteries solved. And this book ends with a *bang*…literally.

But I don't want to give away *too* much…

Until next time, all my best,

Michelle

EXPECTANT PRINCESS, UNEXPECTED AFFAIR

BY
MICHELLE CELMER

Published in Great Britain 2011
by Mills & Boon, an imprint of Harlequin (UK) Limited,
Eton House, 18-24 Paradise Road, Richmond, Surrey TW9 1SR

© Michelle Celmer 2010

ISBN: 978 0 263 88313 8

51-0811

Harlequin (UK) policy is to use papers that are natural, renewable and
recyclable products and made from wood grown in sustainable forests. The
logging and manufacturing processes conform to the legal environmental
regulations of the country of origin.

Printed and bound in Spain
by Blackprint CPI, Barcelona

Bestselling author **Michelle Celmer** lives in southeastern Michigan with her husband, their three children, two dogs and two cats. When she's not writing or busy being a mom, you can find her in the garden or curled up with a romance novel. And if you twist her arm really hard you can usually persuade her into a day of power shopping. Michelle loves to hear from readers. Visit her website, www.michellecelmer.com, or write her at PO Box 300, Clawson, MI 48017, USA.

To mothers and fathers, brothers and sisters, family and friends. Cherish your loved ones and keep them close. You never know what tomorrow will bring...

One

Though she had always considered her reserved nature one of her best qualities, there were times when Princess Anne Charlotte Amalia Alexander wished she could be more like her twin sister.

She sipped her champagne and watched from across the ballroom as Louisa approached one of the guests: a tall, dark and handsome gentleman who had been eyeing Louisa all evening. She smiled, said a few words, and he kissed her proffered hand.

It was so easy for her. Men were naturally drawn to her delicate beauty and enthralled by her childlike innocence.

But Anne? Men considered her cold and critical. It was no secret that people in society, men in particular, often referred to her as *The Shrew*. Usually she didn't let that bother her. She liked to believe that they felt threatened by her strength and independence. However, that was little consolation on a night like this one. Everyone around her was dancing and drinking and socializing, while she stood by herself, alone in her principles. But with her father's failing health, was it so hard to fathom that she just didn't *feel* like celebrating?

A waiter carrying a tray of champagne passed by and she snagged a fresh glass. Her fourth for that night, which was precisely three more than she normally drank.

Her father, the king of Thomas Isle, who should at least be able to attend the charity event they were holding in his honor, was too weakened by heart disease to even make an appearance. Her mother refused to leave his side. It was up to Anne, Louisa and their brothers, Chris and Aaron, to act as hosts in the king's absence.

Getting hammered probably wasn't in her or the rest of the family's best interest. But didn't Anne always do as she was told? Wasn't she always the rational, responsible twin?

Well, almost always.

She knocked back the champagne in two swallows, deposited her empty glass on another passing tray and grabbed a fresh one. She would drink this one slower, she promised herself, but already she could feel the alcohol warming her belly and she began to get a soft, fuzzy feeling in her head. It was…nice.

She downed glass number five in one long swallow.

"You're looking lovely, Your Highness," someone said from behind her.

She turned to the voice, surprised to find Samuel Baldwin, son of the prime minister of Thomas Isle, greeting her. Sam was the sort of man a women looked at and instantly went weak in the knees. At thirty he was more cute than handsome—at least she thought so— with naturally curly, dark blond hair that never seemed to behave and deep dimples in both cheeks when he smiled. He was several inches taller than her own five foot eight, with a lean, muscular build. She had spoken to him a time or two, but nothing more than a casual hello. The gossip mill pegged him as one of the island's most eligible bachelors, and he had been groomed since birth to take over his father's position.

He bowed in greeting, and as he did, a lock of that unruly hair fell across his forehead. Anne resisted the urge to reach up and brush it back, but couldn't help wondering what it would feel like to run her fingers through it.

She would normally greet him with cool indifference, but the alcohol was doing funny things to her head because she could feel herself smiling. "How nice to see you again, Mr. Baldwin."

"Please," he said, "call me Sam."

Out of the corner of her eye Anne saw Louisa on the dance floor, her mystery man holding her scandalously close, gazing into her eyes. A pang of jealousy soured Anne's stomach. She wanted a man to hold her close and look at her as though she were the only one in the room, as if he couldn't wait to get her alone so he could ravage her. Just this once she wanted to feel…wanted. Was that really too much to ask for?

She finished her champagne in one gulp and asked, "Would you care to dance, Sam?"

She wasn't sure if his look of surprise was due to her barbaric behavior, or the actual invitation. For a dreadfully long and horrifying instant, she thought he might turn her down. Wouldn't that be ironic considering all the dance invitations she had declined over the years? So many, in fact, that men had stopped asking altogether.

Then a grin curled his mouth, his dimples a prominent dent in each cheek, and he said, "I would be honored, Your Highness."

He offered his arm and she slipped hers through it. Then he led her out onto the crowded dance floor. It had been so long since she'd danced that when he took her in his arms and began to waltz, what used to be second nature suddenly felt clumsy and awkward. Or maybe that was the champagne making her knees soft…or the spicy scent of his aftershave making her light-headed. He smelled so delicious, she wanted to bury her face in the crook of his neck and breathe him in. She tried to recall the last time she'd been this close to a man she found so sexually appealing.

Maybe a little *too* long.

"Black suits you," Sam said, and it took her several seconds to realize he was talking about her gown, a floor-length, sequined number she had purchased off the rack in Paris. She didn't know if the color suited her so much as it had suited her mood when she'd picked it out. Now she wished she had worn something brighter and more cheerful. Like Louisa in her trademark pink, who, come to think of it, looked a bit like the Good Witch of the North. Which Anne supposed would make her the Wicked Witch of the West.

"Yes," she told Sam. "All that's missing is the pointy black hat."

It was the sort of remark that might put a man off. Instead Sam laughed. A deep, throaty laugh that seemed to vibrate through her, causing delicious friction that warmed her insides. "Actually, I was thinking that it brings out your milky complexion."

"Oh, well, thank you."

A slow song began, and Anne couldn't help noticing how Louisa's mystery man drew her in even closer. A little *too* close.

"Do you know that man dancing with my sister?" she asked Sam, gesturing with her chin.

"Garrett Sutherland. He's the richest landowner on the island. I'm surprised you don't know him."

The name was definitely familiar. "I know *of* him. I've heard my brothers mention him."

"It looks as though he and your sister are quite… friendly."

"I noticed that, too."

He watched Anne watching her sister. "You look out for her?"

She nodded and looked up at him. "Someone has to. She can be very naive, and far too trusting."

He grinned, his dimples so adorable she wanted to rise up and press a kiss to each one. "Then who looks after you?"

"No one needs to. I'm entirely capable of looking out for myself."

He tightened the arm around her back, tucking her

closer to his chest, and his smile went from teasing to sizzling. "Are you sure about that, Highness?"

Was he *flirting* with her? Men never teased and flirted with her. Not unless they wanted their head handed back to them on a platter. Samuel Baldwin was a brave man. And she realized, she *liked* it. She liked the weight of his hand on her back and the way it felt when her breasts skimmed the wall of his chest. She'd never been what anyone could call a sexual woman—not that she didn't enjoy a quick, meaningless roll in the hay now and then—but being close to Sam awakened feelings in her she never knew were there. Or was it more the champagne than the man?

No. No amount of alcohol had ever given her this warm, shivery, feverish ache. This primitive longing to be taken and…possessed. To rip Sam's clothes off and put her hands all over him. She wondered what he would do if she wrapped her arms around his neck, tugged his head down and kissed him. His lips looked so soft and sensual and she was dying to know what they would feel like, how they would taste.

She wished she possessed the courage to do it, right here, right now, in front of all these people. She wished she could be more like Louisa, who was now walking arm in arm with her dance partner, out the doors and onto the patio, seemingly oblivious to the hundred or so pairs of eyes following their every move.

Maybe it was about time Louisa learned to fend for herself. For tonight at least. From this moment forward, she was on her own.

Anne turned her attention to Sam and smiled. "I'm

so pleased you could attend our benefit. Are you having a good time?"

"I am. I was sorry to hear that the king wasn't well enough to attend."

"He has to have a procedure done and adjustments made to his heart pump so he must stay in tip-top shape. Being in a large crowd could expose him to infection. His system is very vulnerable."

Her siblings all seemed to think he was going to be fine, and the heart pump he had been attached to for the past nine months was going to give his damaged heart the time it needed to heal, but Anne had a bad feeling it was a waste of time. Lately he'd begun to look so pale and he had so little energy. She worried that he was losing his will to live.

Though the rest of the family was hopeful, deep down Anne knew he was going to die and her instincts were telling her that it would be soon.

A sudden feeling of intense grief welled up inside her, and hard as she tried to push it back down, tears sprang to the corners of her eyes and a sob began to build in her throat. She never got upset, at least not when other people were around to see it, but the champagne must have compromised her emotions because she was on the verge of a meltdown and she couldn't do a single thing to stop it.

Not here, she begged. *Please not in front of all these people.*

"Anne, are you okay?" Sam was gazing down at her, his eyes so full of concern and compassion, it was almost too much.

She bit down hard on her lip and shook her head, and he seemed to know exactly what to do.

He swiftly whisked her off the dance floor, while she struggled to maintain her composure. "Where to?" he whispered, as they exited the ballroom, into a foyer full of people socializing and sipping drinks. She needed to be somewhere private, where no one would see the inevitable breakdown. A place where, when she finally pulled herself together, she could fix her makeup and return to the party as though nothing were out of the ordinary.

"My room," she managed.

"Upstairs?" he asked, and she nodded. She was biting her lip so hard now she tasted blood.

The staircase was roped off and two security officers stood guard, but as they approached one unhooked the rope to let them pass.

"Her Highness was kind enough to offer me a tour of the castle," Sam told them, which really wasn't necessary. Then she realized he'd said it not for the guards' sake, but for the guests who were watching them. She would have to remember to thank him. But the fact that he cared about her reputation, that he would be so kind as to help her avoid embarrassment, brought the tears even closer to the surface. They were halfway up to the second floor when her eyes started to leak rivers of warm tears down her cheeks, and when they reached her door and he ushered her inside, the floodgates burst.

She thought for sure he would leave her alone, but after she heard the door close Sam's arms went around her, pulling her tight against him. The idea that he cared enough to stay, when normally she felt so isolated in her grief, made her cry even harder.

Anne clung to him, sobbing her heart out against his chest, both mortified and desperately grateful that he was there.

"Let it out, Annie," he whispered, rubbing her back and stroking her hair. No one but Louisa had called her Annie, and it made her feel close to him somehow, which made no sense because she barely knew him. Still it felt as if they had shared something special. Something intimate.

As spontaneous and intense as the emotional outburst had been, it was surprisingly short-lived. As the sobs subsided, Sam handed her his handkerchief and she dabbed her eyes.

"She cries," he said, sounding amazed.

"Please don't tell anyone," she whispered against his jacket.

"They wouldn't believe me if I did."

Of course they wouldn't. She was the ice princess, *The Shrew*. She didn't have feelings. But the truth was she felt just as deeply as anyone else, she was just damned good at hiding it. But she didn't want to be the ice princess anymore. At least, not tonight. Tonight she wanted someone to know the woman underneath.

Sam cradled her face in his palms and gently tipped it up to his, wiping the last of her tears away with his thumbs. She gazed up into eyes as clear blue as the ocean, and she could swear she felt something shift deep inside her.

She wasn't sure if he made the first move, or she did, or they met halfway, but suddenly their lips were locked, and in that instant she had never wanted a man more than she wanted him.

Any man who accused Princess Anne of being cold and unfeeling had obviously never kissed her. She tasted sweet and salty, like champagne and tears, and she put her heart and soul, her entire being into it.

Though Sam wasn't quite sure who kissed whom first, he had the feeling he might have just unleashed some sort of wild animal. She clawed at his clothes, yanking his jacket off his shoulders and down his arms, tugging his bow tie loose. She fumbled with his belt, unfastened his pants, and before he could manage to catch his breath, slid her hand inside his boxers and wrapped it around him. Sam cursed under his breath, a word that under normal circumstances he would never dare utter in the presence of royalty, but he was having one hell of a tough time reconciling the princess he knew with the wild woman who was now walking backward toward her bed, unzipping her dress and letting it fall to the floor. She plucked a jewel-encrusted comb from her hair and he watched as it spilled down over her shoulders like black silk. She grinned wickedly, tempting him with eyes the color of the sky just before a storm—smoky gray and turbulent.

Though under normal circumstances he would find it juvenile and downright rude, when his mates dared Sam to ask Princess Anne, *The Shrew,* to dance, he'd had just enough champagne to take the bait. But never in a million years did he expect her to ask him first. Nor did he expect to find himself in her bedroom, Anne undressed to her black lace strapless bra and matching

panties. And as she draped her long, lithe body across
the mattress, summoning him closer with a crooked
finger and a seductive smile, he guessed it wouldn't be
long before she wore nothing at all.

"Take your clothes off," she demanded as she reached
around behind her to unhook her bra. Her breasts were
small and firm and he could hardly wait to get his hands
on them, to taste them. He ripped his shirt off, losing a
button or two in his haste, then stepped out of his pants,
grabbing his wallet for later. That was when he realized
the mistake he'd made and cursed again.

"What's wrong?" Anne asked.

"I don't have a condom."

"You don't?" she said, looking crestfallen.

He shook his head. It wasn't as if he came to these
events expecting to shag, and even if he had, he would
have anticipated taking the woman in question home,
where he kept an entire box in his bedside table
drawer.

"I've got it covered," Anne told him.

"You have a condom?"

"No, but I have it covered."

In other words, she was on birth control, but that
wouldn't protect either of them from disease. But he
knew he was clean, and it was a safe bet to assume she
was, too. So why not? Besides, Anne was wearing a look
that said she wouldn't be taking no for an answer.

He dropped the rest of his clothes in a pile and joined
her. As she dragged him down onto the bed, ravaging
his mouth with a deep, desperate kiss, rolling him onto

his back and straddling him, he had the feeling this was a night he wouldn't soon forget.

They had barely gotten started and it was already the best sex he'd ever had.

Two

September

I've got it covered, Anne thought wryly as she dragged herself up from the bathroom floor, still weak and shaky, and propped herself against the vanity over the sink. What the bloody hell had she been thinking when she told Sam that? Had she not bothered to even consider the consequences? The repercussions of her actions?

Well, she was considering them now. And she had no one to blame but herself.

She rinsed her mouth and splashed cold water on her face and the wave of nausea began to pass. The family physician, whom she had sworn to total secrecy, had assured her that she'd feel better in her second trimester. But here she was in her fifteenth week, three weeks past that magical date, and she still felt like the walking dead.

But it was worth it, she thought, as she laid a hand over the tiny bump that had begun to form just below her navel.

It was hard to believe that at first, when she learned she was pregnant, she wasn't even sure that she wanted to keep it. Her initial plan had been to take an extended vacation somewhere remote and warm, live in exile until it was born, and then give it up for adoption. Then Chris's wife, Melissa, had given birth to their triplets and Anne cradled her tiny niece and nephews in her arms for the first time. Despite never having given much thought to having children—it had always seemed so far off in the future—in that instant she knew she wanted her baby. She wanted someone to love her unconditionally. Someone to depend on her.

She was going to have this baby and she was going to raise it herself. With support from her family, of course. Which she was sure she would get just as soon as she told them. So far only her twin sister, Louisa, knew. As for Sam, he obviously wanted nothing to do with her.

Their night together had been like a fantasy come to life. She'd heard her sister talk for years about destiny and finding one true love. And in fact, Louisa's dreams had come true at the ball—she was now married to her mystery man, Garrett Sutherland. But until Sam kissed Anne, until he made love to her so passionately, until, exhausted, they fell asleep in each other's arms, Anne hadn't truly believed in love. But now that she did, it would seem that Sam didn't share her feelings.

She had been sure that it had been as special for him as it had been for her, that they had connected on some deeply visceral level. Even when she had woken up alone and realized that at some time in the night he had slipped away without saying goodbye, she wouldn't let her hopes be dashed. She kept waiting to hear from him. For weeks she stayed close to the phone, willing it to ring, hoping to answer and hear his voice. But the call never came.

She shouldn't have been surprised, really. Sam was a politician, and everyone knew that politics and royalty did not mix well. Not if Sam wanted to be prime minister someday, and that was what she'd heard. By law, no member of the royal family was permitted to hold a position in government. Could she honestly blame him for choosing a career he had spent his entire life preparing for over her? That was why she had made the decision not to tell him about the baby. It was a complication that neither of them needed. And one she was quite sure he didn't want despite the scandal it would cause for her.

She could see the headlines now. *Princess Anne Pregnant with Secret Love Child.*

No matter how liberal the world had become in such matters, she was royalty and held to a higher standard. The stigma would follow her and, even worse, her child, for the rest of their lives. But at this point, she saw no other options.

Feeling half-human again, she decided she should get back to the dining room and try to choke down a few bites of dinner. Geoffrey, their butler, had just begun to serve the first course when her stomach lurched and she'd had to excuse herself and dash to the loo.

She gave one last furtive look in the mirror and decided that short of a total makeover, this was as good as it was going to get. She opened the door and almost collided with her brother Chris, who was leaning against the wall just outside.

Bloody hell.

His grim expression said that he had heard her retching, and he wanted to know what would cause her to be so ill.

"Let's have a talk," he said, jerking his head toward the study across the hall.

"But, supper…" she started to say, and he gave her that *look*.

"*Now,* Anne."

Since arguing would be a waste of time, she followed him. With their father in poor health, Chris was acting king, and technically the head of the family. She was duty-bound to follow his lead. And didn't she always do as she was told? Wouldn't everyone be surprised when they learned of her predicament.

She could lie and tell him that she had a flu bug, or a mild case of food poisoning, but at the rate her tummy was swelling, it wouldn't be long before it was impossible to hide anyway. But she wasn't sure if she was ready for the truth to come out just yet.

Or maybe he already knew. Had Louisa blabbed? Anne would kill her if that was the case.

Anne stepped into the study, and, shy of her mother, father and the triplets, the entire family was there!

Aaron and his wife, Liv, a botanical geneticist, sat on the couch looking worried. Louisa and her new husband, Garrett, stood across the room by the window. Louisa wore a pained expression and Garrett looked as though he wanted to be anywhere but there. Melissa, Chris's wife, stood just inside the door, looking anxious. Not five minutes ago they had all been in the dinning room eating supper.

Her first instinct was to turn and walk right back out, but Chris had already followed her in and shut the door.

What a nightmare.

"I don't suppose I have to tell you why I asked you here," he said.

Ordered was more like it. Now she was sorry she'd agreed.

"We're very concerned," Melissa said, walking over to stand beside Chris. "You haven't been yourself lately, Anne. For the last couple of months you've been pale and listless. Not to mention all the times you've dashed off to the loo."

So they didn't know. Louisa had kept her secret.

"It's obvious something is wrong," Aaron said. He normally wasn't one to butt into other people's business, so she knew he must have been genuinely concerned. Maybe waiting so long to tell everyone had been an error in judgment. She didn't honestly think that anyone really noticed the changes in her or for that matter cared about them.

"If you're ill—" Melissa began.

"I'm not ill," Anne assured her.

"An eating disorder is a disease," Chris said.

Anne turned to him, amused because Louisa had suspected the same thing at first. "Chris, if I were bulimic, I would be dashing off to the loo after supper, not before."

He didn't look as though he believed her. "I know something is wrong."

"It all depends on how you look at it, I guess."

"Look at what?" Melissa asked.

Just tell them, dummy. "I'm pregnant."

All through the room jaws dropped. Except Louisa's, of course.

"If this is some kind of joke, I'm not amused," Chris said.

"It's no joke."

"Of course!" Melissa said, as though the lightbulb had just flashed on. "I should have realized. I just never thought…"

"I would be careless enough to go out and get myself in trouble?" Anne asked.

"I…I wasn't even aware that you were seeing anyone," Aaron said.

"I'm not. It was a one-time encounter."

"Maybe this is a silly question," Chris said. "But are you sure? Have you taken a test? Seen the family physician?"

She lifted the hem of the cardigan she'd been wearing to hide the evidence and smoothed her dress down over her bump. "What do you think?"

Had his eyes not been fastened in they might have fallen out of his head. "Good God, how far along are you?"

"Fifteen weeks."

"You're *four* months pregnant and you never thought to mention it?"

"I planned to announce it when the time was right."

"When? After your water broke?" he snapped, and Melissa put a hand on his arm to calm him.

"There's no need to get snippy," Anne said.

Ironic coming from her, his look said, the princess of snip. Well, maybe she didn't want to be that way any longer. Maybe she was tired of always being on the defensive.

"This isn't like you, Anne," Chris said.

"It's not as if I went out and got knocked up on purpose, you know." Although he was right. She had been uncharacteristically irresponsible.

I've got it covered. Brilliant.

"This is going to be a nightmare when it hits the press," Melissa said. Being an illegitimate princess herself, she would certainly know. Until recently she'd lived in the U.S., unaware that she was heir to the throne of Morgan Isle.

"And what about the Gingerbread Man?" Louisa asked, speaking up for the first time. "I'm sure he'll use the opportunity to try to scare us."

The self-proclaimed Gingerbread Man was the extremely disturbed man who had been harassing the royal family for more than a year. He began by hacking their computer system and sending Anne and her siblings twisted and grisly versions of fairy tales, then he breached security on the palace grounds to leave an ominous note. Not long after, posing as housekeeping staff, he'd made it as far as the royal family's private waiting room at the hospital. Hours after he was gone, security found the chilling calling card he'd left behind. An envelope full of photographs of Anne and her siblings that the Gingerbread Man had taken in various places so they would know that he was there, watching.

He would sometimes be silent for months, yet every time they thought they had heard the last of him, he would reappear out of the blue. He sent a basket of rotten fruit for Christmas and an e-mail congratulating Chris and Melissa about the triplets before her pregnancy had even been formally announced.

His most recent stunt had been breaking into the florist the night before Aaron and Liv's wedding in March and spraying the flowers with something that had caused them to wilt just in time for the ceremony.

Anne was sure he would pull something when he learned of her pregnancy, but she refused to let him get to her. She wouldn't give him the satisfaction. "I don't care what the Gingerbread Man does," she said, lifting her chin in defiance. "Personally, I'm all for drawing him out into the open so he makes a mistake and gets caught."

"Which we have agreed not to do," Chris said sternly.

Aaron asked the next obvious question. "What about the father of the baby? Is he taking responsibility?"

"Like I said, it was a one-night thing."

Chris frowned. "He didn't offer to marry you?"

This was where it was going to get tricky. "No. Besides, he's not a royal."

"I don't give a damn who he is. He needs to take responsibility for his actions."

"Liv and Garrett aren't royals. And I'm only half-royal," Melissa added.

"It doesn't matter. He's out of the picture," Anne insisted.

"And that was his choice?" Aaron asked.

Anne bit her lip.

"Anne?" Chris asked, and when she remained silent he cursed under his breath. "He doesn't know, does he?"

"Trust me when I say, he's better off."

Melissa made a clucking noise, as though she were thoroughly disappointed in Anne.

"That is not your decision to make," Chris said. "I don't care who he is, he has a right to know he's going to have a child. To keep it from him is unconscionable."

She knew deep down that he was right. But she was feeling hurt and bitter and stubborn. If Sam didn't want her, why should he be allowed access to their child?

"Sam may be a politician, but he's a good man," Chris said.

Once again, mouths fell open in surprise, including her own. She hadn't told anyone the father's identity. Not even Louisa. "How did you—"

"Simple math. You don't honestly think Melissa and I could go through months of infertility treatments and a high-risk pregnancy without learning a thing or two about getting pregnant? Conception would have had to have occurred around the time of the charity ball. And do you really think that Sam's sneaking out in the middle of the night would go unnoticed?"

No, of course not. They were under a ridiculously tight lockdown these days. "You never said anything."

"What was I supposed to say? You're a grown woman. As long as you're discreet, who you sleep with is your business." He put both hands on her shoulders. "But now, you need to call him and set up a meeting."

"Why, so you can have a *talk* with him?"

"No. So *you* can. Because it's not only unfair to Sam, it's unfair to that baby you're carrying. He or she deserves the chance to know their father. If that's what Sam wants."

"He's right," Louisa said. "Put yourself in Sam's place."

"You should definitely tell him the truth," Aaron said.

She fiddled with the hem of her sweater, unable to meet Chris's eyes, knowing he was right. If not for Sam, then for the baby's sake. "I'm not sure what to say to him."

"Well," Melissa said. "I often find it's best to start with the truth."

Sam had just ended a call with the Secretary of State of DFID, or what the Brits called the Department for International Development, when his secretary, Grace, rang him.

"You have a visitor, sir."

A visitor? He didn't recall any appointments on the calendar for this afternoon. This was typically his time for any calls that needed to be made. Had Grace scheduled another appointment she'd forgotten to mention? Or maybe she had entered information incorrectly into the computer again.

He was sure at one time she had been an asset to his father's office, but now she was at least ten years past mandatory retirement.

"Do they have an appointment?" he asked her.

"No, sir, but—"

"Then I don't have time. I'll be happy to see them after they schedule an appointment." He hung up, wishing he could gently persuade his father to let her go, or at the very least assign her to someone else. But she had been with the office since the elder Baldwin was a young politician just starting out and he was as fiercely loyal to her as she was to him. Sam may have suspected some sort of indiscretion had it not been for the fact that she was fifteen years his father's senior, and they were both very happily married to other people.

There was a knock at his office door and Sam groaned inwardly, gathering every bit of his patience. Did Grace not understand the meaning of the word *no?* "What is it?" he snapped, probably a bit more harshly than she deserved.

The door opened, but it wasn't Grace standing there. It was Anne. *Princess* Anne, he reminded himself. Spending one night in her bed did not give him the privilege of dispensing with formalities.

"Your Highness," he said, rising from his chair and bowing properly, even though he couldn't help picturing her naked and poised atop him, her breasts firm and high, her face a mask of pleasure as she rode him until they were both blind with ecstasy. To say they'd slept together, that they'd had sex, was like calling the ocean a puddle. They had transcended every preconceived notion he'd ever had about being with a woman. It was a damned shame that they had no future.

He must have picked up the phone a dozen times to call her in the weeks following their night together, but before he could dial he'd been faced with a grim reality. No matter how he felt about her, how deeply they had connected, if he wanted to be prime minister, he simply could not have her.

He had accepted a long time ago that getting where he wanted would involve sacrifice. Yet never had it hit home so thoroughly as it did now.

"Is this a bad time?" she asked.

"No, of course not. Come in, please."

She stepped into his office and shut the door behind her. Though she was, on most occasions, coolly composed, today she seemed edgy and nervous, her eyes flitting randomly about his office. Looking everywhere, he noticed, but at him.

"I'm sorry to just barge in on you this way. But I was afraid that if I called you might refuse to see me."

"You're welcome anytime, Your Highness." He came around his desk and gestured to the settee and chair in the sitting area. "Please, have a seat. Can I get you a drink?"

"No, thank you. I'm fine." She sat primly on the edge of the settee, clutching her purse in her lap, and he took a seat in the chair. She looked thinner than when he'd last seen her, and her milky complexion had taken on a gray cast. Was she ill?

"Maybe just a glass of water?" he asked.

She shook her head, her lips folded firmly together, and he watched as her face went from gray to green before his eyes. Then her eyes went wide, and she asked in a panicked voice, "The loo?"

He pointed across the room. "Just through that—"

She was up off the settee, one hand clamped over her

mouth, dashing for the door before he could even finish his sentence. It might have been comedic had he not been so alarmed. He followed her and stood outside the door, cringing when he heard the sounds of her being ill. There was obviously something terribly wrong with her. But why come to him? They barely knew one another. On a personal level at any rate.

He heard a flush, then the sound of water running.

"Should I call someone for you?" he asked, then the door opened and Anne emerged looking pale and shaky.

"No, I'm fine. Just dreadfully embarrassed. I should have known better than to eat before I came here."

"Why don't you sit down." He reached out to help her but she waved him away.

"I can do it." She crossed the room on wobbly legs and re-staked her seat on the settee. Sam sat in the chair.

"Forgive me for being blunt, Your Highness, but are you ill?"

"Sam, we've been about as intimate as two people can be, so please call me Anne. And no, I'm not ill. Not in the way you might think."

"In what way, then?"

She took a deep breath and blew it out. "I'm pregnant."

"Pregnant?" he repeated, and she nodded. Well, he hadn't seen that coming. He'd barely been able to look at another woman without seeing Anne's face, but it would seem she'd had no trouble moving on. And what reason had he given her not to? Maybe that night hadn't been as fantastic for her as it was for him. It would explain why she had made no attempt to contact him afterward.

But if she was happy, he would be happy for her. "I hadn't heard. Congratulations."

She looked at him funny, then said, "I'm four months."

Four months? He counted back and realized that their night together had been almost exactly—

Sam's gut tightened.

"Yes, it's yours," she said.

He *really* hadn't seen *that* coming. "You're sure?"

She nodded. "There hasn't been anyone else. Not after, and not a long time before."

"I thought you said you had it covered."

"I guess nothing is one hundred percent guaranteed."

Apparently not.

"If you require a DNA test—"

"No," he said. "I trust your word." What reason did she have to lie?

They were going to have a baby. He and the princess. He was going to be a *father*.

He had always planned to have a family someday, but not until he was a bit more established in his career. And not until he met the right woman.

"You're probably wondering why I waited so long to tell you," she said.

Among other things. "Why did you?"

"I just…I didn't want to burden you with this. I didn't want you to feel…obligated. Which I realize now was totally unfair of me. And I apologize. I just want you to know that I don't expect anything from you. I'm fully prepared to raise this baby on my own. Whether or not you want to be a part of its life is your choice entirely."

What kind of man did she take him to be? "Let's get one thing perfectly clear," he told her. "This is my *child,* and I'm going to be a part of it's life."

"Of course," she said softly. "I wasn't sure. Some men—"

"I am *not* some men," he told her firmly. "I hope that won't be a problem for you or your family."

She shook her head. "No, of course not. I think it's wonderful. A child should have both its parents."

He leaned back in the chair, shaking his head. "I'm… *wow.* This is quite a surprise."

"I can relate, believe me. This was not the way I imagined starting a family."

"I suppose some sort of announcement will have to be made." He could just imagine what his friends would say. For weeks after the ball they had tried to bully him into explaining his and the princess's sudden absence from the party, but he'd refused to say a word. Now everyone would know. Not that he was embarrassed or ashamed of what he'd done. "You know that the press will be brutal."

"I know. When they learn you're the father and that we're not…together, they won't leave us alone."

If that was some sort of hint as to the future direction of their relationship, he hated to disappoint her, but he was not about to give up everything he had worked so hard for, his lifelong dream, for a one-night stand.

He cared for Anne, lusted after her even, but a marriage was absolutely out of the question.

Three

"The press will just have to get used to the idea of us being friends," Sam told her.

"I hope we can be, for the baby's sake."

"And your family? How do they feel about this?"

"So far only my siblings know. They were surprised, but very supportive. My father's health is particularly fragile right now, so we've decided to wait to tell him and my mother. I have to admit that *you're* taking this much better than I expected. I thought you would be angry."

"It was an accident. What right would I have to be angry? You didn't force me."

"Didn't I?"

He wouldn't deny that she had started it, and she had been quite…*aggressive*. But he had been a willing participant. "Anne, we share equal responsibility."

"Not all men would feel that way."

"Yes, well, I'm not all men."

There was a short period of awkward silence, so he asked, "Everything is okay? With the pregnancy, I mean. You and the baby are healthy?"

"Oh yes," she said, instinctively touching a hand to her belly. "Everything's fine. I'm right on schedule."

"Do you know the sex of the baby?"

"Not for another month, at my next ultrasound." She paused, then said, "You could go, too. If you'd like."

"I would. Are you showing yet?"

"I have a little bump. Want to see?" She surprised him by lifting up the hem of her top and showing him her bare tummy. But why would she be shy when he had seen a lot more than just her stomach?

Her tummy had indeed swelled and was quite prominent considering how thin she was. He wasn't sure what possessed him, but he asked, "Can I touch it?"

"Of course," she said, gesturing him over.

He moved to the settee beside her and she took his hand, laying it on her belly. She was warm and soft there, and the familiar scent of her skin seemed to eat up all of the breathable air. His hand was so large that his fingers spanned the top of her bump all the way down to the top edge of her panties.

Maybe this wasn't such a good idea. Knowing they couldn't be together didn't make him want her any less. And knowing that it was his baby growing inside her gave him an almost irrational desire to protect her, to claim her as his own.

And hadn't he felt the same way the night they had made love?

"Have you felt it move?"

"Flutters mostly. No actual kicks yet. But press right here," she said, pushing his fingers more firmly against her belly, until he hit something firm and unyielding. She looked up at him and smiled, her mouth inches from his own. "You feel it?"

Did he ever, and it took all of his restraint not to lean in and capture her lips. He breathed in the scent of her hair, her skin, longing to taste her again, to…*take* her. But a sexual relationship at this stage, with her all hormones and emotions, could spell disaster.

She seemed to sense what he was thinking, because color suddenly flooded her cheeks and he could see the flutter of her pulse at the base of her neck. Without realizing it, he had started to lean in, and her chin had begun to lift, like the pull of a magnet drawing them together. But thank goodness he came to his senses at the last second and turned away. He pulled his hand from her belly and rose to his feet. His heart was hammering and she'd gone from looking pale and shaky to flushed and feverish.

"This is not a good idea," he said.

"You're right," she agreed, nodding vigorously. "I wasn't thinking."

"It would be in our best interest to keep this relationship platonic. Otherwise things could get confusing."

"Very confusing."

"Which could be a challenge," he admitted. Total honesty at this point only seemed fair, as she had been forthcoming with him. "It's obvious that I'm quite attracted to you."

"There does seem to be some sort of…connection."

That was putting it mildly. It was taking every bit of restraint he could gather to stop himself from taking her, right there in his office. Pregnant or not, he wanted to strip her naked and ravish her, drive into her until she screamed with release. The way she had that night in her bedroom. He'd never been with a woman so responsive to his touch, so easy to please. He couldn't help wondering if her pregnancy had changed that. He'd often heard that it made women even more receptive to physical stimulation. And maybe it was true, because he could clearly see the firm peaks of her nipples through her clothes. Her breasts looked larger than they had been before, too. Rounder and fuller. What would she do if he took one in his mouth…?

He swallowed hard and looked away, turning toward his desk, so she might not notice how aroused he was becoming. "You mentioned an ultrasound. Do you know the time and date, so I can mark it on my calendar?"

She rattled off the information and he slid into his chair behind the safety of his desk and made himself a note.

"Maybe we could have dinner this Friday," she said, then added quickly, "A platonic dinner, of course. So we can discuss how we plan to handle things. Like the press and custody."

That would give him three days to think this through and process it all. He always preferred to have a solid and well-considered plan of action before he entered into negotiations of any kind.

However, he wasn't sure he was ready to be thrown

in the mix with her family just yet. Not that he didn't feel as though he could hold his own. He just felt these matters were private, between himself and Anne, and in no way concerned her family.

"How about we eat at my place," he said. "Seven o'clock?"

"If you don't mind your residence being swarmed with security. We're still on high alert."

He frowned. "Is the royal family still being harassed?"

"Unfortunately, yes."

All he knew of the situation was what he'd read in the papers. "So it's serious," he said.

"More than anyone realizes, I'm afraid. There have been threats of violence against the family. I should probably warn you that once we're linked together, you could become a target, as well."

He shrugged. "I'm not worried. As far as the baby goes, I'm assuming that until you've told your father, there will be no announcement to the press."

"Of course not."

"I do intend to tell my family, but they can be trusted to keep it quiet."

"Of course you should tell them. Do you think they'll be upset?"

Her look of vulnerability surprised him. He didn't think she was afraid of anything. Or cared what anyone thought of her. But hadn't he learned that night at the ball that she wasn't nearly as tough as she liked people to believe? "I think they'll be surprised, but happy," he told her.

He just hoped it was true.

* * *

Sam stopped in to see his parents that evening to break the news. When he arrived they had just finished supper and were relaxing out on the veranda with snifters of brandy, watching the sun set. Despite his father's career in politics, and his mother's touring as an operatic vocalist, they always made time for each other. After forty years they were still happily married and going strong.

That was the sort of marriage Sam had always imagined for himself. He had just never met a woman he could see himself spending the rest of his life with. Until Anne, he admitted grudgingly. How ironic that when he finally found her, he couldn't have her.

He wasn't quite sure how they would react to learning that they would be grandparents to the next prince or princess of Thomas Isle, but under the circumstances, they took it pretty well. Probably in part because they had been vying for grandchildren for some time and Sam's older brother, Adam, had yet to deliver.

"I'm sure I'm going to sound old-fashioned," his mother said, "but ideally we would like to see you married."

"Mother—"

"However," she continued. "We understand that you need to do what you feel is right."

"If I married Anne, I would be considered a royal and I would never be prime minister. That isn't a sacrifice I'm willing to make." Of course, with that in mind, he shouldn't have slept with her in the first place, should he? He suspected that was what his mother was thinking.

"You would be giving your child a name," his father pointed out.

"I don't need to be married to do that. He had my name the moment he was conceived."

"He?" his mother asked, brows raised.

"Or she."

"Will you find out?"

"I'd like to. And I think Anne would, too. She has an ultrasound in four weeks."

"Maybe I could invite her for tea," she suggested, and at Sam's wary look added, "I should be allowed to get to know the mother of my future grandchild."

She was right. And he was sure Anne would be happy to oblige her. Didn't pregnant women love to talk about their condition with other women? Especially the grandparents? "I'll mention it to her."

"You know that this is going to be complicated," his father said. "They think differently than we do."

"They?"

"Royals."

"Not so different as you might expect," Sam said. "Not Anne, anyway. She's actually quite down-to-earth."

"I've only spoken briefly with the princess," his mother said. "But she seemed lovely."

There was a "however" hanging there, and Sam knew exactly what she was thinking. What they were *both* thinking. He couldn't deny he'd thought the same thing before his night with Anne. "I know you've probably heard things about her. Unfavorable things. But she isn't at all what you would expect. She's intelligent and engaging." And fantastic in bed…

"It sounds as if you're quite taken with her," his mother not-so-subtly hinted.

He was. Probably too much for his own good. He just hoped that once Anne began to look more pregnant, and especially after the baby was born, it would be easier for him to see her only as the mother of his child and not a sexual being.

"I have every hope that Anne and I can be good friends, for the child's sake, but that is as far as it will ever go."

He knew they were disappointed. This wasn't the sort of scenario his parents had envisioned for him, and honestly neither had he. He had assumed that it would have been like it had been for them. He would meet a woman and they would date for a reasonable period of time, then marry and have a family. Sam would eventually become prime minister, and his wife would have a rewarding and lucrative career that still allowed her time to put her family first.

So much for that plan.

"As long as you're happy, we're happy," his mother said.

Sam hoped she really meant it. Even though they gave no indication that Sam was disappointing them, he couldn't help but feel that he'd let them down. That he had let *himself* down.

Even worse, was he letting his child down?

What had happened was an accident, but ultimately the person who would pay for it would be the baby. The baby would be the one relentlessly dogged by the press. And being a royal, the stigma of illegitimacy could potentially follow him or her for life. Was it fair to put the baby through that for his own selfish needs?

It was certainly something to consider.

He had just arrived home later that evening when he got a call on his cell phone from Prince Christian's assistant, with a message from the prince. It was odd enough that she would call at almost 10:00 p.m., but how had the prince gotten his private cell number? The prince's calls typically went through Sam's office line.

Silly question. As acting king, he probably had access to any phone number he wanted.

"His Royal Highness, Prince Christian, requests your presence in the royal family's private room at the Thomas Bay yacht club tomorrow at one-thirty," she said.

Oh did he? That was an odd setting for a business meeting. Unless it had nothing to do with business. "And the nature of this meeting?" he asked her.

"A private matter."

Well, so much for believing that this would stay between Sam and Anne. He should have anticipated this. Prince Christian probably considered it his obligation to watch his sister's back. That didn't mean Sam would let him intimidate or boss him around.

"Tell the prince that I would be happy to meet him at three."

There was a brief pause, as though the idea of someone actually refusing an invitation from the prince was beyond her realm of comprehension. Finally she said, "Could you hold, please?"

"Of course."

She was off the line for several minutes, then came back on and said, "Three will be fine. The prince asks that you please keep this meeting to yourself, as it is a sensitive matter."

This suggested to Sam that Anne probably had no idea a meeting was being arranged and the prince preferred it to stay that way. He didn't doubt that the prince would try to persuade him to marry Anne. Truth be told, if Sam had a sister in a similar situation, he might do the same thing.

But this was the twenty-first century and people had children out of wedlock all the time. On occasion, even royalty. Prince Christian's wife, Princess Melissa of their sister country, Morgan Isle, was an illegitimate heir. In fact, with two illegitimate heirs, and a former king who reputedly lacked the ability or desire to keep his fly zipped, the royal family of Morgan Isle was positively brimming with scandal. By comparison the royal family of Thomas Isle were saints. Would a little scandal be so terrible?

But was it fair to the baby, who had no choice in the matter? Wasn't it a father's responsibility to protect his child?

But at what cost?

Sam slept fitfully that night and had trouble concentrating at work the next day. It was almost a relief to leave the office early, even though he doubted his meeting with the prince would be a pleasant exchange.

He arrived five minutes ahead of time, and the prince was already there, sitting in a leather armchair beside a bay of windows that overlooked the marina. He rose to greet Sam.

"Your Highness." Sam bowed his head then accepted Prince Christian's hand for a firm shake.

"I'm so glad you accepted my invitation," he said.

The Prince requests your presence sounded more like an order than an invitation. "I wasn't aware it was optional."

"I'm sorry if you were given that impression. I just thought it would be appropriate, in light of the situation, if we had a friendly chat."

Friendly? Sam doubted that.

The Prince gestured to the chair opposite him. "Please have a seat. Would you like a drink?"

A few too many glasses of champagne had gotten Sam into this mess. Had he been sober, he probably never would have approached the princess, much less danced with her. "Nothing for me, thanks."

They both sat.

"No disrespect intended, but if the *situation* you're referring to somehow involves my being the father of your sister's child, we have nothing to discuss, Your Highness."

His blunt statement seemed to surprise the prince. "Is that so?"

"It is."

"I'm afraid I disagree."

"This is between me and Anne."

"No one wishes that were the case more than I. Unfortunately, what Anne does affects our entire family. I had hoped you would do the right thing, but I understand that's not the case."

"Of course I'll do the right thing. But I'll do what *I* feel is the right thing."

"And may I ask what your idea of the right thing is?"

"As I said, that is between me and the mother of my child."

His expression darkened. He obviously didn't like that Sam wasn't falling into line. But Sam would be damned if he was going to let the prince, or any member of the royal family, walk all over him.

Prince Christian leaned forward slightly. "I won't see my sister's reputation, not to mention that of her child, decimated, because you couldn't keep out of her knickers."

What was that phrase the Americans used? It takes two to tango? "If blaming me for this situation makes you sleep better, I can live with that."

"You're being unreasonable."

"On the contrary, I'm being very reasonable. I'm considering your sister's privacy."

"This concerns more people than just you and Anne. You know that our father isn't well. A scandal like this is more than his heart could take."

So now not only was Sam decimating reputations, but he was essentially killing the king? "I'm sorry to hear that, but I'm still not talking to you."

"I could make your life unpleasant," Prince Christian said ominously. "If I feel that you're disrespecting my sister's name, I will lash out at you in any way I see fit."

So much for their *friendly* chat. He couldn't say he was surprised.

Sam shrugged. "Knock yourself out, Your Highness. I'm still not discussing my and Anne's private matters with you."

For a long moment Prince Christian just stared at him, and Sam braced himself for the fireworks. But instead of exploding with anger, the prince shook his head and laughed. "Christ, Baldwin, you've got a pair."

"I just don't respond well to threats or ultimatums."

"And I don't like giving them. But I have an obligation to look out for my family. The truth is, if it weren't for my father's fragile state, we wouldn't be having this conversation. He's in extremely poor health and it would make him very happy to see his oldest daughter married before she has a child."

He found what Prince Christian was doing utterly annoying, but in a way Sam actually felt sorry for him. "I'm truly sorry to hear that your father isn't well. I hold him in the highest regard."

"And I sympathize with your situation, Sam. I honestly do. It's common knowledge that you intend to follow in your father's footsteps and I believe you have the fortitude to pull it off. But marrying my sister would make that impossible. For what it's worth, you've built a reputation as one hell of a foreign affairs advisor. If there *were* a marriage, you would be offered a powerful and influential position within the monarchy."

After serving in, and being around, government for most of his life, the idea of taking a position with the monarchy was troubling to say the least. Not that they weren't on the same side when it came to serving the people of the country. But in Sam's eyes it had always been something of an "us against them" scenario.

Not to mention that, while he enjoyed foreign affairs, he had set his sights higher.

"Have you given any thought to how difficult it could be for your child, being illegitimate?"

"That's *all* I've been thinking about." And the more he thought about it, the more he came to realize that marrying Anne might be the wisest course of action. They may not have planned this pregnancy, but it had happened, and from now on he would have to put the welfare of his child above all else. Including his political ambitions.

"What's it like?" Sam asked. "Being a father?"

The prince smiled, his affection for his children undeniably clear. "It's exhilarating and terrifying and more rewarding than anything I've ever done. Ever *imagined*. I have these three perfect little human beings who are completely helpless and depend on me and their mother for everything they need to survive. It can be overwhelming."

"And if someone gave you a choice? Give up the throne or your children would live a life of disgrace and shame."

"No question. My children come first."

As it should be.

"You know that my wife was born out of wedlock," the prince said.

Sam nodded.

"She didn't find out that she was a royal until she was in her thirties, but it was *still* extremely difficult for her. To lay that on a child? As if life as a royal isn't tough enough already. Kids need stability, and consistency."

Things that would be much harder to give a child who

was being bounced back and forth between two parents, two households, all while being under the microscope of the press.

Sam had grown up in an ideal situation and had always hoped to provide the same for his own children. Didn't his child deserve that?

He had gone from flirting with the idea of marrying Anne to seriously considering it. And now, after talking to the prince, there seemed to be little question in his mind.

He could give it more thought, mull it around in his head for a while just to be sure, but he knew deep down the decision was already made.

He was going to marry the princess.

Four

Sam's home was not at all what Anne had expected.

She'd pictured a modern-style mansion or a seaside condo with every amenity a wealthy bachelor could want. Instead, as her driver pulled up the long gravel drive, what she got was a scene straight out of *Hansel and Gretel*.

Sam lived in a quaint cottage tucked deep in the forest and nestled under a canopy of towering pines and lazy oaks so dense only dappled sunshine dotted its sagging roof. It was quiet, and secluded, and utterly charming. Not to mention a security *nightmare*.

"Maybe we should have had dinner at the palace," she told her bodyguard, Gunter, who sat in the front seat beside her driver.

"Is no problem," he replied in a thick Russian accent. He checked his reflection in the side mirror, running a hand through his blond brush cut. Preening, she thought with a quiet smile. Physically Gunter bore a striking resemblance to Arnold Schwarzenegger in his early *Terminator* days, with a face that, Anne hated to admit, was far prettier than her own. Women swooned in his presence, never suspecting that a man so ridiculously masculine and tough lived with a cat called Toodles and a life partner named David. He had a killer fashion sense and was more intuitive than most women she knew. In fact, he had guessed that she might be pregnant before anyone in her family had even noticed. She had been in serious denial and Gunter showed up for duty with a pregnancy test.

"Is good you should know, yes?" he'd said, then he'd sat on her bed waiting while she took the test, then listened to her vent after it came back positive.

He was also ex-KGB and could snap a man's neck like a twig without breaking a sweat.

The car rolled to a stop and Gunter got out to open her door.

"I do sweep," he said, as he helped her out.

"He's the father of my child. Is that really necessary?"

Gunter just gave her one of those looks and she knew it wasn't even worth arguing. She blew out an exasperated breath for good measure and in her best annoyed tone said, *"Fine."*

The door to the cottage opened as they started up the walk and there stood Sam, looking too adorable for words, wearing dark blue slacks and a sky-blue button-up shirt with the sleeves rolled to the elbows.

He smiled, both dimples showing, and she caught herself hoping that the baby looked just like him.

Out of the corner of her eye she noticed Gunter's brows lift, almost imperceptibly, and she could swear she heard him say, *Nice,* under his breath.

Up until that instant she had only been a little nervous about seeing Sam, but suddenly her heart was going berserk in her chest and her hands were trembling.

"Hi," she said as she stepped up to the tiny, covered porch complete with a rickety rocking chair and a terra-cotta pot overflowing with yellow and purple petunias.

Sam leaned casually in the doorway, the sweet smile not budging an inch, taking in her taupe cotton skirt and yellow silk sleeveless blouse. It was the most cheerful outfit she could dredge up that still fit. Only lately had she realized just how dark and dreary her wardrobe had become over the past few years. She swore that when she got around to buying maternity clothes they would be in only bright and cheerful colors. She was turning over a new leaf so she could be someone her baby would respect and be proud of. The way she respected her own mother.

Sam's eyes traveled very unplatonically down her body then back up again, clearly liking what they saw. "You look beautiful."

"Thank you. You look nice, too." Talk about swooning. Being close to him did funny things to her head. Neurons misfired and wires crossed, creating total and utter chaos.

You're only here to talk about the baby, she reminded herself, *not to indulge your ridiculous crush.*

Beside her Gunter softly cleared his throat. Right. The sweep.

"Would you mind terribly if Gunter did a quick security check of the house?" Anne asked Sam.

It was the kind of request that might insult some people, but Sam just shrugged, gestured inside and said, "Have at it, Gunter."

Gunter pinned her with a look that said, *Don't move,* but she knew the drill.

"Wouldn't want to meet him in a dark alley," Sam said, after he disappeared inside. "Gunter. German, right?"

"On his mother's side, but he was raised in Moscow." Anne peered past him into the cottage. It was just as quaint and old-fashioned as the exterior, with older but comfortable-looking furniture and more knickknacks that even Gunter would deem appropriate for a man. And it smelled a little like...old people.

"Your house is lovely," she said. "Not at all what I expected."

"Needless to say, I'm exceedingly secure in my masculinity."

"I guess so."

He laughed. "I'm sorry but no man is that secure. The truth is, it's my grandmother's place."

Which explained the geriatric bouquet. "You live with her?"

"Only in spirit. She passed away three years ago."

"Oh, I'm so sorry."

"I'm just staying here temporarily. While my place is being worked on."

"You're remodeling?"

"You could say that, although not by choice. I've had a leak in the roof for a while, but when my bedroom and kitchen ceilings started to droop, I decided it was time to finally do something about it. But then I figured, since I would be gone anyway, it only made sense to update the kitchen while I was at it. So, three days' worth of work turned into more like three weeks." He gestured inside. "Can I give you the tour?"

"I can't, not until I get the all clear."

"Right," he said. "Just in case I have an assassin hiding under the davenport."

"I know, it's ridiculous."

His expression turned serious. "Not at all," he said, then he reached out and placed a hand over her baby bump. The gesture was so surprising, so unexpected, that her knees went weak. His eyes locked on hers, clear and intense, and his mouth was close. Too close. "Not if it keeps you and Sam Junior safe."

Hadn't they agreed that it would be prudent to keep a safe physical distance? That when they got too close they— Wait, what did he say? "Sam who?"

He grinned and gave her belly a gentle pat before he moved his hand away. "Sam Junior."

"So you think it's a boy?"

"That's the beauty of it. It works for a boy or a girl. Samuel or Samantha. Either way we call it Sam."

She folded her arms across her chest. "It would seem you have it all figured out."

He pinned his eyes on her, his gaze so intense she swore she could feel it straight through to her bones. "I'm a man who knows what he wants, Your Highness."

His eyes said he wanted her, but she knew he was

probably only teasing. But if Gunter hadn't reappeared at that very second, she might have melted into a puddle on the doorstep.

"Is all clear," Gunter said, stepping onto the porch and gesturing her in. As Sam closed the door, Anne knew that Gunter would stand on the porch, in a military stance, unmoving until it was time to leave.

"Ready for that tour?" Sam asked and she nodded. Although, honestly, there really wasn't that much to see. The front room had just enough space for a couch, glider and a rickety television stand with a TV that was probably older than her. The kitchen was small but functional, with appliances that dated back to the dark ages. But if the flame under the pot on the stove, and the hum of refrigerator, were any indication, they were both still working. The loo was also tiny, with an antique sink and commode and an antique claw-foot tub.

Next he took her into the bedrooms. The smaller of the two was being used as an office and the larger was where Sam slept. As they stood in the doorway, Anne couldn't help thinking that the last time they had been in a bedroom together they had both been out of their brains with lust for each other. It seemed like so long ago, yet she recalled every instant, every detail in Technicolor clarity.

"Sorry it's a bit of a mess," he said.

The bed was mussed and there were clothes piled over a chair in the corner. The entire house had something of a cluttered but cozy feel. And though the entire square footage was less that her sleeping chamber at the castle, she felt instantly at home there.

"I was under the impression your family had money,"

she said, feeling like a snob the instant the words were out. "I didn't mean that the way it sounded."

"That's okay," he said with a good-natured smile. "The money came from my grandfather's side. My grandmother grew up here. After her parents died, she and my grandfather would spend weekends here. After my grandfather died, she moved back permanently and stayed until she died."

"I can see why she moved back," she told him as they walked back to the kitchen. "It's really lovely."

"It's not exactly the castle."

"No, but it has loads of charm."

"And no space."

She shrugged. "It's cozy."

"And it desperately needs to be updated. Did you see that tub?"

She gazed around. "No, I wouldn't change a single thing."

He looked at her funny. "You're serious."

She smiled and nodded. She really liked it. "It's so… peaceful. The minute I walked in I felt completely at home." She could even picture herself spending time here, curled up on the couch reading a book or taking long walks through the woods. Although, until the Gingerbread Man was caught, that would never be allowed.

"I'm glad," he said, flashing her the sexy grin that made her knees go weak. "Would you like something to drink? I have soda and juice."

"Just water, please."

He got a bottle from the fridge and poured it into a

glass with a wedge of lime. As he handed it to her, their fingertips touched.

"Something smells delicious," she said.

"Chicken soup. My grandmother's recipe."

Not your typical summer food, but that was okay. "I didn't know you could cook."

He grinned and wiggled his brows. "I am a man of many talents, Your Highness."

Oh, did she know it. Although under the circumstances many of those talents were best not contemplated. "What else can you make?"

"Let's see," he said, counting off on his fingers. "I can make coffee. And toast. I can heat a pizza. Oh, and I make a mean tray of ice cubes. And did I mention the toast?"

She smiled. "So in other words, you eat out a lot?"

"Constantly. But I wanted to impress you and I figured the soup might be good since you haven't been feeling well."

It was sweet of him to consider her temperamental stomach. He was so considerate and…nice. And oh, how she wished things could be different, that they could at least try to make a go of it, try to be a family. She wanted it so much her chest ached. It was all she had been able to think about since their talk in his office the other day. He was, by definition, the man of her dreams.

But some things just weren't meant to be.

"I think maybe it was stress making me feel sick," she said. "Since I told you about the baby, I've felt much better. I'll get nauseous occasionally, but no more running to the loo. I've even gained a few pounds, which I know will make my physician happy."

"That's great." He lifted the lid off the pot of soup and gave it a stir with a wooden spoon. "The soup is ready. But would you prefer to talk first and get it out of the way? So we can relax and enjoy dinner."

"I think that would be a good idea."

He gestured to the front room. "Shall we sit on the sofa?"

She nodded and took a seat, and he sat beside her, so close that his thigh was touching hers. Was this his idea of platonic?

He had given no indication that he would be difficult, or make unreasonable demands when it came to the baby, but she still wasn't sure what to expect. Sam, in contrast, sat beside her looking completely at ease. Did the man never get his feathers ruffled? When she had fallen apart at the ball he had snapped into action and rescued her from imminent public humiliation. When she told him about the baby he had been calm and rational and even sympathetic. She had never seen, or even heard of him ever losing his temper.

She, on the other hand, always seemed to be irritated and cranky about one thing or another. She could learn a lot from Sam. Although, if he knew the truth, if he knew that this little "accident" could have easily been prevented, he might not be so understanding. She would just have to be sure that he never found out.

"Before we get started," she said, "I just want to tell you again that I appreciate how well you've taken all this. I know things could potentially get complicated at some point, with custody and financial issues, and even different parenting styles. I just want you to know that I'm going to try my best to keep things civilized. I know I don't have a reputation for being the most reasonable woman, but I'm going to try really hard."

Sam's expression was serious. "Suppose I thought of a way to make things exponentially easier on both of us. On all three of us, actually."

She couldn't imagine how, but she shrugged and said, "I'm all for easy."

"I think you should marry me."

He said it so calmly, so matter-of-factly, that the meaning of his words took several seconds to sink in. Then she was sure that she must have heard him wrong, or he was playing some cruel joke. That any second he was going to laugh and say, "Gotcha!"

"I know it's fast," he said instead. "I mean, we barely know each other. But, for the baby's sake, I really think it's the logical next move."

My God, he was *serious*. He wanted to marry her. How was that even possible when only a few days ago it supposedly hadn't been an option?

"But…you want to be prime minister."

"Yes, but that isn't what's best for the baby. I'm going to be a father. From now on, I have to put his or her best interests first."

She had a sudden, unsettling thought. "My family isn't making you do this, are they? Did they threaten you?"

"This has nothing to do with your family." He took her hand and held it between his two. "This is what I want, Annie. What I think is best for everyone. We have to at least try, for the baby's sake."

She was thrilled to the center of her being…and drowning in a churning sea of guilt. If she had just acted responsibly, if she hadn't lied about being protected, they wouldn't be in this situation. He wouldn't be forced to give up everything that he had worked so hard for.

What if it was a decision he regretted someday and he grew to resent her and the baby? But what if he didn't? What if they fell in love and lived a long and happy life together?

She folded her other hand over his two. "Sam, are you *sure* about this? Because once we're married, that's it. A divorce can only be granted with the consent of the king."

"Let's try this another way," he said, then he dropped down on one knee in front of her and produced a diamond ring from his pants pocket.

She could hardly believe that this was really happening. It was a real, honest-to-goodness proposal.

He took her hand, looked deep in her eyes. "Will you marry me, Annie?"

There was only one answer she could give him. "Of course I'll marry you, Sam."

Grinning, he slid the ring on her finger. It was fashioned from white gold with a round cut diamond deeply set and surrounded by smaller stones. Despite its shine it was clearly an antique, not to mention exquisitely beautiful.

"Oh, Sam, it's amazing."

"It was my great-grandmother's," he said.

"We must have the same size finger," she said, turning her hand to watch it sparkle. "It's a perfect fit."

"I had it sized."

"But how did you know what size to make it?"

"Princess Louisa."

"You asked my sister?"

"Is that okay?"

"Of course. I just can't believe she didn't say anything. She's horrible at keeping secrets."

"I guess she wanted our moment to be special."

"It is." She threw her arms around his neck and hugged him and he hugged her back just as hard. It felt so good to hold him, to be close to him. It felt like… coming home. And she realized, she was truly happy. The happiest she had been in a long, *long* time. Maybe ever.

It was astonishing how, out of such a complicated situation, something so fantastic could arise. Ideally, he would have slipped sentiments of love somewhere between the rationale, but she was sure that would come later. Not that she believed it would be all smooth sailing. She knew that marriages took work and this one would be no exception. But they seemed to be off to a fairly good start under the circumstances.

"I know he's not well, but if at all possible, I'd like to be there when you tell the king and queen," Sam said. "I'd like to do this by the book and have the chance to ask for your hand."

His words made her practically burst with joy, because he would be giving her father something he had always looked forward to. "We'll go to them tomorrow," she said, already excited at the prospect, because she knew that her parents would be thrilled for her. Even if Sam was a politician. And they would be so excited about the baby.

"Needless to say, we should have the wedding soon," he said. "I was thinking next week."

That was really soon, but he was right. The sooner the better. It would have to be a small ceremony, if for no other reason than her father's health. It was the reason Louisa had kept her own wedding small and intimate, despite having always dreamed of a huge, traditional affair.

Not one to like being in the spotlight, Anne would be quite content with small and simple. That didn't mean there weren't a million things to do to prepare.

Her mind was suddenly flooded with all the plans they had to make and the short amount of time they had to make them. Where would they have the ceremony and who would they invite? And would the king be well enough to walk her down the aisle? And what about a honeymoon? Where would they—

That thought brought her mind to a screeching halt.

What about the honeymoon? And even more important, the *wedding night?*

Suddenly she was ultra-aware of Sam's arms around her, his body pressed against hers. The heat of his palms on her back and the spicy scent of his aftershave.

Suddenly her heart was beating so hard and fast she was sure Sam must have felt it through her clothes and skin. And all she could think about was getting him naked again. Touching him and kissing him all over. He must have been able to read her mind, because his breath hitched and his arms tightened around her.

"So, I guess this means that we don't have to keep our relationship platonic any longer," she said.

"Funny," he said. "But I was just thinking the exact same thing."

Thank God. Because frankly, a marriage without sex would be bloody awful.

She turned her face into the crook of his neck and kissed the side of his throat, could feel the heavy thump-thump of his pulse against her lips, and knew that he was just as aroused as she was. "We could make love right now if we wanted to."

"We could," he agreed, groaning when she nipped him with her teeth. She felt as though she wanted to eat him alive. Swallow him whole. She lifted her head, and the second she did he captured her lips with his own, but instead of the slick, ravenous kiss she was expecting, *hoping* for even, his lips rubbed softly, almost sweetly over hers. He kissed her chin and her throat, working his way down.

"Take me into your bedroom," she urged, sliding her hands up to tangle in the curls at his nape, feeling so hot she could burst into flames. "Right now."

"God knows I want you," he said, brushing his lips over her collarbone. "I've wanted you since that night. It's all I've been able to think about."

"You can have me. Right now."

He trailed his way back up to her mouth and whispered against her lips, "Or we could wait until we're married."

She groaned her disappointment. She wasn't even sure she *could* wait. "I feel as though I might go out of my mind if I can't have you right now."

"All the more reason to wait," he said, sounding far

too rational. "Think of how special it would be on our wedding night."

She opened her eyes to look at him and smiled. "Isn't that supposed to be *my* line?"

He grinned. "Poke fun all you want, but you know I'm right."

Yes, he was right. Not that anything about their relationship up to this point could be called conventional. She might have worried that he just didn't want her, and was trying to let her down gently, but the tent in his pants and the color in his cheeks said he was just as aroused as she was.

"Is that really what you want?"

He took her hands from around his neck and held them, his expression earnest. "I think we should wait."

It was clear that this wasn't an easy decision for him to make, and if she pushed the issue he would probably cave and make passionate love to her all night long. She didn't really understand why this was so important to him, but it clearly was. Besides, what was a few more days?

She would respect his wishes and wait for her wedding night, she decided grudgingly. But that didn't mean she had to like it.

Five

Anne was barely home for five minutes that evening when Louisa knocked on her bedroom door. It was nearly eleven—well past Louisa and Garrett's usual bedtime. Garrett had taken over management of all the royal family's vast farmlands so their brother Aaron could go to medical school, so he rose well before sunrise every morning. Not to mention that Louisa and Garrett were still newlyweds. They were constantly holding hands and touching. Sharing secret smiles and longing glances, as though they couldn't wait to be alone.

Anne would even admit to being jealous a time or two. But soon it would be her turn.

"You're up late," Anne said, pretending she had no idea why Louisa was so eager to speak to her, keeping her hand casually behind her, so she wouldn't see the ring.

"I just wondered how your date went," Louisa said, stepping into the room and closing the door behind her.

"Technically it wasn't a date," Anne said, walking to the bed and sitting down with her hands under her thighs. "We just had things to discuss."

Louisa sat beside her. "What did you talk about?"

"The baby mostly."

"That's it?" Louisa hedged.

"Pretty much," she said, then added casually, "Oh, and he asked me to marry him."

Louisa squealed so loudly Anne was sure the entire castle heard her. "Oh my God! Congratulations! What did you say?"

She shrugged. "I told him I would think about it."

Louisa gasped in horror, looking as though she wanted to throttle her. "You didn't!"

"Of course not." She grinned and pulled her hand from under her leg, flashing Louisa the ring. "I said yes."

Louisa threw her arms around Anne and hugged her. "I am so happy for you, Annie. You and Sam are going to be perfect together."

"I really hope so," Anne said.

Louisa held her at arm's length. "You will. If you believe it, it'll happen."

She wished that were true, that it were that easy. "I just keep thinking about you and Aaron and Chris. You all found the perfect person for you—you're all so happy."

"And you will be, too."

"It just seems as though every family has at least

one person who goes through life always ruining relationships. What if I'm that person? I've always been so negative. What if I don't deserve to be happy?"

"After all we've been through with our father, don't you think we *all* deserve some happiness? Besides, nothing is predetermined. Your life is what you make of it."

"That's what I'm worried about. Up until now, I've made a mess of it. Especially my love life."

"That was just bad luck. You just happened to meet a string of jerks. But anyone who knows Sam will tell you he's a great guy. And he'll be a fantastic husband and father."

Anne didn't doubt that at all. She never would have accepted his proposal otherwise. It was herself she was worried about. For the first time in her life she had a real shot at happiness—and she was terrified that she would find a way to screw it up.

"I'm sure you're right," she told Louisa.

"Of course I am," she said, as if there was never a doubt. Her relentless optimism never ceased to amaze Anne.

After Louisa went back to her room, Anne changed into her softest pajamas and crawled into bed, but her mind was still moving a million miles an hour and she was practically bursting with excitement. Thinking that a cup of tea might soothe her nerves, she climbed out of bed and put on her robe. The halls of the castle were silent but for the muffled wail of a baby crying from Chris and Melissa's room. Five months from now Anne could look forward to the same. She *and* Sam, she reminded herself with a smile.

She expected the kitchen to be empty and was surprised, when she switched on the light, to find their butler, Geoffrey, sitting at the butcher-block table. He squinted at the sudden bright light.

"I'm sorry," Anne said. "I didn't mean to startle you."

"No need to apologize," he said. His jacket was draped over the back of his chair and his tie hung loose around his neck. In front of him sat a bottle of scotch and a half-full highball glass. "What brings you down here at this late hour, Your Highness?"

"Couldn't sleep. I thought I would make some tea."

"You should have called down," he scolded. "I'd have brought it to you."

"I didn't want to bother you."

He rose and gestured to an empty chair. "Sit. I'll make it for you."

Because this was Geoffrey's domain, and he could be a little territorial, she did as he asked. She gestured to his drink and said, "Rough day?"

"Worse than some, better than others." He put the kettle on to boil. "How about you?"

"Actually, I had a very good day."

He pulled a cup down from the cupboard and dropped a tea bag in. "Would that have something to do with a certain young man and that ring on your finger?"

"It might." She should have realized he would notice the ring. Geoffrey didn't miss a thing. He may have been getting up in years, but he was still sharp as a tack. He had been with the family since before she was born and in some ways she had come to think of him as a second father. As far as she knew he had no family of his own, no one to care for him if he ever became incapacitated. But after so many years of loyal service, he would always have a place at the castle with the royal family.

"I suppose you heard about the baby."

"I might have," he said cryptically, but knowing him, he'd probably suspected all along.

"Are you disappointed in me?"

"If you had murdered someone, I would have been disappointed in you. A child is a blessing."

"Yes, but I know you have...*traditional* values."

He poured boiling water into her cup then set it on the table in front of her. "Then I suppose you'll be surprised to learn that I was once in a similar situation."

Surprised? For a moment she was too stunned to even respond. She never knew him to have a girlfriend, much less a pregnant one. He'd never spoken of any family. "I—I had no idea."

He sat across from her. "It was many years ago. Before I came to work here."

"You have a child?"

He nodded. "His name is Richard."

"Why didn't you ever say anything?"

He shrugged, swirling the amber liquid in his glass. "It isn't something I like to talk about."

"Do you see him?"

He shook his head, looking remorseful. "Not for many years."

"What happened?"

He downed the last of his drink then poured himself another. She wondered if the alcohol was responsible for his sudden loose tongue. He looked so sad. And when had he gotten so old? It was as though the lines on his face had appeared overnight. Or maybe she just hadn't wanted to see them.

"His mother was a cook for my previous employer," he told her. "We had an affair and she became pregnant. I did the responsible thing and married her, but it didn't take long to realize that we were completely incompatible. We stayed together for two years, then finally divorced. But working together was unpleasant for both of us, so we decided it would be best if I left and found a new job. That was when I came to work here."

"When did you stop seeing your son?"

"When he was six his mother remarried. At first I was jealous, but this man was good to Richard. He treated him like his own son. A year later he was offered a position in England. I objected at first, but my ex pointed out what was obvious. I didn't have time for my son and his stepfather did. She convinced me that it would be best if I let him go."

"That must have been devastating for you."

"It was the hardest thing I've ever done. I tried to keep in touch with phone calls and letters, but we drifted apart. I think he just didn't need me any longer."

He looked so sad that tears burned the corners of Anne's eyes. She reached out and placed a hand on top of his. Learning this was such a shock. Had she never considered that he had a life that she knew nothing about? Had she believed his life hadn't really begun until he'd come to work for them? That his world was so small and insignificant? "I'm so sorry, Geoffrey."

Even his eyes looked a bit misty. "I was saddened,

but by then I had you and your siblings to chase around. Only now I fear I made a terrible mistake by letting him go."

He looked so sad it made her want to hug him. "You did what you thought was best. And that doesn't mean you can't try to contact him now. Do you have any idea where he lives? What he does for a living?"

"The last time I talked to his mother, he was serving as a Royal Marine Commando."

"Goodness! That's impressive."

"She bragged that he was some sort of computer genius. But that was more than ten years ago."

"You could at least try to look him up."

He rubbed his thumb around the rim of his glass. "What if I do, and I don't like what I find?"

She wondered why he would think a thing like that. He should at least try to find him.

Geoffrey swallowed the last of his drink and looked at his watch. "It's nearly midnight. I should turn in. And so should you, young lady."

She smiled. He hadn't called her that in years. "Yes, sir."

As he walked past her to his quarters behind the kitchen he patted her shoulder. She was struck by how his capable hands were beginning to look wrinkled and bony.

She looked down and realized she hadn't taken a single sip of her tea, and now it had gone cold.

The king had been out of the public eye for such a long period of time that Sam was genuinely stunned when he saw him the following afternoon. Though he knew the king was in ill health, never had he expected him to look so pale and fragile. Practically swimming in too-large flannel pajamas and a bulky robe—that Sam was sure had probably fit him at one time—the king looked painfully thin and small. A mere shell of the larger-than-life figure he used to be. And it was obvious that the months of sitting at his side had visibly taken their toll on Anne's mother. The queen looked utterly exhausted and beaten down. Her features, once bright and youthful, now looked drawn and tired, as though she had aged a decade in only months.

But the grief they suffered did nothing to dampen their joy when Sam announced his intention to marry Anne and asked them for her hand. Though the king may have been physically fragile, when it came to his mental faculties, he was clearly all there. "I had hoped you would do the right thing, Sam," the king told him. "For my grandchild's sake."

"Of course you'll want to have the wedding soon," the queen told Anne. "Before you're really showing."

For a moment Sam felt slighted, since they had agreed to tell her parents together, then he glanced over at Anne, saw her stunned expression, and realized that she hadn't said a word.

So much for the news being too much for the king's heart to take, Sam thought wryly. His children obviously underestimated him.

"I'm going to kill Louisa!" Anne growled, looking as though she would do just that. "Or was it Chris who snitched?"

Sam folded his arms across his chest and casually covered his mouth to hide a grin. So this was the feisty side of Anne he had heard so much about. He kind of liked it.

"No one said a word," the queen assured her. "They didn't have to. I know my daughter."

"And though I may be an invalid," the king added, shooting a meaningful look Sam's way, "I stay well-informed as to what goes on in my castle."

Things like Sam sneaking out of his daughter's bedroom in the wee hours of the morning.

The king chuckled weakly. "Don't look so chastened. I was a young man once, too, you know." He looked over at his wife and smiled. "And there was a time when I did my fair share of sneaking around."

The queen reached over and took his hand and they shared a smile. It was clear that despite all they had been through, or maybe because of it, they were still deeply in love. Sam hoped that someday it would be like that for him and Anne.

"Why didn't you say anything?" Anne asked, looking genuinely distressed.

"Sweetheart," her mother said. "You've always been one to take your time and work things through. I assumed that when you were ready for us to know, you would tell us. And if you needed my guidance, you would have asked for it."

"You're not upset?" Anne asked, looking a bit like a naughty child who feared a sound lashing for misbehaving.

"Are you happy?" the king asked her.

She looked over at Sam and smiled. "I am. Very happy."

"Then what do I have to be upset about?"

"Well, the baby—"

"Is a blessing," the queen said.

Their casual attitude toward the situation surprised Sam, but then, after all they had been through, and knowing the king was living on borrowed time, what point would there be to make a huge fuss and create hard feelings?

Sam had always respected the king, but never so much as he did now. And despite what his father believed about them thinking *differently,* they seemed to be exceptionally well grounded in reality.

"I assume that you intend to live here, at the castle," the king said.

Anne glanced nervously his way. Where they would live hadn't yet come up, but Sam knew what was expected. "Of course, Your Highness."

"And of course you will work for the royal family."

Sam nodded. "I would be honored."

"Have you thought about what colors you would like for your wedding?" the queen asked Anne.

"Yellow, I think," Anne said, and she and her mother drifted off to discuss wedding plans while Sam spoke to the king about his future position in the monarchy. He assured Sam that his talents would not be wasted, nor would they go unrewarded. Sam's inheritance guaranteed him a financially sound future, so salary wasn't an issue, but he was happy to know they valued his service. And relieved that under the circumstances, this entire situation was running as smoothly as a well-oiled machine.

So well that, were he not such a positive thinker, he might be waiting for the other shoe to fall.

* * *

The following Friday, with only the royal family, Sam's parents and a few close friends in attendance, Sam and Anne were wed in a small, private ceremony in the garden on the palace grounds. The weather couldn't have been more ideal. Sunny and clear with a temperature in the low seventies.

Louisa was the matron of honor and Sam's older brother, Adam, flew in from England to be his best man. A musician and composer, Adam couldn't have been less interested in politics, yet the artist in him understood Sam's lifelong passion, and his desire to follow in their father's footsteps.

"You're sure you want to do this?" he asked Sam just before the ceremony was about to begin. "If you're doing this to salvage the princess's reputation—"

"I'm doing this because my child deserves to have parents who are married."

"A one-night fling does not make for a lasting relationship, Sam. You barely know her. If the royal family is forcing you into this—"

"This is my choice, and mine alone."

Adam shook his head, as though Sam were a lost cause. Then he grinned and said, "My baby brother, a *duke*. Who would have thought?"

Sam appreciated his brother's concern, that after all these years Adam was still looking out for him. But Sam had already put the political chapter of his life behind him. He'd spent the last two days cleaning out his office at work since, as of that morning, he had been given the official title of duke and by law could no longer serve in government. His secretary, Grace, had tearfully said goodbye, telling him what an exceptional boss he'd been and how she would miss him. She said she was proud of him.

"I know I haven't been the most efficient secretary and I appreciate your patience with me."

Of course he felt guilty as hell for all the times he'd gotten frustrated and snapped at her or regarded her impatiently.

After he and Anne returned from their honeymoon Sam would take up his new position with the monarchy. He couldn't say he was thrilled by the prospect, but he was trying to keep an open mind and a positive attitude. At least they didn't try to force him into their agricultural business. A farmer, he was not. He didn't know the first thing about managing farmland and raising crops. Nor did he have any inclination to learn.

His new goal was to surpass his new position as foreign affairs director and when Chris officially became king, become his right hand.

The music began, and Sam looked up to see Anne and her father taking their places. She wore a crème-colored floor-length dress with layers of soft silk ruffles. But even that did little to disguise the fact that she was pregnant. Not that everyone there didn't already know. He would swear that since she had come to see him last week her tummy had nearly doubled in size. But as far as he was concerned it only made her look more ravishing.

Her hair was piled up on her head in loose curls with soft wisps trailing down to frame her face. And of course she wore a jewel-encrusted tiara.

Everyone stood to receive her, and Sam watched,

mesmerized as she walked slowly toward him, looking radiant. She seemed to glow from the inside out with happiness.

It was obvious, the way the king clung to her arm as he walked her down the short path, that it was taking every bit of strength he could muster to make the short trip. But he did it with grace and dignity.

Here we go, Sam thought, as the king linked his and Anne's hands together. It was the end of life as he once knew it. But as they spoke their vows and exchanged rings, instead of feeling cornered or trapped, he felt a deep sense of calm. He took that as a sign that he truly was doing the right thing. Maybe not just for their child, but for the two of them, as well.

Following the ceremony, drinks and hors d'oeuvres were served under a tent on the castle grounds. After a bit of mingling, Sam stood by the bar, watching his new wife. She was chatting with his brother and Adam seemed quite taken with her. Under the circumstances Sam might have expected some tension between their families, but everyone seemed to get along just fine. Almost *too* well.

Price Christian stepped up to the bar to get a drink, and told Sam, "Nice wedding."

Sam nodded. "It was."

He got his drink then turned to stand beside Sam. "I've never seen my sister so happy."

She did look happy. And Sam was glad that his family had the chance to see this side of her, the one so unlike what they had read in the press and heard about through the rumor mill. He liked to think of this Anne as *his*

Anne, the real woman inside, whom he had rescued from an existence of negativity and despair.

They had done a lot of talking this week in preparation for their wedding and she'd opened up about some of the past men in her life. The ones who had used and betrayed her. After all she had been through, it was a wonder she hadn't lost her ability to trust entirely.

She saw him watching her and flashed him a smile.

"Your sister deserves to be happy," Sam told the prince.

"I think so, too." Then he added with a wry grin, "And if you ever do hurt her, I'll have to hurt you back."

Sam was quite sure, despite the prince's smile, it was said only partly in jest. "I'll keep that in mind, Your Highness."

From across the tent a baby's cry split the quiet murmur of conversation and they both turned to see Princess Melissa wrestling with two squirming bundles.

"I guess that's my cue," the prince said. He started to walk away, then stopped and said, "By the way, since we're family now, you can drop the 'Your Highness' thing and just call me Chris."

"After all these years of addressing you formally, that might take some getting used to."

"Tell me about it," Chris said with a grin before he walked off to rescue his wife.

Sam felt a hand on his arm and turned to see Anne standing there.

She slipped her arm through his and tucked herself

close to his side and said excitedly, "Can you believe it, Sam? We're *married*."

"Strange, isn't it?"

"Do you think it's odd that I'm so happy?"

"Not at all." He leaned down to brush a kiss across her lips. "I would be worried if you weren't."

"How soon do you think we can sneak out of here? I'm guessing that we could squeeze in some alone time before we leave for our honeymoon."

He was about to say, *as soon as possible,* when an explosion pierced his ears and shook the ground beneath his feet. Startled cries from the guests followed and Anne screeched in surprise. Sam instinctively shielded her with his body and looked in the direction of the sound as a ball of fire and smoke billowed up from the north side of the castle. At first he could hardly believe what he was seeing—his first instinct was to get Anne somewhere safe as quickly as possible—but before he had an instant to act, the entire area was crawling with security.

"What the bloody hell is going on?" Anne demanded, shoving past him to see, and when she saw the flames and smoke darkening the clear blue afternoon sky, the color drained from her face.

Security was already rounding everyone up and guiding them in the opposite direction, away from the blast.

"It's him," Anne said, looking more angry than afraid, watching as acrid smoke began to blow in their direction. "The Gingerbread Man did this."

Threatening e-mails and occasional pranks were an

annoyance, but this was a serious escalation. He was obviously out of control. If it was even him. "For all we know it could be an accident," he told her.

"No," she said firmly. "It's him. And this time he's gone too far."

Six

As Anne had suspected, the explosion had been deliberate.

The device had been hidden in the undercarriage of a car that belonged to Sam's aunt and uncle. The police bomb squad still had investigating to do, but as far as they could tell, the bomb had been detonated remotely.

Four other cars had been damaged in the blast and the castle garage had taken a serious hit. Four of the five doors would need to be replaced and the facade would require repair. Thankfully, no people had been seriously hurt. He'd had the decency to do it when there weren't a lot of people close by. Or maybe that had just been dumb luck. A few maintenance people walked away with mild abrasions and first-degree burns, but it could have been so much worse.

Sam's poor aunt and uncle, whose car had been sabotaged, were beside themselves with guilt. They felt responsible, even though Anne and her siblings assured them repeatedly that they were in no way being blamed. There was only one person responsible for this.

The Gingerbread Man.

They knew this for a fact now because shortly after the explosion he'd sent an e-mail to Anne via the security office.

Sorry I couldn't make it to your wedding.
Heard it was a blast.

"This has got to stop!" she told Chris, who sat slumped in a chair in the study, nursing a scotch. The wedding guests had all been driven home in the royal fleet—since their own cars had been casualties of the explosion—and most of the family had gone up to bed. Only she, Sam and Chris stayed behind to talk. Or in her case, castigate. She was so filled with nervous energy she hadn't stopped pacing, hadn't stopped moving in hours. "Someone could have been seriously hurt. Someone could have *died!*"

"You think I don't know that?" Chris said, looking exhausted. "We're doing all that we can. What else would you have me do?"

"You know what I think we should do," she said, and his expression went dark.

"That is *not* an option."

"What's not an option?" Sam asked from his seat on the settee. He had been so understanding about this, considering his wedding day had literally gone up in smoke. But she had warned him that being with her could potentially suck him into this mess. And so it had. She shuddered to think what would have happened if the Gingerbread Man had waited until the guests were leaving to sink the plunger. She was sure Sam had considered the same possibilities.

"She wants us to try to draw him out so we can catch him," Chris said.

"Draw him out *how?*"

"I assume by using one of us as bait."

Sam turned to look at her. "You're not serious."

"Maybe I trust our security team to do their job. Besides, no one else has had a better idea. How long are we supposed to go on like this? Living like prisoners, in fear of what he'll do next. He's obviously escalating the violence."

"Obviously," Chris snapped. He rarely lost his cool, so Anne knew that he was much more upset about this than he was letting on. "And now we know what he's capable of. He's not just some twisted stalker. He made a bomb. He's more dangerous than *any* of us anticipated."

"Okay," she acknowledged. "Maybe luring him out wouldn't be such a hot idea after all."

"I think that, in light of what happened, it would be best if you two canceled your honeymoon."

"What!" she screeched, indignation roiling up in her like a volcano. "You can't be serious."

"I'm very serious."

"But you're the one who suggested we go there, because it would be safe."

She and Sam had been invited by Chris's brother-in-law, King Phillip of Morgan Isle—the sister to Thomas Isle—to use their family hunting lodge. In fact, they should have been on a boat to the other island hours ago. If things had gone as planned, they would already be celebrating their honeymoon.

"I thought it would be the safest place for you, but—"

"Louisa went to Cabo for her honeymoon and no one gave her a hard time," Anne reminded him.

"Circumstances have changed."

"Chris, he *ruined* my wedding. I refuse to let him ruin my honeymoon, too. We'll have plenty of security there. We'll be *fine*."

He still looked hesitant.

"The location was kept so hush-hush that by the time he figures out where we are, and comes up with his next diabolical plan, we'll be back to the castle."

"All right," he finally agreed. "As long as you promise not to take any unnecessary risks."

"Of course." Did he think that she was a complete dolt? She wanted the man caught and brought to justice, but not so badly that she would endanger the life of her child.

Chris looked at Sam, who nodded and said, "We won't."

Is that how it would be now? Her family looking to her husband to keep her in line?

She realized she was clenching her fists and forced herself to relax. Getting this worked up wasn't good for her or the baby. What she needed was an outlet for all this tension and stress. And she didn't have to look far to find one.

She gazed over at Sam. Her *husband*. He was still wearing his wedding clothes but he'd shed the jacket and loosened his tie. The hair that had been combed back from his face earlier now fell forward in soft curls across his forehead. He looked too adorable for words and she couldn't wait to put her hands all over him.

Her wedding day may have been decimated, but they still had their wedding night. After four months of missing his touch, and a torturous week of waiting for this very night, she was determined to make it a memorable one.

"I'm exhausted," she announced, forcing a yawn for added effect, when in reality she was so awake she was practically buzzing. "Are you ready for bed, Sam?"

He nodded and rose from the settee.

"I'll arrange to have the boat ready for your trip to Morgan Isle at 10:00 a.m.," Chris told her.

"Thank you," she said, taking Sam's hand, leading him out of the study and up the stairs to her room. Make that *their* room. Most of Sam's clothes and toiletries had been moved in earlier that morning, which had necessitated her clearing a place in her closet for him. Sharing her space again would require some getting used to. Louisa and Anne had shared a bedroom until they were thirteen and Anne could no longer stand the frilly pink bedcovers and curtains, the childish furnishings. Furnishings Louisa had still used until a few months ago.

What Anne really hoped was that when this Gingerbread Man business was behind them, she and Sam could spend time at his grandmother's cottage. Away from her family and the confines of her title. A place where she could just be herself. A place where, unlike the castle, portraits of her relatives didn't stare accusingly from every hallway. And where she could make herself a cup of tea without feeling like an intruder in the kitchen. Where she could make love to her husband and not worry that someone on the opposite side of the wall would hear her.

Privacy. That was what she wanted. A place of her own.

"I need to apologize," Sam said.

She looked over at him. "For what?"

"Until today, I really didn't take this Gingerbread Man thing very seriously. It seemed more an annoyance than a serious threat. But when that car exploded, I swear I saw my life flash before my eyes."

She squeezed his hand. "I'm sorry I dragged you into this."

He looked at her and smiled. "I'm not. I just want you to be safe."

Which he had proven. The first minute or so after the blast was a bit of a blur, but the one thing she did remember with distinct clarity was the way he had used his own body as a shield to protect her. She could say with much certainty that in a similar situation, the men who had come before him would have ignored her entirely and saved their own asses.

And now it seemed only fair to reward him for his chivalry. Right?

They reached her room—*their* room—and the instant they were inside with the door closed, she launched herself at him. He let out a startled "Oof!" as she threw her arms around his neck and crushed her lips to his.

But it didn't take him long to recover from his surprise, before his arms went around her and he leaned in, took control of the kiss. In that single joining of their mouths, the tangling of their tongues, they seemed to unleash months of pent-up sexual frustration. She curled her fingers through his hair and sucked on his tongue, wishing she could crawl inside his skin, anything to be *closer* to him.

When they came up for air they were both breathing hard and he was wearing a slightly confused expression. "I thought you were exhausted."

"What was I supposed to say? Let's go upstairs so you can shag me silly?"

A slow smile curled his lips. "Is that what I get to do?"

"If you want to," she said, already knowing by the look in his eyes the answer was yes. She pulled the pins from her hair, shaking it loose and letting it spill down over her shoulders. His eyes raked over her and she could swear she actually felt his gaze caressing her skin.

"Unless you'd rather just go to sleep," she teased.

To answer her, he wrapped an arm around her waist, tugged her against him and kissed her. And kissed her.

And *kissed* her.

A part of her wanted to drag him to the bed, rip off his clothes, impale herself on his body and ride him to ecstasy. The other part wanted to take her time, draw out the anticipation and make this last.

She broke the kiss and backed out of his arms, wearing a come-and-get-me smile as she unzipped her dress and pulled it over her head. All she wore underneath was a beige lace bra and matching panties.

"Take it all off," he ordered, transfixed as she unhooked her bra and dropped it on the floor.

"They're bigger," she said, cupping her breasts in her palms.

"I don't care what size they are, as long as they're attached to you."

How was it that he always knew the exact right thing to say?

She gave each one a gentle squeeze, careful to avoid her nipples. They had been especially sensitive since the second month of her pregnancy. Sometimes just the brush of her pajama top made them hard and tingly, almost to the point of pain.

"The panties, too," he demanded.

She slid them down, anticipating the slow smile that curled his mouth when he realized what she was hiding—or more to the point *wasn't* hiding—underneath.

"I think I just died and went to heaven," he said.

"It was Louisa's idea," she told him, touching her fingers to the smooth skin from the recent Brazilian wax that her sister had *insisted* would drive Sam wild. If the look on his face was any indication, she was right.

"Louisa, huh?" He shook his head. "She just doesn't seem the type."

No kidding. For someone who had clung to her virginity until her engagement several months ago, Louisa seemed to know an awful lot about sex. "She said it enhances sensation."

"I guess we'll have to test that theory."

She was counting on it. She backed toward the bed and Sam watched as she pulled back the covers and draped herself across the mattress, letting her legs casually fall open. Giving him a view of the full package.

He started to walk toward her but she shook her head and said, "Uh-uh," and he stopped in his tracks. She gestured to his clothes. "Your turn to undress. Take it all off."

If there were a land speed record for disrobing, he probably broke it. And he had the most beautiful body she had ever seen. Long and lean and perfect. Simply looking at him made her feel all hot and fidgety and anxious.

"Lie down," he ordered.

She scooted over and lay back against the pillows. Sam crawled in and settled down beside her. She was so ready for him she ached, but she didn't want to rush this. She wanted to savor every second. Sam seemed content just lying there looking at her, lightly caressing the tops of her breasts, the column of her throat.

"You are so beautiful," he said, his eyes already shiny and heavy-lidded with arousal. He cupped her breasts, testing their weight in his hand, then he leaned over and licked the dark crest of one. She knew her nipples were sensitive, she just hadn't realized *how* sensitive until he nipped one with his teeth. Her body jerked violently, as though he were holding a live wire to her skin, and a strangled moan ripped from her throat.

He lifted his head, looking equal parts alarmed and intrigued. "What just happened?"

"I don't know," she said, her voice unsteady with shock and arousal. "I've never felt anything like that."

"Was it bad?"

"Not exactly. It felt…*electric*." Pleasure and pain all wrapped up in one.

"Should I stop?"

She shook her head. "Do it again."

"You're sure?"

She bit her lip and nodded. He lowered his head to try again and she grabbed his shoulders, bracing herself. But nothing could have prepared her for the assault of sensation as he sucked her nipple into his mouth. There was a tremendous, almost unbearably intense throb between her thighs, as if her breasts had somehow been hardwired directly to her womb. A moan rolled up from deep in her chest and her nails dug into his flesh. Then he did the same to the opposite side and she nearly vaulted off the bed, so far gone that she was on another planet.

Sam released her nipple and gazed down at her, looking fascinated, like a child who had just been handed a new toy. "Wow."

No kidding. This was completely crazy. He'd barely touched her and already she was hovering on the verge of an orgasm. Her body was so alive that if he so much as looked at her cross-eyed, she was going to lose it.

"If you do that again, I'll come," she warned him.

"Seriously?"

She nodded.

He looked like he wanted to, if for no other reason than to see if she really would. He even started to lean forward, then seemed to change his mind at the last second. Instead he pushed himself up, pressing her thighs apart and kneeling between them.

She thought he would enter her right away, but he leaned forward instead and licked her. Whether it was the bare skin enhancing things, or her fragile sexual state making it especially erotic, she couldn't really say. And didn't really care. All she knew was that it felt so out-of-this-world fantastic she actually forgot to breathe.

"I've been fantasizing about being with you since that night in your room," he said, pressing a kiss to her swollen belly. "I haven't been able to even look at another woman. I've only wanted you."

She threaded her fingers through his hair as he kissed and nibbled his way up her body, driving her mad. She was sure that was exactly what he intended. When he finally lowered himself on top of her, she was half out of her mind from wanting him and desperate for release.

He eased into her, one slow, steady, *deep* thrust, and a burst of electricity started deep in her core and zinged outward until only the boundaries of her skin kept it from jumping from her body to his.

His eyes locked on hers as he pulled back, then he rocked into her again, only this time she arched her hips up to meet him halfway and there were no words to describe the shocking pleasure, the sensations building inside her. It robbed her ability to think, to reason. All she could do was feel.

Every thrust drove her higher, closer to nirvana, then Sam clamped his mouth over her breast and her body finally let go. Pleasure flooded her senses in a violent rush, sinking in like a wild animal, feral and out of control.

Through a haze she heard Sam moan, heard him

say her name, felt his breath hot on her neck as his body locked and shuddered. In that instant nothing else mattered. It was just the two of them, just her and Sam against the world. Two souls twining and fusing in an irreversible bond.

She knew without a doubt that she loved him. And not just because he'd given her the best orgasm of her life. They were soul mates. She had known it the minute he'd taken her in his arms on the dance floor the night of the charity ball.

But she couldn't tell him. Not yet. The time just didn't feel right.

Sam started kissing her neck, nibbling her ears, whispering how delicious she tasted and she felt herself being dragged back under, into that deep well of desire. And before she even had a chance to catch her breath, he was making love to her all over again.

Seven

Considering it was owned by royalty, the hunting lodge on Morgan Isle was just about as stripped down and bare bones as it could be. It was a log cabin shell with a small kitchen, great room, two bathrooms—one on each floor—and four small, sparsely furnished bedrooms. Two upstairs, two down. And of course there were the obligatory stuffed dead animals all over the place.

There was no television or radio. No phone. Sam even insisted that he and Anne surrender their cell phones to Gunter, and made it clear that shy of a catastrophic disaster or urgent family matter, they were not to be disturbed. He didn't want a single thing to distract them from his primary goal. Get Anne naked and keep her that way for the next six days. And she seemed to have the same thing in mind. When he'd commented on her conspicuous lack of luggage—she'd brought only one small bag—she'd shrugged and said, "It's our honeymoon. What do I need clothes for?"

It was nice to know they were on the same page, since last night had been, by far, the hottest sex of his entire life. He'd been fantasizing about being with her for months, but the scenarios he'd created in his mind had paled in comparison to the real thing. And though he enjoyed getting off as much as the next man, nothing could have been more satisfying than watching Anne writhe and shudder in ecstasy. He'd made her come six times—*six times*—which under normal circumstances should have earned him some sort of accolade. But the truth was, he'd barely had to work at it.

He'd been with women who were difficult to please. But with Anne it didn't make a difference what position they happened to be in—if he was on top or she was, or if he took her pressed up against the shower wall, which he'd done twice. All he had to do was play with a nipple—a suckle or a pinch—and she went off like a rocket.

They probably could have gone for seven, but by then she was exhausted and clenching her legs together, begging him to let her sleep. And he'd figured it was only fair to let her reserve some of her strength for the actual honeymoon.

It was a cool day, so while she took a shower, Sam changed into jeans and a sweater and built a fire in the stone fireplace in the great room. He checked the cupboards and refrigerator and found they were stocked with enough food to last a month.

He was just putting on a kettle for tea when Anne appeared at the top of the stairs, her hair wet and twisted up, held in place with a clip, wearing a black silk robe. Sam couldn't help wondering if she wore anything underneath.

"I know this is a hunting lodge," she said. "But do there have to be so many *dead* things mounted on the walls?"

"Personally, I've never understood the appeal in killing defenseless animals," he told her, watching as she walked down the stairs. When she got the kitchen where he stood, she stopped, looked him up and down and smiled.

"What?" he asked.

"I've never seen you dressed so casually."

"It happens every now and then."

"I like it." She crossed the room to him and rose up to kiss him on the cheek.

She smelled clean and girly and looked delicious enough to eat. He was tempted to scoop her up and carry her off to bed that very instant, or even better, make love to her right there in the kitchen. The butcher-block table looked just the right height for fooling around, although it was pretty rough and scarred from many years of use. He didn't want her getting splinters in her behind. Besides, they had all week. It had been a hectic few days and it would be nice to just relax for a while. Maybe even take a nap. Anne had slept like the dead last night but Sam had tossed and turned, worrying about this Gingerbread Man business.

If something had gone wrong with that bomb, if they had hit a pothole and it had detonated too soon, his uncle and aunt—two of the sweetest people he knew—could have been blown to kingdom come. He agreed with

Anne that something needed to be done, but also saw Chris's point, and he was right, it wasn't worth putting someone's life at risk.

He and Chris would have to have a serious talk when Sam and Anne returned to Thomas Isle. Maybe it was time they considered a new course of action.

"Is everything okay?" Anne asked, her brow wrinkled.

"Of course. Why do you ask?"

"You sort of drifted off there for a second."

He smiled and kissed her forehead. "Just thinking about what a lucky man I am."

She wrapped her arms around his waist and snuggled against him. "I feel lucky, too."

"I was making tea. Would you like a cup?"

"I'd love one. Can I help?"

"You could find some honey. I think I saw it in the cupboard above the coffee maker."

She rooted around in the cupboard while he took two cups and a box of tea bags out.

Suddenly she gasped and stepped back, clutching her belly. "Oh my God!"

Thinking she'd hurt herself, or something was wrong with the baby, he was instantly at her side. "What's the matter? What can I do?"

She looked down at her stomach. "I think I just felt the baby kick."

"You did?"

She nodded excitedly. "When I was pressed up against the cupboard. I've felt flutters before, almost like butterflies in my stomach, but this was different. Like a poke." she said, demonstrating with her index finger on his stomach. "But from the inside. If you press down maybe you can feel it, too."

She unbelted her robe and pulled it open and—*bloody hell*—was naked underneath. She took his hand and pressed his palm firmly over her belly.

"I don't feel anything," he said.

"Shh, just wait a minute." She leaned into him, resting her head against his shoulder.

Looking down, he realized he must have gotten a little carried away last night. She had a few faint love-bites on her breasts. He was willing to bet that he'd find some on her neck as well, and maybe one or two on her inner thighs.

Maybe it was wrong, but with her pressed up against him, smelling so sexy, her skin soft and warm, her breath hot on his neck, he was getting a hard-on. And he definitely wasn't feeling the baby kick. Maybe it was too soon.

He started to move away but she held his hand firmly in place. "Just wait."

He was convinced he *wouldn't* feel anything, and when he actually did—a soft little bump-bump against his palm—he was so startled he almost pulled his hand away.

Her eyes darted up to his. "Did you feel it?"

He laughed in amazement. "I did."

She smiled. "That's our baby, Sam."

He felt it again. Another bump-bump, as if the little guy—or girl—was in there saying, *Hey, here I am*.

He'd heard that for men, feeling their baby move for the first time often made the experience more real, which he'd always thought was total bollocks. It felt bloody well real to him the moment she broke the news. But now, after experiencing it, he suddenly realized what they meant. That was *his* baby. No longer just a concept, but something he could feel.

He kept his hand there, hoping it would happen again, but after several minutes more Anne said, "He must be asleep again."

Sam smothered his disappointment and reluctantly pulled his hand away. The kettle had begun to boil, so Anne belted her robe and turned the burner off.

"Why don't we have our tea by the fire?" she suggested.

While he fixed it, she pilfered a fluffy down comforter from one of the beds and spread it out on the floor. He carried their cups over and set them on the hearth.

Anne let her hair down and flopped onto her back, the sides of her robe slipping apart over her belly. Instead of readjusting it, she tugged the belt loose and let the whole thing fall open. He certainly couldn't accuse her of being modest. Even that first night, during the ball, she hadn't been shy about taking it all off. And he could never get tired of looking at her body.

He sat cross-legged facing her, thinking that if the baby started to kick again he would be right there to feel it.

She closed her eyes and sighed contentedly. "The heat from the fire feels nice."

But a little too warm for the sweater he was wearing, so he pulled it up over his head and dropped it on the floor beside him. Anne was looking up at him, smiling.

"What?"

"You have a beautiful body. I like looking at it."

"The feeling is mutual."

"Does it bother you that I'm getting fat?"

He rolled his eyes. "You are *not* getting fat."

"You know what I mean," she said. "My belly is going to get huge."

"And it will look beautiful that way," he assured her, pressing a kiss just above her navel.

"You know, I already found a stretch mark. By the time I give birth I could be covered in them."

He examined her stomach but didn't see anything but smooth, soft skin. "I don't see any stretch marks."

"It's there."

"Where?"

She reached down, feeling around the lowest part of her belly. "Right here…see?"

He leaned in to get a closer look and saw what was, at best, a microscopic imperfection that may or may not have been an actual stretch mark. "It's tiny."

"Yes, but it will probably get bigger, until it's huge."

He seriously doubted that, but her concern surprised him a little. She'd never struck him as the type to be hung up on body image. She seemed so comfortable in her own skin. "You could be covered with them and I wouldn't think you were any less beautiful." He stroked the offending area. Her skin was warm and rosy from the heat coming off the fire. "In fact, I happen to think it's sexy."

She pushed herself up on her elbows. "And I think you're full of bunk."

"I mean it. If I found it off-putting, would I do this?"

He leaned down and kissed the spot, just a soft brush of his lips, and heard her inhale sharply.

When he lifted his head she had that heavy-lidded sleepy look that she got when she was turned on. And seeing her that way gave him an instant erection.

"See," he said.

"I think there might be another one," she said.

"Another stretch mark?"

She nodded solemnly.

"Really?" He manufactured concern. "Where?"

"This one is lower."

"How low?"

"Oh, a couple of inches, maybe."

He knew for a fact that there wasn't one *there,* but he stifled a smile. "I didn't see it."

She put a hand on the back of his head and gently pushed it down. "I think you should look closer."

Enjoying the game, he leaned in and pretended a thorough inspection, close enough that he was sure she could feel the whisper of his breath on her skin. He wasn't sure what the Brazilian wax was doing for her, but he sure was enjoying it.

After a minute or so he shrugged and said. "Sorry, I just don't see it."

He tried to straighten up and she not-so-gently shoved his head back down.

"Look *again.*"

He smiled to himself. "Wait…oh yes, I see it now. Right here." He pressed a kiss right at the apex of her puffy lips, paused, then swept his tongue between them.

Anne moaned and curled her fingers in his hair.

For a brief moment he considered torturing her a bit longer, but the sweet taste of her, her tantalizing scent drew him in like a bee to a flower. Unfortunately his jeans didn't have a lot of give, and he was so hard that a few more minutes of bending over like this was going to do mortal damage. He stretched out beside her in the opposite direction, relieving the pressure, and in a millisecond Anne was tugging at his belt. She worked with impressive speed and in seconds had his erection out of his pants…and into her mouth. It felt so damned fantastic, he might have swallowed his tongue if wasn't already buried in her.

Her mouth was so hot and wet and soft, and the damp ribbons of her hair brushing his stomach and thighs was unbelievably erotic. But when she reached into his jeans and cupped him…well, everything after that was a bit of a blur. A jumble of wet heat and intense pleasure, moans and whimpers that at times he wasn't sure were from him or from her. Or both. Too soon he felt his control slipping, but he never came first. It was against his personal code of conduct. He considered it selfish and impolite. Fortunately, he knew exactly what to do.

When he'd reached the point of no return, he slid a hand up to her breasts, took her nipple between his fingers and squeezed. She moaned, and her body started to quake, which sent him right over the edge with her. He would have cursed in blissful agony if his mouth hadn't been otherwise occupied. Afterward, she collapsed beside him and they lay side by side on the blanket, still facing opposite directions, breathing hard. He felt limp, as though every last bit of energy had been leeched from his body, and the heat from the fire was making him drowsy. Maybe now would be a good time for that nap.

His eyes drifted closed, but he felt Anne sit up beside him.

She gave him a shove. "Hey, wake up."

"I'm tired," he mumbled.

"But I'm not finished with you."

"I can't function. I need rest."

That didn't seem to deter her, because a second later he felt her tugging his jeans down and pulling them off. Now he was exhausted and *naked*. Did she really think that was going to help?

He opened one eye and peered up at her. She flashed him a wicked smile and, starting at his ankles, began kissing and licking her way up his body, and despite his fatigue, he was getting hard again. Apparently she wasn't taking no for an answer this time. And it looked as though that nap would have to wait.

If the perfect honeymoon included staying perpetually naked, eating hastily prepared meals on the floor by the fire and making love on a whim, Sam considered it safe to deem the first three days of their honeymoon a success. In fact, he would be a bit sorry when they had to return to real life.

He lay limp on the blanket in front of the fire, listening to the sound of the shower running overhead. He knew he should probably get up and throw something together for breakfast, as he'd promised Anne he would—the woman had a ravenous appetite lately—but he was so comfortable and relaxed he simply couldn't make himself move. Maybe food could wait, and instead he would pull her back down with him and make love to her one more time first. In the past three days he had mapped and memorized every inch of her, each curve and crevice. There wasn't a place on her body he hadn't caressed and kissed. In fact, it was quite possible that he knew her body better than his own.

What continued to astonish him was that, discounting those four months apart, technically, they had known each other the sum total of less than two weeks. Yet he had never felt so comfortable with a woman. With *anyone,* actually. It was as if they had known one another all their lives. He'd dated his share of women but he had never come close to finding one he could imagine spending the rest of his life with. One who was everything he had ever imagined a wife should be. He was beginning to wonder if he might have found his soul mate. And all because a few intoxicated mates had dared him to ask her to dance.

It was funny how fate worked.

A firm knock on the front door startled him. Sam cursed and pulled himself to his feet, grabbing a throw from the back of the davenport and wrapping it around his waist. As he crossed the room, the words *this better be important* sat on the tip of his tongue, ready to assault whoever was standing on the other side of the door.

The cool air rushing in didn't chill him even close to as much as the look on Gunter's face did. He didn't look upset, exactly. Gunter didn't show emotion. But there was something in his eyes that told Sam this wasn't going to be good news.

"Is urgent call from Prince Christian," Gunter said,

holding out Sam's cell phone. Sam's heart lodged somewhere south of his diaphragm.

"Thank you," he said, taking the phone. Gunter nodded and backed out the door, shutting it behind him. Deep down Sam knew, even before he heard Chris's solemn tone, what the prince was going to say.

"I'm afraid I have some bad news. The king passed away last night."

Sam cursed silently. "Chris, I'm so sorry."

"We'll need you and Anne back at the castle as soon as possible. I'm sure she'll want to see him one last time. Before…"

"Of course."

"Gunter will take you to an airfield not far from the lodge and a chopper will be waiting there. I've already arranged for your things to be brought back separately."

Chris certainly was on top of the situation, and Sam suspected that seeing to all the details was the only thing holding him together.

"Do you want me to tell her, or would you rather do it?" Chris asked.

"I'll tell her."

"Tell me what?" Anne asked.

Sam turned to find Anne standing behind him, wearing her robe, her hair still damp. He hadn't even heard her come down the stairs.

"We'll see you soon," Chris said and disconnected.

"Who was that?" Anne asked as he snapped the phone closed.

"Chris."

"What did he want?" she asked, though her expression said she already suspected.

"I'm afraid he had bad news."

She took a deep breath. "My father?"

He nodded.

"He's gone, isn't he?"

He took her in his arms and held her. "I'm so sorry."

She pressed her cheek against his chest and he could feel that it was already damp. "I'm not ready for this."

"I know." Even if they were ill, and suffering, was anyone ever ready to lose a parent?

Eight

Everyone was surprised to learn that it wasn't a heart attack. The king had just gone to sleep, and sometime in the night his heart had simply stopped beating. According to the physician, he hadn't suffered or felt a thing.

The only solace Anne could take was that he was finally at peace. The last few years had been so hard, and he'd put up one hell of a fight, but he had made peace with the fact that it was his time. Even if his family wasn't ready, he had been.

Chris and Aaron were somber and, like typical men, kept their feelings to themselves. Louisa cried constantly the first day, then miraculously seemed to pull herself together. The worst part was watching her mother cope, knowing that she must have been falling to pieces on the inside, but forcing herself to be strong for her children.

Anne was simply heartbroken. Her father would never know her children, and they would never see firsthand what a wonderful father, and grandfather, what a wonderful *man* he was. It just didn't seem fair that someone with so much to live for should be taken far too soon.

When she checked her e-mail the day of the funeral, reading condolences from friends and relatives, she found one from the Gingerbread Man, too. It said simply, *Boo Hoo.*

Anne had been so furious that she actually picked her laptop up and hurled it at the wall.

Those first few days after the service, she walked around in a fog, functioning on autopilot during the day and falling apart at night in the privacy of their bedroom, crying herself to sleep in Sam's arms while he stroked her hair and murmured soothing words. He was truly a godsend, taking care of her while dealing with the stresses of a new job.

But as the days passed it started to get easier. She began to focus not on her loss, but her new marriage and the baby who seemed to grow exponentially every day. Gradually everyone seemed to get back to their lives. Within a few weeks she and Sam had fallen into a comfortable routine. Before she knew it the day arrived when it was time for her ultrasound.

She drank what felt like *gallons* of water, and by the time they got to the royal family's private wing at the hospital she was in misery. Thank goodness the specialist was in the room and ready for them. When she lay back and exposed her belly he looked a little surprised.

"You're quite large for twenty-one weeks."

"Is that bad?" Sam asked, looking worried.

"Every woman carries differently," the doctor said as he squeezed cold goo on her belly, and used the wand thingy he was holding to spread it around. Images appeared on the screen immediately.

"Hmm." He nodded, his brow furrowed. "That would explain it."

Anne's heart instantly skipped a beat. She simply couldn't handle any more bad news.

"Is something wrong?" Sam asked.

"Not at all. So far everything looks great. I'll have to take a few measurements, but development seems to be just where it should be. For both of them."

At first Anne was confused, thinking he meant her and the baby, then the meaning of his words sank in and she was dumbstruck.

"Are you saying that there are two babies?" Sam asked. "We're having twins?"

The doctor pointed to the screen. "This is baby A, and over here is baby B."

"But there was only one heartbeat," Anne said.

"It's not uncommon for the hearts to beat in unison, making it difficult to differentiate between them. I'm sure your doctor explained that because you're a twin it was more likely you would have twins."

"Of course, but…"

"I guess that explains why you're so big already," Sam said, sounding surprisingly calm about this. In fact, while she was stunned, he looked as though he couldn't be happier.

"Would you like to know the sex of the babies?"

the doctor asked. She and Sam said "yes" in unison, then laughed because they were obviously very much in agreement.

"We'll see if we can get them to cooperate," he said, trying different angles. Then he pointed to the screen. "See there. This is baby A. There's the left leg, and the right, and see that protrusion in between?"

"A boy!" Sam said, beaming.

Baby B didn't want to cooperate, so he had Anne turn on her side, so the babies would shift position. "There we go!" the doctor finally said, pointing out both legs again, and there was no little protrusion this time.

"A girl," Anne said excitedly, squeezing Sam's hand. "One of each!"

The doctor took the measurements he needed and announced that everything looked wonderful. Her children were healthy, Sam was beaming with pride, and Anne could say with certainty that it was one of the happiest days of her life. After all that had happened lately, she figured they deserved it.

When the doctor was finished Anne dashed to the loo to empty her bladder before it burst. When she met Sam in the waiting room, he had an odd look on his face.

What if the idea of having twins had finally sunk in and he'd realized it was more than he bargained for? What if he was overwhelmed by the responsibility?

"What's wrong, Sam?"

"The doctor and I had an interesting discussion while you were gone."

"What kind of discussion? Is something wrong with the babies?"

"I voiced some concerns about you being on birth

control when you conceived. I was afraid it might cause complications or defects."

Anne's breath hitched. "What did he say?"

"He checked your chart."

Oh God. Anne's heart sank so hard and fast it left a hollow feeling in her chest. "Sam—"

"I want the truth, Anne. That night, when you said you had it covered, did you mean it, or did you lie to me?"

It felt as though the entire room had flipped on its axis and she had to grab the wall to keep from pitching over. "I can explain—"

"Did. You. *Lie.*" He was angry. Not just angry, but seething mad. This man who had never so much as raised his voice looked as though he wanted to throttle her.

She had to force the words past the lump of fear blocking her throat. "Yes, but—"

The door opened and Gunter stuck his head in to tell them the car was ready.

"Sam," she said, but he silenced her with a sharp look and said, "When we get home."

The ride back to the castle was excruciating. Sam sat silently beside her, but she could feel his anger. It seemed to fill the car, until it became difficult to breathe. Or maybe that was her guilty conscience.

There had to be a way to fix this. To make him understand.

When they got back they went straight to their room and Sam closed the door firmly behind him. Then he turned to her and in a voice teeming with bitterness said, "I should have known."

"Sam…" She tried to touch his arm but he jerked it away.

"I was raised on the principle that royals are never to be trusted, that they always have an agenda. I knew it that night, and still I ignored my instincts."

It crushed her that he would ever think of her that way. Yet she couldn't deny she slept with him knowing they were unprotected. "It's not what you think. I didn't have any agenda. I wasn't trying to trap you."

"So, you just wanted sex."

He made it sound so sleazy. He had been there, too, he knew damn well how deeply they had connected. He had wanted her, too. "I wanted you, Sam, and I honestly didn't think I would get pregnant. The timing was completely off."

"So what you're saying is, with no regard to anyone but yourself and your own selfish needs, you took a chance. You didn't even have the decency to stop and consider the repercussions of your actions, and how it might affect me."

When he said it that way, it *was* pretty awful.

"I'm sorry," she said in a whisper, because suddenly she couldn't seem to draw in a full breath, as though his animosity was leeching all the oxygen from the air.

"You're *sorry*," he said, spitting out a rueful laugh. "You stole *everything* from me and all you can say is you're sorry?"

"I made a mistake. I know. But I love you, Sam."

"You love me?" he said, astonished. "Playing Russian roulette with my future? Lying to me? You call that *love?* I think there's only one person here that you give a damn about, Your Highness, and that's you."

He couldn't be more wrong. She hated herself right now. For not having the guts to tell him the truth right away. "Sam, I just wanted—"

"You wanted to screw me," he said. "And I guess you succeeded because as far as I can see, I am thoroughly screwed."

He yanked the door open and stormed out, slamming it behind him.

Anne's heart was pounding and she was trembling so hard her legs wouldn't hold her upright. She slid down the wall to the floor, her legs finally folding under her like a marionette whose strings had been cut.

Sam was right. Everything he said about her was true, and he had every right to be furious with her. But was he mad enough to leave her? To demand a divorce?

Maybe after he had some time to cool down and think things through, he would remember how happy he'd been and how good they were together.

And what if he didn't? What then?

The worst part was that she had no one to blame for this mess but herself. And the happiest day in her life had just turned into her worst nightmare.

Anne didn't know where Sam went, but she learned from Gunter that he took his own car and left without a bodyguard. Which, considering the Gingerbread Man's escalating violence, probably wasn't the smartest idea, but she was in no position to be telling him what to do.

He had arranged to take the afternoon off for the ultrasound, so she knew he probably wasn't at the office. He could be anywhere. And even if she did know where he went, there was nothing she could do about it. She needed to give him space, time to think things through.

She wasn't the least bit hungry, but with two babies growing inside her, she knew skipping meals wasn't an option. But since she didn't feel like facing her family—and any questions—she asked Geoffrey to bring her dinner to her room. She was so beside herself she couldn't choke more than a few bites down.

To kill time while she waited for Sam, she started a list of all the baby things they were going to have to get. They would need two of everything. And they were going to have to think about names. It still amazed her that she was having twins, and she realized her family didn't even know yet. But that was the kind of news she and Sam should announce together.

A little later Louisa knocked on her door and Anne called for her to come in.

"I'm not disturbing you, am I?" Louisa asked, peeking her head in and looking around for Sam.

"I'm alone."

She stepped inside. "Oh, where's Sam?"

If she told Louisa they'd had a fight, she would have to tell her why, and she was too ashamed to admit how badly she had screwed things up.

"He had a thing with his parents," she said, keeping it vague. "I was supposed to go, but I wasn't feeling well."

Louisa frowned. "Are you all right?"

"Fine, just normal pregnancy stuff."

She flopped down on the bed beside her. "Is that why you didn't come down for dinner?"

"I had Geoffrey bring me a tray."

"Mother ate with us again."

"That's good," Anne said. For months now, since their father became so ill, he and their mother shared dinner in their suite. And right after the funeral she continued to eat alone, until they all finally talked her into coming back down to the dining room.

"She told Chris that she thinks he and Melissa and the triplets should move into the master suite. Since he is king now. And there's five of them and just one of her."

"What did he say?"

"At first he said no, but she insisted, so he said he would think about it. Maybe she just has too many memories there."

"She shouldn't rush into anything. It hasn't even been a month. She needs to give herself time to grieve."

"I agree, but try telling her that. And people wonder where we got our stubborn streak."

One of the babies rolled and Anne placed a hand on her belly.

"Kicking?" Louisa asked, putting a hand beside Anne's. She loved feeling the baby move.

"More like rolling."

"I wish I were pregnant, too," she said, looking sad.

"It'll happen. It's only been a few months. Sometimes it takes a while." And sometimes it worked on the first shot, whether she wanted it to or not.

"Well, it's certainly not for a lack of trying. Last night alone—"

"Please," Anne interrupted. "Spare me the gory details. I believe you."

Louisa grinned. "I'm pushing thirty. If I'm going to have six kids, I have to get the ball rolling. Besides, don't you think it would be fun if we were pregnant together?"

"We still could be. I've got nineteen weeks to go." Although maybe less, because the doctor said it wasn't uncommon for twins to come as much as four weeks early. That meant she and Sam could be parents in only *fifteen* weeks.

"Well, if not this time then the next," Louisa said with a shrug. But Anne didn't tell her there wouldn't be a next time. She hadn't even been sure she wanted *one* child. Two kids, especially since she was having one of each gender, was going to be her limit.

She wanted so badly to tell Louisa about the ultrasound. It was right there on the tip of her tongue, dying to come out, but she restrained herself. She and Sam should tell everyone together and she didn't think it was fair to deprive him of that. And she didn't want to give him yet another reason to be mad at her.

After Louisa left—probably to work on making that baby with Garrett—Anne picked up a novel she'd been meaning to start. Even though it was written by one of her favorite authors, she just couldn't concentrate. Her mind kept wandering and her eyes drifting to the clock on the bedside table.

It was going on eleven. Where could he be?

At midnight she finally changed into her pajamas and crawled into bed, but she couldn't sleep. It was after one when Sam finally opened the bedroom door and stepped inside.

Her heart stalled, then picked up double-time.

He went to the closet to change, the light cutting a path though the darkness. Then the light went out and she heard him in the bathroom. The shower turned on and she lay in the darkness listening and waiting. Finally the bathroom door opened, the light went out and he walked to the bed. She could smell the scent of soap and shampoo as he climbed in beside her.

For a long moment she lay silent, afraid to make a sound, afraid that he was still angry. She waited to see if he made the first move, but after several minutes he hadn't said a word. Maybe he thought she was asleep.

She rolled on her side facing him and asked, "Can we talk about this?"

"There's nothing to talk about."

"Sam…" She laid a hand on his arm but he shrugged it away. "Please."

"Nothing you could say or do will erase what you did to me."

His words cut deep and she realized he wasn't even close to being ready to forgive her. "I understand. So long as you know that when you're ready to talk, I'll be here."

He sat up suddenly and switched on the light, blinding her for a second. When her eyes adjusted she saw that he looked tired, and angry and…betrayed. "You don't get it. I know what you did, and why you did it, and nothing you can say will ever change it. You stole my life from me. It's done. I'm not just going to get over it."

Her heart sank. He didn't even want to try to forgive

her? To understand her side of it? He was just going to give up?

She had grown to love Sam, but obviously for him, she was as easily discarded as a used tissue. "So what are you saying? That it's over?"

"We both know that isn't an option. Like you said, once we're married, that's it. Royals don't do divorce."

Her relief was all encompassing. And it must have shown because he added hastily, "Don't think for a second that I'm doing this for you. I'm staying married to you for my children. That's it."

Yes, but as long as he was still there, still a part of her life, he would eventually have to forgive her. He couldn't stay mad forever.

"I didn't tell anyone our news yet," she said. "About the twins. I thought we should announce it together."

"You needn't have bothered waiting. I already told my parents. Tell your family whenever and whatever you want. It really doesn't matter to me."

His words cut so deep, she wouldn't have been surprised to find blood on her pajamas.

With that he switched off the light and lay back down, turning his back to her. A clear indication that the conversation was now over. Though her stubborn, argumentative side wanted to push, she forced herself to let it go. She just needed to give him time. Eventually he would remember how happy they'd been, how good they were together.

Sam may have never said he loved her, but she knew he did. She could feel it. And people didn't fall out of love instantly. The fact that he was feeling so angry and betrayed was a sure sign that he cared deeply for her. Otherwise it wouldn't matter what she had done to him.

It simply had to work out. Because the alternative was not an option.

Nine

How had Sam gotten himself into this mess?

He sat at his desk, in his new office—which he couldn't deny was far larger and more lavish than even his father's, with a secretary on the other side of the door who had already proven herself more than competent—contemplating the disaster that was now his life.

Their marriage was supposed to be perfect. And it had been. They had been happy. Right up until the instant he learned that it was all a lie.

People had always accused him of being too laid-back and easygoing. Too trusting, especially for a politician. But he had always considered it one of his strengths. Now it would seem that everyone had been right, and his ignorance had finally come back to bite him in the ass.

However, that wasn't a mistake he intended to make again.

All he'd ever wanted was a marriage like his parents had. He wanted a partner and a soul mate. He wasn't naive enough to believe there wouldn't be occasional disagreements or spats. That he could live with. But what Anne had done to him was unforgivable. And not just the part when she lied about the birth control. She'd had a chance to redeem herself and tell him the truth when she came to tell him about the baby. Instead she had lied to him again. And she kept lying.

Now he was trapped in a marriage with a wife he could never trust. Never love, even if he'd wanted to. And he had been close. So close that the thought of his gullibility sickened him.

At least something good had come out of this miserable union. Three things actually. His son and his daughter. He would never consider a child anything but a blessing—no matter the circumstances of its conception—and he would never hold them responsible for their mother's deception.

The third good thing was his job with the royal family. He'd always been a people person, and in his new position as foreign ambassador, communication was the main thrust of his position. He actually looked forward to going to work every morning. Even before it meant getting away from his wife. So of course the last thing he wanted to do was put that position in jeopardy. And despite what Anne had done to him, he didn't doubt her family would take her side. Sam could easily find himself working out of an office the size of a closet pushing papers. Or even worse, they might delegate him to work in their agricultural department, possibly picking weeds in the fields, so he figured it was in his best interest not to let anyone know that he and Anne were, for all intents and purposes, estranged.

But it wasn't easy to play the doting newlywed husband when he was so filled with resentment. And though he hadn't yet discussed it with Anne, he was quite sure she would agree to the charade. She owed him that at least.

It had taken him hours to finally fall asleep last night, and when he woke this morning he almost reached for her, the way he usually did. Making love in the mornings had become a part of their regular routine.

Then he remembered what she had done and rolled out of bed instead.

He didn't doubt that he would miss the sex. When it came to sexual compatibility, they were off the charts. But he couldn't abide by having sex with a woman whom he no longer respected. One he didn't even like.

She had still been sleeping, or pretending to, when he left for work. He usually ate breakfast with the family, but he'd had no appetite this morning. Now it was barely eight-thirty and he'd already been in the office forty-five minutes. But it was better than being at home. With her.

At nine Chris knocked on his door. "I hear congratulations are in order."

Sam must have looked confused, because Chris added, "Twins?"

"Oh, right!" Of course, Anne must have told them this morning.

Chris laughed. "Don't tell me you forgot."

"No, I just…" He shook his head. "Busy morning. And I didn't sleep well last night."

"As the parent of triplets, I can tell you it's not quite as daunting as it sounds. Not yet anyway. Get back to me when they're teenagers."

"It was definitely a surprise, but we're both thrilled." At least, she had seemed thrilled. Until the walls caved in on them.

"And like Anne said, you get one of each, so you don't have to go through this again."

A wise decision in light of the situation. Not that he'd have wanted more than that anyway. Two was a nice tidy number. It seemed to suit his parents fairly well. Although he was sure his mother would have liked a little girl to spoil. He was sure a granddaughter would be the next best thing. And he was happy to be able to give her that.

"Of course," Chris added, "I understand some women enjoy being pregnant. Melissa was carrying three, so it wasn't the easiest of pregnancies. But Anne seems to be doing well."

Sam wasn't sure how Anne felt about being pregnant. Other than a few halfhearted gripes about stretch marks and occasional complaints about heartburn, if she had reservations, he didn't hear about them. Even when she was getting sick she didn't grumble about it. Truth be told, she was fairly low maintenance for a princess. "I imagine it will get uncomfortable closer to her due date. Her only concern at this point seems to be stretch marks."

"That was a big issue for Melissa, too. But it's kind

of an inevitability with multiples, I think. Mel has a list of plastic surgeons she's considering already."

"I guess that means you're stopping at three?"

"Neither of us wants to take another spin on the fertility roller coaster."

It struck Sam as ironic that Chris and Melissa had worked so hard to have a child, while Sam and Anne, who weren't even trying, hit the jackpot the first time. Maybe she had been thinking the same thing that night. Not that it was an excuse to put his future on the line without his knowledge. If she had been honest and said that she wasn't taking birth control, but the timing was off and she most likely wasn't fertile, he might have said what the hell and slept with her anyway. But that would have been *his* choice. She had deprived him of that.

Chris's cell phone rang, and when he looked at the display said, "It's Garrett."

He answered, and not ten seconds into the conversation Sam could see by his expression that something was wrong.

He listened, nodding solemnly, then asked, "Were there any injuries?"

Sam sat a little straighter is his chair. Had there been another incident?

"How bad?" Chris asked. He listened for another minute, his expression increasingly grim, then said, "I'll be right over."

He shut his phone and told Sam, "I have to get to the east field greenhouse facility."

Sam knew that was the heart of the royal family's vast organic farming business. When an unidentifiable blight infected the crops there last year, it put the economic fate of the entire island in jeopardy.

"Did something happen there?" he asked.

"Yeah, it just blew up."

It was a bomb identical to the one detonated at Anne and Sam's wedding, activated remotely from God only knew where, and was hidden in the men's loo. The force actually shot a commode through the roof and it had come crashing down on a car parked in the lot several hundred feet away. Thankfully an *empty* car. But half a dozen people were injured in the blast, two of them with third-degree burns, and one with shrapnel to his eye that could possibly cost him his sight. The greenhouse itself had sustained hundreds of thousands of pounds' worth of damage.

A busload of school children had been scheduled to tour the facility only an hour later and Anne shuddered to think what would have happened if he'd detonated the bomb then. That alone was cause for great relief as the family gathered in the study after dinner the following night to discuss the investigation. The only other bright spot in this tragic situation was that this time the Gingerbread Man had made a crucial error. He'd allowed himself to be caught on surveillance. And not just the top of his head this time. This was a straight-on, up-close-and-personal view of his face.

He'd entered the facility the previous day posing as a repairman. He had the proper credentials so no one seemed to think twice about letting him in. He wore a cap, and kept his head down so that the brim covered his face. It was sheer dumb luck that, on his way out, someone carrying a large piece of equipment bumped into him in the hallway, hitting his cap and knocking it off his head. For a split second he jerked his head up and just happened to be standing under a surveillance camera. If they had planned it, it couldn't have been more eloquent.

"He's not the monster I expected," Louisa said, looking at the still shot of his face that had been taken from the tape. It had already been distributed to the authorities and would run on the national news. Someone would recognize him, meaning it was only a matter of time before he was identified and apprehended.

"He looks…intense," Liv said, taking the photo from Louisa to study it. "It's his eyes, I think. There's an intelligence there."

"If he's so intelligent," Aaron quipped, "why did he make a mistake?"

"Intelligent or not, it was inevitable that he would eventually screw up," Chris said, taking the photo, giving it another quick look, then setting it on the bar before he walked over to sit next to their mother on the settee. "This nightmare is almost over."

"This would have pleased your father," she said with a sad smile. "It's about time we had some good news. We should have a toast, to celebrate. Don't you think?"

"I'm all for a little celebrating," Aaron said.

"I'm sure we could scrounge up a bottle or two of champagne," Chris said, ringing Geoffrey.

"Champagne please, Geoffrey," their mother said, when he stepped into the room.

Geoffrey nodded and said, "Of course, Your Highness."

"Water for me," Anne told him.

"Me, too," Melissa added as he walked to the bar.

"I thought you stopped nursing," Louisa said.

"I did. But champagne makes me groggy and I have to be up for a 2:00 a.m. feeding."

That would be her and Sam in a few months, Anne thought, and she could only hope their situation had improved by then. And as much as she wanted the Gingerbread Man caught, it was difficult to feel like celebrating.

All evening Sam had acted as if nothing was out of the ordinary, but she knew that was for her family's sake. They had agreed that it would be best if they kept up the ruse of being happily married newlyweds. The kind who no longer had sex. Or *spoke*. At least she would be spared the humiliation of having to admit that barely a month after their wedding they were already having issues.

There was a sudden crash behind the bar and everyone turned simultaneously to look.

"My apologies," Geoffrey said, leaning down to clean up the glass he'd dropped. Anne was standing close by so she walked around to help him, picking up some of the larger pieces. She noticed, as he swept the smaller shards into a dustpan, that his hands were shaking, and when he stood, his face looked pale.

She took his hand. It was ice cold. "Are you okay?"

"Arthritis," he said apologetically, gently extracting it from her grasp.

She helped him pour the champagne and when everyone had a glass they toasted to the new lead in the investigation.

"I have an excellent idea," their mother said. "You kids should play poker. It is Friday."

Everyone exchanged a look. Friday used to be poker night, but since the king's death they hadn't played.

"We could do that," Chris said.

"I'm in," Aaron piped in, then he turned to Sam. "Do you play?"

"Not since college, but I'm pretty sure I remember how."

Like sharks smelling fresh blood in the water, Chris and Aaron grinned.

"Count me in, too," Garrett said.

"I think I'll head down to the lab instead," Liv said.

"You don't play poker?" Sam asked her.

"We don't let her," Aaron said, shooting her a grin. "She cheats."

Liv gave him a playful shove, her cheeks turning a bright shade of pink. "I do not!"

"She counts cards," Aaron said.

"Not on purpose," she told Sam. "It's just that when it comes to numbers I have a photographic memory."

"How about you, Anne?" Chris asked. "You up for a game?"

Though Anne normally played, she figured it might be a better idea to give Sam some space. Maybe relaxing with her brothers, not to mention a few drinks, would make him forget how angry he was with her. "I don't think so."

"Why don't you help me get the triplets ready for bed," Melissa suggested. "For practice. After that, having two babies will feel easy."

"I'd love to."

"I'll help, too!" Louisa said excitedly.

"I thought we could watch a movie," their mother said.

"Of course," Louisa said with a bright smile, though Anne guessed that deep down she preferred to help Melissa.

Everyone went their separate ways and Anne followed Melissa to the nursery.

"Have you decided if you're taking the master suite?" Anne asked her.

"I don't know. It just seems like it should belong to the queen."

"Have you forgotten that you *are* the queen?" When Chris became king, Melissa automatically became queen, and their mother was given the title of Queen Mother. Which was technically more of a lateral move than a demotion.

"It's just really hard to fathom," Melissa said. "Three years ago I didn't even know I was a royal. But I can't deny it would be nice to have all the space."

Instead of going into the nursery, Melissa walked past it to her and Chris's bedroom and opened the door.

Anne stopped, confused. "I thought…"

"The nanny put them to bed already. I wanted to talk to you, and I didn't want to say anything in front of everyone else." She gestured Anne inside.

Anne got a sinking feeling in her chest. Was she so transparent that Melissa had figured out something was wrong? Or had she heard Anne and Sam fighting the other night?

They sat on the sofa by the window and Anne held

her breath. If Melissa did ask about Sam, what would Anne say? She didn't want to lie, but she had promised Sam, for the sake of his job, not to tell anyone.

"I wanted to talk to you about something. About Louisa."

Anne felt a mix of relief and confusion. "Louisa? What did she do?"

"Oh, she didn't do anything. It's just…something happened." She stopped and sighed.

"What happened?"

"Chris and I are going to be making an announcement, and I'm afraid she's going to be upset. I talked to your mother, but she suggested I talk to you. You know Louisa better than anyone. I thought maybe you could think of a way that we could…soften the blow."

"What could you possibly have to say that would make her so up—" She gasped when she realized there really was only one thing. "Oh my God! Melissa, are you *pregnant?*"

She bit her lip and nodded. "I took a test today."

"Already?" She laughed. The triplets were barely four months old.

"This obviously wasn't planned. I was all ready to schedule my tummy tuck. After the fertility hell we went through, and the in vitro, I didn't think I could even get pregnant naturally. Not to mention that you're not supposed to be able to get pregnant while you're nursing. As far as I can tell, it had the opposite effect on me. If we had known it was even a possibility we would have been a lot more careful."

"How far along are you?"

"Probably four or five weeks."

"So your children will be almost exactly a year apart."

"Don't remind me," she groaned.

"Six babies born within a year." Anne shook her head in disbelief. "We're going to have to build another wing onto the castle."

"Which is why I'm worried about Louisa. She's so desperate to get pregnant. Have you looked at Garrett lately? The poor guy is exhausted."

"Yeah, but he's always smiling."

"Still, she's so…fragile. I'm afraid this might put her over the edge."

That was a common misconception. But Louisa was a lot tougher that she let people think. "First off, Louisa is not that fragile. And second, if the tables were turned, you know she wouldn't hesitate to announce her news to the entire world. Even if that meant hurting someone's feelings."

Melissa nodded. "You've got a point."

"Louisa has never been a patient person. When she wants something, she doesn't like to wait for it. But she and Garrett have only been trying for a couple of months. It can take time. She's going to have to accept that."

"So you really think I shouldn't worry?"

"I do. And if she does get upset, she'll get over it."

"Thank you," she said, taking Anne's hand and giving it a squeeze.

They talked about Anne's pregnancy for a while, and she pretended that everything was okay. That she wasn't miserable and scared. It had only been two days, but what if Sam really couldn't forgive her? Could she stay with a man who resented her so? Would she even want to?

When he came to bed that night she was already under the covers but wide-awake. He didn't say a word. He just crawled in beside her, facing away. She wasn't sure how relaxing the game had been, but she could tell from the whiff of alcohol that he'd been drinking. Still, he didn't even kiss her good-night. On top of that, she had a case of heartburn that wouldn't quit and her back was aching. She slept in fits and starts, and finally crawled out of bed around six-thirty and wandered down to the kitchen for a glass of milk.

She was surprised to find Chris there, still in his pajamas, drinking coffee and reading the paper.

"You're up early," she said, pouring herself a glass of milk.

"It was my morning for the 4:00 a.m. feeding," he said, setting the paper aside. "Then I couldn't get back to sleep. I'll be very happy when the triplets are sleeping through the night."

"Isn't that what you have nannies for?"

"Only to assist. Mel and I agreed that if we were going to have children, we wouldn't rely on the hired help to do all the dirty work."

"Excuse me, Your Highness."

They both turned to see Geoffrey standing in the doorway to his residence behind the kitchen. He looked terrible. His hair was mussed, his eyes red and puffy, as though he hadn't slept a wink all night. Though she had never once seen him emerge in anything but his uniform, he was wearing a velour robe over flannel pajamas. The idea that maybe he really was sick made her heart sink. Chris looked concerned, as well.

"I was hoping to have a word with you," Geoffrey said.

"Of course, Geoffrey, what is it?"

He walked over to where they stood. He had a sheet of paper clutched in his hand. The surveillance photo of the Gingerbread Man, she realized. He set it down on the countertop.

"I need to speak with security, about this photo."

"You recognize him?" Anne asked.

Geoffery nodded. "I do."

"Who is he?" Chris asked.

"This man," he said, in an unsteady voice, "is my son."

Ten

His name was Richard Corrigan.

The entire family was shocked and saddened at learning he was Geoffrey's son, but at least now they had a good idea what had started this whole thing.

According to Richard's mother, whom Geoffrey contacted immediately, he had always deeply resented the royal family. Especially the children, whom he felt his father had chosen over him. But his bitterness didn't manifest into violence until recently.

He was Special Forces in the military and highly decorated, until an assignment gone terribly wrong in Afghanistan, where he saw many of his fellow soldiers brutally slain, left him suffering from PTSD. Rather than giving him the counseling he needed, he was discharged from the service instead. Apparently he snapped, and started to blame the royal family for his troubles.

The reference to the nursery rhymes, Geoffrey suspected, dated back to when Richard was small and he would read to him. He admitted that deep down he suspected it might be his son months ago, but he hadn't wanted to believe it. He thought it might be his own guilty conscience playing tricks on him. Only when he saw the photo could he no longer deny the truth.

In his guilt and grief Geoffrey tried to quit, but no one would accept his resignation. He was a part of the family and families stuck together. Chris assured him that when Richard was apprehended, he would see to it personally that he got the psychiatric help he needed.

Unfortunately, after a month, and a worldwide bulletin calling for his capture, he hadn't been arrested. There had been dozens of reported sightings and tips called in, but none of them panned out.

Anne couldn't help thinking that their champagne celebration had been hasty and they may have jinxed themselves irrevocably. And though she wanted to believe that he would be caught before he detonated another bomb and hurt more people, her life in general was in such a shamble, she couldn't help but expect the worst.

It had been a long and miserable month since their fight, but Sam still hadn't come around. It wasn't even that he was bitter or unkind. At least to that she had defenses. What she couldn't bear, what was slowly eating away at her, was the indifference. The silence. They only spoke when it was necessary, and even then she usually got one-word answers from him. He often worked late, or went out for drinks with his friends. He kept up the ruse of their happy marriage in front of her family, for which she was infinitely grateful, but otherwise, he ignored her.

She didn't understand how he could go from being so sweet and attentive to acting as though she didn't exist. Was it really so easy for him to shut her out, to flip his emotions on and off like a light switch?

In a month he hadn't so much as kissed her, and though she had tried a few time to initiate sex, she was met with icy indifference. She suspected that given the choice, he would opt to not share a bed with her any longer. What was the point when he had drawn a very distinct and bold invisible line down the center of their mattress? But it was her experience that men could only go so long without sex before they explored alternative options, and she couldn't help worrying that it was only a matter of time before he came home smelling of another woman's perfume.

For that reason alone, and despite the indignity of his perpetual cold shoulder, she continued to try to seduce him. She waited until nights when she knew he was in a particularly good mood, when his defenses might be down. She kept thinking that if they made love, reminded him how good it used to be, it would make him want to forgive her.

She kept telling herself that if she was persistent, eventually he would give in, and if she kept him sexually satisfied, he wouldn't think about straying. Even if he couldn't love her, at least he would be faithful.

Then she began to wonder if he was refusing her advances not because of their fight, but because he was completely turned off by her body. Maybe, with her huge belly and expanding hips, she disgusted him to the point that he couldn't stand to even touch her. Maybe their fight had been a convenient excuse to act on feelings he'd been having as far back as their honeymoon.

With the seed planted, the idea began to fester, until she became convinced Sam was disgusted by her body. Until the sight of her own reflection in the mirror disturbed and humiliated her. She stopped undressing in front of him and began showering with the lights off so she wouldn't have to look at herself.

She had never been one of those women with body issues. She had always been comfortable in her own skin, and didn't particularly care what anyone thought. Being in the public eye, Anne found that people didn't hesitate to voice their very critical opinions. Now it consumed her thoughts. She dressed in baggy clothes and oversize sweaters to hide the grotesque curves.

She had herself so convinced that she was hideous that she gave up on trying to seduce Sam. She threw in the towel and resigned herself to the inevitable. Eventually he was going to find someone else to satisfy him sexually. They were going to be one of *those* couples. The kind who kept up the ruse of their marriage for appearances, even when rumors of infidelity became common knowledge. In public people would stare and whisper behind her back. Sam's friends would be polite to her face and snicker when she was out of earshot.

"Poor Princess Anne," they would say. "Too naive to realize she's been played the fool."

The possibility was like the final hit to the spike that he had slowly been driving through her heart.

Anne had been going to bed earlier and earlier lately, so when Sam came home late from work one evening, he wasn't surprised to hear that at nine, she had already gone upstairs.

After a quick bite in the kitchen, and a short conversation with Chris about the conference call they had both stayed late for, Sam headed upstairs. He expected Anne to be asleep already, but the bed was empty. He walked into the closet to change out of his suit and heard the shower running. The bathroom door was open a crack, and he had to fight the urge to peek inside, to get a glimpse of her.

Despite everything that had happened, he was still sexually attracted to Anne, still desired her with an intensity that sometimes had him taking cold showers to control his urges and waking in the middle of the night in a cold sweat.

Lying beside her every night, not touching her, was a special kind of torture. It had taken more strength than he thought he possessed to keep turning down her overtures. But he didn't feel it was fair to make love to her, to give her hope that things might change, when he knew that wasn't true.

He knew he was making her miserable, and despite what she probably believed, that wasn't his intention. Since they were stuck with each other, he had hoped they would reach an understanding, find some middle ground where they could coexist peacefully. But his life was anything but peaceful.

It had been almost two weeks since she'd initiated sex; she'd even gone so far as to stop undressing in front of him, which he'd thought would be a relief. Instead, the longer he went without seeing her, or touching her, he wanted her that much more. But giving in, making love to her, would just do more damage.

He walked closer to the bathroom door, thinking he would just accidentally bump it with his elbow while he hung up his suit jacket. But when he did, he still couldn't see a thing. The room was black as pitch.

What would possess her to shower with all the lights off?

Puzzled, he walked into the bedroom to drop his watch and phone on the bedside table. Then he remembered that he had to be to work early for another conference call and set the alarm on his phone for six-thirty. He walked back into the closet, tugging his shirt off, and saw that Anne was out of the shower and drying off with her back to him. Seeing her naked again made him hard instantly. She dropped the towel and turned his way, shrieking when she saw him standing there.

At first he thought he'd only startled her, until she reached down and clawed at the ground for the towel she'd just dropped. She fumbled to untwist it, holding it up to cover herself, a look of sheer horror on her face.

She acted as if he were a rapist or molester. The fact that he had seen her frequently, and intimately, naked made her reaction more than a little peculiar. He was so surprised his first instinct was to ask, "What the hell is the matter with you?"

His harsh tone made her flinch. "I…I'm sorry. I didn't know you were here."

What did she think she was doing? Punishing him by not letting him see her undressed? Torturing him? Well, he had news for her. It was torture no matter what she did. Dressed, undressed, he still wanted her.

She fumbled with the towel, trying to cover as much of herself as possible, and something inside him snapped. What right did she have to deprive him of anything? Damn it, she *owed* him.

He reached out, fisted the towel and yanked it away from her. She tried desperately to shield his view with her hands, looking around for something to cover herself, deep red splotches blooming across her cheeks.

She was embarrassed, he realized. Not just embarrassed, but mortified. "Anne, what is the matter with you?"

"I'm fat," she said in a wobbly voice, tears gathering in the corners of her eyes. "My body is disgusting."

Suddenly it all made sense. The reason she didn't undress in front of him. And why she showered with the lights off. She was ashamed of her body. A woman who, six weeks ago, had no issue walking around naked, flaunting herself to him.

If she were anyone else, he might have suspected it was an act, to make him feel guilty for ignoring her. But she'd had weeks to pull that sort of stunt. This was real.

He had finally done it. He had broken her. He'd taken a woman who was sharp and feisty and full of life and he had shattered her spirit. He'd made her hate herself and he hated *himself* for it.

And he could no longer live with himself if he didn't fix it.

When Sam came toward her he looked so furious that, for a terrifying second, she thought he was going to hit her. She even put her hands up to shield herself. But instead he swooped her up in his arms, which, despite her added tonnage, he did effortlessly. Only then, with her hip pressed against his pelvis, did she realize that he was erect.

Was that what it took to arouse him? Exposing and humiliating her?

He carried her into the bedroom and dropped her on the bed, right on top of the covers. She tried to pull the duvet up over herself and he yanked it back into place. Then he started unfastening his pants.

"Wh-what are you doing?" she asked, and cursed herself for sounding so fragile and weak. So afraid. She was tougher than this.

"What does it look like I'm doing?"

"I—I don't want to."

"You've obviously got some warped version of reality and I feel obligated to set you straight." He shoved his pants down and kicked them away. "Not touching you has been the *worst* kind of torture. But I restrained myself. I thought it wasn't fair to lead you on, to make you think that anything was going to change. But I can see now that I've only made things worse."

She was afraid to say a word. To even open her mouth. He got on the bed and lowered himself over her, his familiar weight pressing her into the mattress. It felt so good, she could have cried.

"This changes nothing," he said firmly. "Not about our relationship, or the way I feel about you. You understand that?"

She understood it, even if she couldn't accept it. But she missed him so badly, she didn't care what happened after tonight. She just wanted to touch him, to feel him inside her. There was a huge lump in her throat, and she feared that if she tried to talk she would start to cry, so she nodded instead.

"You are a beautiful woman, Anne. I'm sorry if my actions made you think otherwise." He lowered his head and kissed her. Hard. He centered himself between her legs and drove into her, deep and rough, again and again, almost as if he were trying to punish her. But it was so wonderful, such a relief to know he still wanted her, tears leaked from the corners of her eyes. Almost instantly her body began to shudder with release and Sam wasn't far behind her. She didn't want it to be over so fast, she wanted to be close to him, then she realized, he wasn't finished. She barely had a chance to catch her breath before he began thrusting into her again, still hard. He lasted longer this time, making her come twice before he let himself climax. And after what couldn't have been more than a moment or two of rest, he was ready to go again. It was almost as if his body was making up for lost time and refused to rest until it had its fill of her, and her own body accepted him eagerly.

They eventually fell asleep in a sweaty tangle. Then sometime in the middle of the night she woke to feel his hand between her legs, stroking her. She moaned and pulled him to her, and they made love again.

Eleven

When Anne woke the next morning Sam was already up, and she could hear the shower running. She lay there waiting for him. She had never been so physically satisfied, and was feeling a troubling combination of joy and dread.

Never had sex been as passionate as last night. But what now? Would he go back to ignoring her? Would they only connect at night between the sheets of their bed? And could she live with that? Was it even worth it?

She heard the shower stop, then the bathroom door opened. She heard him moving around in the closet. He came out a few minutes later, a towel riding low on his hips, his hair damp and curly. She held her breath, waiting to see what he would do. If he would talk to her, or move through his morning routine without a word, the way he had been for weeks.

He walked over to his side of the bed, sat on the edge of the mattress. He sat there for thirty seconds or so, not saying a word, then finally turned to face her. "I'm tired of holding on to my anger. It's exhausting and it's not doing either one of us any good."

She braced herself for the disclaimer that she knew would follow. And it did.

"However," he added firmly, "that doesn't change the fact that I'm here—I'm in this marriage—for our children." He caught her gaze. "We're clear on that?"

"Yes." For now maybe. But eventually he would come around. She knew he would. He simply had to. They had taken a huge step last night. Whether he wanted to admit it or not. Before the fight he'd been so close to falling in love. They could get there again. She would just have to be patient.

"That said, there's no reason why we shouldn't try to make the best of it."

"I have been," she reminded him.

"I know. And I've been selfish. But things will be different this time. I promise."

She wanted to believe him. She *had* to.

One of the babies rolled and started kicking her, and she automatically put a hand to her belly.

"Kicking?" he asked.

"Want to feel? You haven't in a long time." Not since the fight.

"I feel them every night. As soon as you go to sleep, they're all over the place. It amazes me that you can sleep through it."

She'd had no idea that he did that, that he felt his children moving inside her while she slept. That had to mean something, right?

He rolled onto his side next to her and laid a hand on her belly.

"We still have to talk about names," she said, watching her skin undulate with kicks and punches. "I was hoping we could use James. For my father."

"We could do that," he said, stroking her belly lower, and maybe it was wrong, but she was starting to get turned-on. "I was thinking Victoria, after my grandmother."

"I like that name," she said, closing her eyes, savoring the sensation of his hands on her skin. Then he slipped his hand between her legs, stroking her. It felt so good a moan worked its way up and past her lips.

"Wet already?" he asked, filling her with his fingers, and she gasped, arching to take them deeper. "I could make you come right now," he said, flicking her nipple with his tongue, causing that deep tug of pleasure in her womb. He could, but she hoped he wouldn't. She wanted to make this last, just in case for some reason, it might be the last time. She wanted to savor every second.

She tugged his towel open and his erection sprang up, so she leaned over and took him into her mouth. Sam groaned and tangled his fingers through her hair, letting his head fall back against the pillow. She knew exactly what to do to set him off, too. The perfect rhythm, the sensitive spot just below his testicles that she knew made him crazy. But when she could feel him getting close, his body tensing, he stopped her. He pushed her onto her back instead and climbed over her. He took her legs and hooked them, one over each of his shoulders, then he thrust inside her. Morning sex was usually slow and tranquil, but this was different. This was hot and sexy and…wild. In no time she was shuddering with release, but he didn't let himself have pleasure, wouldn't give in until she'd climaxed a second time. Would he be so concerned with her pleasure if he didn't care about her? Didn't *love* her?

She could drive herself crazy questioning his motives, so instead she cleared her mind, closed her eyes and just let herself feel.

Afterward Sam collapsed beside her, his chest heaving with the effort to catch his breath. "Bloody hell… that was…fantastic."

She lay on her back beside him, limp, her body buzzing with afterglow. "You probably noticed that my stomach is starting to get in the way."

"I did." He looked over at her and grinned. "Maybe next time we'll have to try it on our hands and knees."

She was going to suggest they try it right now, but then he looked at the time on his phone and cursed.

"You've made me late."

"Don't blame me. You started it."

"Yes, but if you weren't so irresistible, I wouldn't have been tempted."

Two days ago he wouldn't touch her, now she was irresistible? This was just too odd. But she wasn't about to complain. She felt as though she finally had her husband back. The emotional switch had been flipped back on. Now if she could only manage to keep it on, or even *find* the damned switch in the first place, everyone could be happy.

"I have to get ready," he said, pressing a kiss to her forehead before he rolled out of bed.

She listened to the sounds of him getting ready for work, as she had dozens of times before.

Like magic, Sam was back to his old self. He talked to her, teased her and spent time with her. And the sex? Good Lord, it had never been so fantastic. Or frequent. It was as though, despite how many times they made love, he simply couldn't get enough of her. It was a much needed salve to her ego, and at the same time, confused the hell out of her.

He had been quite clear in saying that he was only there for the children, yet he treated their relationship, their marriage, like the real thing. He had done a complete one-eighty, as if the weeks of misery had never happened. Or maybe it had been a terrible nightmare that she had finally woken up from. Whatever the reason, he was back to being the sweet, patient man she had married.

It was all she had ever hoped for, so she should be blissfully happy. Hell, she should be jumping with joy. Instead she was a nervous wreck, walking on eggshells. She was terrified that if she let her guard down she might say or do the wrong thing, and he would fall off the deep end again. Shut her out of his life.

She began to feel there was something wrong with her. Why couldn't she just relax and let herself be happy?

Maybe she really was the family screwup. Maybe she was destined to live her life in perpetual dysfunction. Or was it just that she was afraid the happier she let herself feel, the more it would hurt when the other shoe finally dropped?

Since their wedding, Anne had only seen Sam's parents a couple of times. And that was before their fight. Every time he had gone there since, he had some excuse why he couldn't take her. Although most times he didn't even bother to tell her he was going. She would find out later. It was almost as if he was sheltering them from her, maybe so they wouldn't get attached, and it made her feel terrible. She didn't want them to think that she was avoiding them, or even worse, didn't like them. She wanted a good relationship with her in-laws.

Finally, when they asked her and Sam to dinner one evening in late November, either he had run out of excuses, or he actually wanted her there, because he accepted. But then she found she was nervous. What had he told them about their marriage?

"Do they know?" Anne asked him as they were getting ready to leave, after she had obsessed for an hour about what to wear, trying on a dozen different outfits before she settled on a simple slip dress.

"Know what?" Sam asked.

"About us. How things have been." She hated mentioning it, reminding him—as if he would ever forget.

"I never said anything about it to them," he told her, holding her coat so she could slip it on. "As far as they know, everything is fine. And as far as I'm concerned, everything is."

She wished she could be so confident.

It had begun snowing that morning, the first of the

season, and by the time she and Sam got to his parents' house, a Tudor-style mansion, several inches had fallen, making the roads a bit treacherous.

The first thing his mother did, after they shed their boots and coats and gloves, was take Anne upstairs to show her the nursery and playroom they had already begun to set up for the twins.

"It's beautiful!" Anne told her, running her hand along the rail of one of the cribs. There were two. One with boy bedding and one for a girl. The walls were painted a gender-neutral shade of green, and there were shelves overflowing with toys and books. Many, she told Anne, used to be Sam's and Adam's.

"I haven't even started setting up the nursery," Anne told her. "Once Chris and Melissa move into the master suite, we'll be taking their old room, since the current nursery is right beside it."

"I hope you don't mind that we have a nursery," his mother said.

"Of course not."

"We know that as new parents it will be nice to occasionally have some time to yourselves. We would love to have the twins spend the night here every now and then. But we don't want to overstep our bounds."

"They're your grandchildren. Of course they can stay here."

She looked relieved. "I'm so glad. We weren't sure how you felt."

Because Anne was so absent from their lives. Her mother-in-law didn't say it, but Anne knew that was what she was thinking. And what could Anne say? *"It's not my fault. Your son has been keeping me from you."*

Then she would have to admit they had been having problems, and her mother-in-law would want to know why. Anne would be too humiliated to tell her what she had done to their son. The way she had lied to Sam. They would probably draw the same conclusion he had. They would think she was spoiled and selfish. That she had trapped him.

From now on, she would make an effort to spend more time with her in-laws. She would ask her mother-in-law to tea, or maybe they could go shopping in Paris or Milan. And she could invite them both to dinner at the castle.

"I'm sorry I don't make it over more," Anne said guiltily. "I feel I haven't been a very good daughter-in-law."

"Oh, Anne," she said, touching her arm. "Please, there's no need to apologize. Sam has explained how complicated it is for you with security and such. He said that you and your family are practically prisoners in the castle."

That was true, but it wasn't the reason for her absence. Sam had flat-out lied to his parents, and she couldn't help but think bitterly that dishonesty seemed to be okay if it suited his own needs, but if she wasn't completely candid all the time, it was wrong somehow. Talk about a double-edged sword and she was getting really tired of falling on it.

"I'll be so relieved when the man harassing you is caught," her mother-in-law said. "They should lock him up and throw away the key."

It was odd, but since they learned he was Geoffrey's son, and that he was emotionally disturbed, the profound hatred and resentment she felt before had fizzled out. Instead she felt deeply sorry for him. Not that she didn't want to see him locked up, but only so he could get the help he needed. She could only imagine the horrors he'd experienced in the military. Then to be refused help. It was unconscionable.

"He's a disturbed man who needs psychiatric help," Anne said. "Everyone will be relieved when he's caught."

Sam's father appeared in the doorway. "I thought I would find you two in here. Supper is ready."

She was probably being paranoid, but all through dinner Anne had the feeling that something was up. Sam's parents seemed…anxious. They picked at their food, a traditional English stew that was so delicious Anne actually had seconds. After dessert, they moved to the living room for brandy, or in Anne's case, mineral water. After they were all served, and the maid out of the room, Sam asked his parents, "So, are we going to talk about whatever it is that's bothering the two of you?"

Apparently Anne hadn't been the only one who noticed something was off.

"There is something we need to tell you," his father said, and his wife took his hand.

Anne had a feeling it wasn't going to be good news, and Sam must have shared her impression, because he frowned and asked, "What's wrong?"

"I went for my annual physical a few weeks ago and the doctor discovered that I have an enlarged prostate. They did some tests and they've come back positive for cancer. However," he added swiftly, "I'm in the early stages and he says it's one of the less aggressive types."

"He's not even recommending surgery," his mother said. "He thinks that with a round of radiation your father will be as good as new."

She could feel Sam's relief all but leaking from his pores as he sagged into the sofa beside her. "That's great. It could be much worse, right?"

"*Much* worse."

Sam looked from one parent to the other. "But there's something else, isn't there?"

They exchanged a look, then his father said. "I've decided that, for the sake of my health, it's time that I retire."

"Retire? But you love being prime minister. What will you do?"

"Relax, for a change. The truth is I've grown weary of politics. The long hours and constant conflict. I'm tired of it. I'm stepping down, and until my term ends six months from now, the deputy prime minister will take my place."

The change in Sam's stature was subtle, but Anne felt it right away, and she knew exactly what he was thinking. If it weren't for his marriage, for *her,* Sam would be running to take his father's place. And he would get it, because out of anyone else who might choose to run, he would be the most qualified. He would be prime minister, just as he had always wanted.

But now that was never going to happen. And it was all her fault.

Maybe she imagined it, but she swore she could feel

that emotional switch snap off. And all she could think was, *Oh God, here we go again.*

"I suppose he'll run for your seat after that," Sam said.

"I'm sure he will," his father said, and Anne knew just what Sam was thinking. He had declared more than once that the deputy was a moron.

"I know this will be difficult for you, son," his father said, avoiding Anne's gaze.

"I'm fine," Sam told him, forcing a smile. Another lie. "You shouldn't even be worrying about how his will affect me. All that matters right now is your health. If you're happy, I'm happy for you."

He sounded sincere, but Anne knew better, and in the back of her mind she heard the distinct clunk of that pesky other shoe dropping.

Since the weather was getting progressively worse, they left his parents' house a short time later. Only when they were in the car and on their way back to the castle did Sam let down his guard, and she saw how truly upset he was.

"The deputy is a wanker," he said.

But he was handsome and congenial, and people had been elected on far less.

"Sam," she started to say, but he held up a hand to hush her.

"Please, don't. Not now."

She knew this was going to happen. That it was inevitable. She'd felt it in her bones. Unfortunately, that didn't make the reality of the situation any easier to accept. Although in a very strange way, it was a relief to finally have it over with.

She leaned back against the seat and looked out into the night, watching as fat snowflakes drifted past the car window. She tried to tell herself that this was just a small blip, and in a day or two, everything would be okay.

She told herself that, because the alternative was unimaginable. If he shut her out again, how long would it take this time to drag him back out of his shell?

And this time, did she even want to try?

Twelve

He knew it was selfish and unfair, but Sam couldn't even look at Anne.

The idea of never following in his father's footsteps had been upsetting, but easier to stomach when the prospect seemed so far in the future. Now here it was staring him right in the face. He was forced once again to rehash everything he'd lost. Everything he wanted and would never have. And he blamed her.

On top of that his father had cancer. Sam could only hope he was being honest about the prognosis, and not sugarcoating the truth so Sam wouldn't worry.

With the inclement weather it took twice the normal time to get home. And he used the term "home" loosely, because right now he felt as if he were in limbo. One foot in and one out of his marriage. His life. He needed some time to himself, to work things through and regroup. If there was any possible way he could justify not staying at the castle for a day or two, he would be gone. The construction on his town house had been completed months ago, so he could stay there. But then there was the problem of her family. If he wasn't careful, he would find himself miserable *and* unemployed. At least with a job he enjoyed, he had someplace to escape to.

Otherwise, he was trapped.

Anne was quiet while they got ready for bed, but when they climbed under the covers, she reached for him. Though he felt like a bastard for it, he shrugged away from her. She was only trying to comfort her, trying to be a good wife, but he couldn't let her in. Not yet. The wound was still too fresh.

It'll be better tomorrow, he assured himself. But the next morning, after a long night of tossing and turning, he only felt worse. Anne tried to talk to him, but he shook his head and told her, "I'm not ready," hating himself for the hurt look she didn't bother trying to hide. He wasn't being fair—there had to come a time when he forgave her and moved on—but he couldn't help the way he felt. The bitterness and resentment. He kept telling himself, tomorrow it will better. But it wasn't. Every day that passed he pulled deeper inside his shell.

Only days ago he had been close to forgiving her—to putting it all behind them. Now he felt as though he would be angry with her indefinitely.

It was killing Anne to see Sam so unhappy.

She had hoped that by now he would have come around, but since his father's announcement two weeks ago they had been in a steady free fall. She had tried to be patient and sympathetic. She tried to give him space to work things through. And still he kept telling her that he needed time. She just wasn't sure if she had any left to give.

He was miserable, and she was miserable, and though she loved him, she simply didn't have the strength to fight anymore. Not when it was a one-sided battle. And forcing him to stay with her, when he clearly didn't want to be there, wasn't right. It wasn't fair to him, or her, or even the babies.

She wasn't a quitter, and she had tried damned hard to make it work, but this was a losing battle. She could no longer take his Jekyll and Hyde mood swings. And even if he did come around again, how could she be sure that the next time things got hard, he wouldn't do this again? And again. She couldn't live like this anymore, always on her guard. Waiting for the next disaster.

It was clear that the only way they would ever be happy again was if they were apart. For good.

Making that final decision had been hard, but at the same time a huge burden had been lifted. She felt…free. The really tough part was going to Chris and admitting that, after only a few months, her marriage was over.

"I had the feeling something was wrong," he told her. "But I had hoped you would work it out."

"We tried," she said. Or at least, *she* had. But this whole mess was her fault in the first place, so it didn't seem fair to blame only him. "It just isn't going to work. We're miserable."

"So what you're saying is, you want permission to divorce."

"I understand the position I'm putting the family in and I'm sorry."

He sighed. "A little scandal won't kill us."

"So you'll allow it?"

"If there's one thing we've learned, it's that life is short. You deserve to be happy, not chained to a marriage that isn't working. I can't deny that I'm very fond of Sam. He's done one hell of a job as ambassador."

"But after the divorce, he'll be able to go back to politics. Right?"

"He'll be stripped of his title, so yes, he can hold any office he wants."

Well, she could give him that at least. And telling Chris made it feel so much more...*final*. She had to fight not to give in to her grief, reach deep inside herself to find the old Anne. *The Shrew*. The Anne who didn't need anyone, or care what anyone thought of her. And still, somewhere deep down, she couldn't help but cling to the slender hope that when faced with the real prospect of their marriage ending, Sam would suddenly comprehend everything he was giving up. Maybe he would even realize that he loved her.

She waited until that evening to approach him. He had just come home from work and was in their room changing for dinner. She walked in and shut the door behind her.

"We need to talk," she said.

Without even glancing her way he said, "Now isn't a good time."

"Then I'll talk and you can just listen."

He turned to her, looking pained, and she almost felt

sorry for him. He was miserable and he was doing it to himself. "I'm not ready. I need time."

"Well, I can't do this anymore," she said.

"Do what?"

"This. *Us*. We're both unhappy. I think it would be best…" The words caught in her throat. *Come on, Anne, hold it together.* She squared her shoulders. "I think it would best for everyone if we called it quits."

He narrowed his eyes at her, as though he thought it might be a trick. After a pause he asked, "Is this the part where I have a change of heart and realize I can't live without you?"

Apparently not. She swallowed back the sorrow rising up from deep inside her. This was it. It was really the end. Her marriage was over. "No. This is the part where I ask you to leave, and tell you I want a divorce."

He just stood there, like he was waiting for the punch line. When it didn't come he said, "You're serious."

She nodded.

"So that's it? Just like that, it's over?"

She shrugged, tried to pretend she wasn't coming apart on the inside. "Just like that."

"You're just giving up?"

"It takes two people to make a marriage work, Sam. You gave up a long time ago. And I can't fight for this anymore."

He didn't deny it, because he knew she was right.

"I've already talked to my attorney and he's drawing up the divorce papers immediately."

"You said before that once we're married, that's it."

"I talked to Chris and he's going to allow it. And he assured me that the second it's legal you will be stripped of your title. That should give you plenty of time to set up a campaign and run for prime minister. You'll have everything you've ever wanted."

He still looked hesitant. Honestly, she thought he'd have been packing by now.

"Why are you doing this?" he asked. "Why now?"

"Because I can't live like this anymore. I may have made a terrible mistake, Sam, but I can't pay for it for the rest of my life. I deserve to be happy. To be married to someone who loves me, not a man who tolerates me for the sake of our children."

"I married you for their sake."

Yes, he had, and shame on her for forgetting that. "There's no benefit to their parents being married if everyone is miserable. We'll share custody, and they will grow up knowing both their parents love them very much, even if they don't live in the same household. They'll live perfectly happy lives, like millions of other kids whose parents are divorced."

"And my ambassadorship?"

"Chris is arranging for a replacement as we speak. You are free to pursue a job you actually like. Effective immediately."

"I did like my job," he said.

"But now you can have the one you want."

He was quiet for a long time, as though he was working it through. Processing it. She started to feel the faintest glimmer of hope. Maybe he was beginning to realize what he was about to lose.

But then he nodded and said, "It probably is for the best." Driving the proverbial stake through her heart.

If he loved her, even a little bit, he would want to fight for her.

"I'd like you gone tonight," she said, struggling to maintain her composure. To keep her voice even, her expression cold.

She was *The Shrew,* she reminded herself. She didn't let people hurt her.

"If that's what you want," he said.

No, she wanted to shout. She wanted *him,* the way he had been right after their wedding. The man who had been so sweet and caring when she lost her father. Her *partner.*

She wanted him to love her. But that was never going to happen.

"It's what I want. I'll go so you can pack."

"You're sure about this?"

"I've never been so sure of anything in my life. I just…" She swallowed hard. "I just don't love you anymore."

"It was never about love."

Not for him maybe, but it had been for her. And saying she didn't love him now was a lie.

But this was one lie she was sure he could live with.

Sam was relieved.

He was out of a job, a signature away from divorce, and wouldn't live in the same house as his twin infants. And he was happy about it.

At least, that's what he had been telling himself. Over and over. And he was sure, in time, he might actually start believing it.

He moved back into his town house, with its shiny new kitchen and sagless ceilings. Exactly where he had wanted to be. Only to realize that it didn't much feel like home anymore.

It would just take time to adjust, he kept telling himself. He could get on with his life now. He could follow in his father's footsteps and run for the prime minister's seat. Even though the mere idea of an arduous campaign exhausted him. He hadn't even thought about whom he would hire to run it, much less a platform to run on.

But he had made the right decision, leaving Anne—of course, he hadn't left so much as been kicked out.

And if he was so sure then why, after three days of moping, hadn't he told his parents? It was only a matter of time before the story made it to the press. He couldn't abide by them reading in the newspaper that their son had failed at being a husband.

And that was how he felt. Like a complete failure.

But he couldn't put it off any longer.

"What a nice surprise!" his father said, when Sam popped in unannounced. But as he shrugged out of his coat and handed it to the maid, his father frowned. "Have you been sick?"

"What makes you ask that?"

"Well, it's Wednesday. You're not at work. And forgive me for saying so, but you look terrible."

He must have been a sight with tousled hair and several days' worth of beard stubble. Not to mention his wrinkled clothes. He hadn't unpacked yet and had been living out of a suitcase and boxes. "No, I'm not sick. But I do need to talk to you about something."

"How about a drink?" his father offered.

Figuring he would need the liquid courage, Sam said, "Make it a double."

While he poured, Sam asked, "Is Mom around?"

"She had some luncheon to attend." He shrugged. "One of her charities, I think. I lose track."

He had hoped to tell them both together, but since he was already here… Besides, it might be easier talking to his father first.

He handed Sam his drink. "Shall we sit in the den?"

"Sure." He followed his father down the hall, thinking how, in all the years they had lived there, not much had changed. But Sam had. And he would be the first to admit he was very fond of the familiar. He was a creature of habit, so change made him…edgy. And right now, his entire life felt turned upside down.

When they were seated in the den, Sam on the sofa and his father in his favorite chair, he asked, "So, what's up?"

Sam sat on the edge of the cushion, elbows resting on his knees, swirling the scotch in his glass. "I thought you should know that I moved out of the castle last week. Anne and I are getting a divorce."

"I'm sorry to hear that, Sam. You two seemed so happy."

They were. For a while. Until things got so complicated.

"Can I ask what happened?"

Sam considered telling him the truth. About the night of the twins' conception and the fact that Anne had lied about birth control. Then continued to lie even after they were married. But he realized that really had nothing to do with this.

So, she had made a mistake. Yes, he'd been angry, and he'd felt betrayed. And he'd struggled so damned hard to hold on to to it, to…punish her. When he finally let go, let himself forgive her, it had been a relief.

This was different. This wasn't about what she had done, although at first it had been easier to blame her than to admit what was really bothering him. Because that was the way he liked things. Easy.

But really, he'd only made things more complicated.

"I screwed up," he told his father, taking a long swallow of his drink, but the path of fire it scored in his throat didn't come close to the burning ache in his heart. "I screwed up and I don't know how to fix it. If it even is fixable."

"Do you love her?"

It surprised him how quickly the answer surfaced. "Yeah. I do."

"Have you told her that?"

No. In fact, he'd told her specifically that he *didn't* love her. That he never would. That he was only in it for the kids. "It wasn't supposed to be about love. That wasn't part of the plan."

His father laughed. "In my experience, son, things rarely go as planned. Especially when it comes to love."

Yes, but if it wasn't about love, then it would be easy. No messy emotions to get in the way and complicate things. It was when he started falling in love with her that everything got so confusing.

He downed the last of his drink and set the empty glass on the coffee table. "It shouldn't be this complicated."

"What?"

"Relationships. Marriage. It shouldn't be this hard."

"If it were easy, don't you think it would get... boring?"

"Is it too much to want what you and Mom have?"

"And what do we have?"

"The perfect marriage. You never fought or had problems. It was so *easy* for you. It just...worked."

"Sam, our marriage is *far* from perfect."

"Okay, I know you two have had your little spats, but—"

"Infidelity? Do you consider that a little spat?"

At first he thought his father was kidding, and when he saw that he was, in fact, *very* serious, Sam's jaw dropped. "You cheated on Mom?"

He shook his head solemnly. "Never. I've never once been unfaithful to your mother. Not that I didn't have the opportunity. But I loved her too much. Too much for my own good."

"If you didn't—" The meaning of his father's words suddenly sank in and they almost knocked him backward. "Are you saying that *Mom* was unfaithful to *you?*"

"You remember how much she toured, all the attention she got. Not to mention that she's an incredibly beautiful woman."

Sam could hardly believe what he was hearing. *"When?"*

"You were eight."

"I—I'm *stunned*. I had no idea."

"And we never meant for you to find out. Now I'm beginning to think that sheltering you from the realities of our relationship was a mistake. Marriages take work, son. They're complicated and messy."

"What did you do when you found out?"

"I was devastated. And I seriously considered leaving. I went so far as to pack my bags, but she begged me to forgive her, to give her a second chance. We decided together that we would go to counseling and try to save our marriage. She even took a year off from touring, to prove to me that she was serious. That our relationship came first."

"I remember that," Sam said. "I remember her being home all the time. I just never stopped to think why, I guess."

"Why would you? You were a little boy. And always so happy. So bright and cheerful. We didn't want our problems to reflect negatively on you. Or Adam. Although I think he suspected."

"How could you ever trust her again?"

"It wasn't easy. Especially after she went back to touring. We had a few very rough years. But I think our marriage is better for it. If we could survive that, we can survive almost anything."

Sam felt as if his entire world had been flipped on its axis. His parents' perfect marriage hadn't been perfect at all. He had been holding himself, his own marriage, to such a ridiculously high standard that the instant they hit a snag, he'd felt like a failure, that he wasn't measuring up. He had expected Anne to conform to some cardboard cut-out version of his perfect mother, never knowing that person didn't even exist.

He pinched the bridge of his nose. "I. Am. A *wanker*."

His dad grinned. "You can't learn if you don't make mistakes."

"Well, I've made a monumental one. All of the troubles Anne and I have been having revolve around one thing, my desire to run for the prime minister's seat. And I've been so damned busy focusing on what I can't have, instead of what I do have, I've completely overlooked the fact that I don't want to be prime minister anymore."

When his father announced his retirement, it had been the perfect excuse to push Anne away. So he wouldn't have to admit that he was falling in love with her.

"Are you disappointed?" he asked his father.

He looked puzzled. "Why would I be disappointed?"

"Well, I always planned to follow in your footsteps."

"Sam, you have to walk your own path, make your own footprint. You have to do what makes *you* happy."

"I'm happy as an ambassador. And I'm damned good at it. Or at least, I *was*."

"They fired you?"

He shrugged. "Anne, the job, it was a package deal." And he had blown it.

His entire life Sam had known exactly what he wanted, and he had never been afraid of anything. But now he wasn't just afraid. He was terrified. Terrified that it was too late.

"Do you want her back?" his father asked.

"More than anything. But I'm not so sure she'll give me another chance. Or if I even deserve one."

"Can I give you a bit of advice?"

Sam nodded.

"The most precious things in life are the ones you have to fight for. So ask yourself, is she worth fighting for?"

He didn't even have to think about it. "Yes, she is."

"So what are you going to do?"

There was only one thing he could do. "I guess I'm going to fight."

Thirteen

Sam headed back to his town house to shower and change before he went to see Anne, only to be met at the front door and served with an envelope containing the divorce papers.

He didn't bother to open it, since he had no intention of signing them. But it was clear, when he got to the castle, that she wasn't going to make this reconciliation easy for him.

"I'm sorry, sir," the guard posted at the gate said, when Sam pulled up. "I can't let you in."

"It's very important," Sam told him, but the man didn't budge. "Come on, you *know* me."

When he was part of the family, the guard's expression said. "I do apologize, sir. But I have strict orders not to let you in."

He said he would fight for her, and that was what he

planned to do, even to the detriment of his pride. "Can you just call up and tell her I'm here?"

"Sir—"

"Please, just do me this favor. Call her and tell her that I *need* to see her."

He hesitated, then stepped back into his booth and picked up the phone. Sam breathed a sigh of relief. If Anne knew he was out here waiting, that he needed to talk to her, surely she would let him in.

The guard spoke into the phone, nodded a few times, then hung up. Sam waited for him to reach for the lever that would open the gate and wave him past. Instead, he stepped back out of the booth and over to Sam's car window. "If you require an audience with the princess, it was suggested that you contact her personal assistant or the palace social secretary."

Now she was being ridiculous. They were still *married* for God's sake. And had she forgotten that she was pregnant with *his* children?

He pulled out his cell phone and dialed her private number. It rang three times, then went to voice mail. He tried her cell phone next. This time it went straight to voice mail. He listened to the generic message, and after the tone said, "Anne, this is ridiculous. Pick up the phone."

He disconnected, then immediately dialed again. Again, he got her voice mail. Either she was rejecting his calls, or the phone was off, but he knew that she always kept her phone on, so he was guessing it was the latter.

He texted her a message: CALL ME!!!!!!

He waited, but after a moment she hadn't replied, and his phone wasn't ringing.

"Sir," the guard said firmly. "I'm going to have to ask you to leave."

"Hold on."

He tried Louisa's phone with no luck, then Melissa's, then as a last-ditch effort, he called Chris's office line, but his secretary fed him some garbage about His Highness being out of the office.

He was being stonewalled.

He texted her again: I'm not giving up. I'm going to fight for you.

"Mr. Baldwin." A second, more threatening-looking guard with a holstered sidearm appeared at his window. "I'm going to have to insist that you leave right now."

Sam could insist that he was staying, and demand to see Anne, but it would most likely land him in jail. He could try to sneak onto the grounds, but with Richard Corrigan still at large, Sam would no doubt be shot on sight.

"All right, I'm going," he grumbled.

She'd completely shut him out. And hadn't he done the exact same thing to her? Hadn't he shut her out emotionally?

He couldn't help thinking that he was getting a taste of his own medicine. That didn't mean he had any intention of giving up.

She had told him she was tired of being the only one fighting to save their marriage. Well, if it was a fight she wanted, that was what she was about to get.

"Sam again?" Louisa asked, when Anne's cell rang for the *bazillionth* time that morning. They were in

Louisa's room, on the Internet, registering for baby things in preparation for Anne's shower in January.

"Who else?" Anne grabbed it and rejected the call. He had been calling and texting and e-mailing incessantly. "I'm going to have to change my bloody number. And my e-mail address."

Louisa bit her lip.

"What?" Anne said.

She pasted on an innocent look and said, "I didn't say a word."

"No, but you want to. I can tell."

Louisa had seen Sam leave with his suitcases that night a week ago—although it felt more like a month—and Anne had finally broken down and told her everything that happened.

"It's just that he's very…persistent," Louisa said gently. "Maybe you should talk to him."

According to his numerous texts—which Anne had grudgingly read but refused to answer—and all the messages he had left on her phone, he loved her, and he wanted to fight to make their marriage work. But she didn't have any fight left in her.

"I have nothing left to say to him."

"You're having his babies, Annie. You can't ignore him forever."

She didn't plan to. She would talk to him eventually, but not until she felt it was safe. Not until she woke in the morning without that sick, empty feeling in her heart, until she could go more than five minutes without seeing his face or hearing his voice in her head. Not until she could face him and not long to throw herself into his arms and hold him.

She needed time to get over him.

Her phone buzzed as a text came through.

I'm not giving up. I love you.

Apparently he'd forgotten that this wasn't about love. Besides, he didn't really love her. He just didn't like losing. But this time he wouldn't charm his way back into her heart. Not when she knew he would only break it again.

"You know I love you, Annie, and I'm always on your side…" Louisa began.

"But?"

"Don't you think you're being just a little…unfair?"

"Unfair? Was Sam being fair when he ignored me for *weeks?"*

"So you're getting revenge? Giving him a taste of his own medicine?"

"No! That's not what I meant."

"Just call him. Tell him it's over."

"I did tell him. The night I kicked him out."

"Well, apparently the message didn't get through, and until you level with him, he's going to keep thinking there's hope. I don't have to tell you what that's like."

She hated that Louisa's words made so much sense.

Her phone started ringing again. Louisa picked it up and handed it to her. "Talk to him. If not for yourself, then do it for me."

She hesitated, then took the phone and Louisa walked out, leaving her alone. She took a deep breath, terrified that when she heard his voice, she was going to melt.

You are *The Shrew,* she reminded herself. A cold-hearted bitch who doesn't need anyone.

Now, if she could just make herself believe it.

* * *

Anne had ignored so many of his calls that when she finally did answer, he forgot what he was going to say. But that wasn't a problem, because she didn't give him a chance to say a word.

"I only accepted your call to ask you to please stop bothering me. I don't want to talk to you."

"Then I'll do the talking and you can listen."

"Sam—"

"I am so sorry for the way I treated you. I love you, Annie."

"It's not supposed to be about love," she said, throwing his words back in his face. Not that he blamed her.

"I know, but I fell in love with you anyway. And it scared the hell out of me."

"Why?"

"I thought that loving you would be too hard. Turns out, loving you was the easy part. The hard part was pushing you away."

"I can't be with someone who flakes out on me every time things get hard. Every time I make a mistake."

"I know my track record up until now hasn't been great, and I'm sorry, but if you give me another chance, I swear it will be different this time."

"That's what you said the last time."

"This time I mean it."

"I want to believe you. I truly do. But I just can't take the chance. The way things were, I just…I can't do that again."

"Annie—"

"It's over, Sam. Please don't call me again."

The line went dead, and Sam stared dumbfounded at the phone.

She was turning him down?

And why shouldn't she? Why should she believe a word he said? Had he just assumed, after the way he had treated her, that he could simply pour his heart out and she would beg him to come home?

A part of him wanted to be angry. He wanted to believe that she was only doing this to be stubborn. To get revenge. But that wasn't Anne's style. She'd loved him, and she had done everything she could to try to make their marriage work. She stuck by him, even when he was treating her like a pariah. And what thanks had she gotten? Absolutely none. He hadn't been the least bit grateful. He hadn't even *tried* to make it work.

The truth was, he didn't deserve her. And maybe they would both be better off if he just let her go.

Anne's feet were swollen and sore and her back ached something special, so the last place she wanted to be was standing out in the freezing cold in front of a crowd of doctors, nurses and television media. But Melissa was in the throes of twenty-four-hour morning sickness, so Chris asked Anne to accompany him to the ground-breaking ceremony for the new pediatric cancer center at the hospital.

They stood on the platform, in the brisk wind, waiting for the hospital administrator to finish his spiel. She kept her hands tucked in her coat pockets, probably looking to everyone like she was just trying to stay warm, when in fact, she clutched her cell phone in her right hand, waiting to feel the buzz alerting her to an incoming call or text message. But as it had been the past two weeks, it remained stubbornly silent.

There had to be something wrong with her. For days Sam had called nonstop and all she had wanted was for him to leave her alone, but now that he had, she longed to hear his voice.

She kept thinking about what he'd said the last time they talked, wondering if he actually meant it this time. He'd told her that he loved her and she was starting to believe him. But she was still too afraid to accept it, to face the possibility that he might just hurt her all over again.

But if he called, if *he* made the first move…again. Why would he when she had asked him to leave her alone? But if he loved her, would he really give up that easily? And was she forgetting all the texts and phone calls that she had refused to answer?

She shivered and hunched her shoulders against a sudden burst of icy wind.

"Whose brilliant idea was it to do this in December?" she grumbled under her breath.

"It's almost over," Chris assured her softly. "Just hang in there."

She glanced over at him, irritable and cold, and wanting to do something really childish, like stick her tongue out at him. She did a swift double take when she noticed a tiny red spot on the lapel of his coat. Had that been there earlier? At first she figured it was some sort of stain, or a stray fleck of lint. Then it moved.

What the—?

She was sure her eyes were playing tricks on her, then the spot moved again, from his lapel to the left side of his chest. It was a light, she realized, like a laser pointer—

It hit her then, what it could be, and her heart clenched. She knew there was no time to alert Gunter, who stood behind her. She had to do something. Now.

Time screeched to a halt, then picked up in slow motion, the seconds ticking by like hours as she yanked her hands free from her pockets and reached up, shoving Chris as hard as she could. She saw his stunned expression the same instant she felt her arm jerked back painfully, and felt herself being pulled over. She braced for the pain of the hard platform as she landed, but instead she landed on a person. Gunter, she realized. He rolled her over to her side away from the crowd and shielded her with his enormous body. Then someone shouted for a medic and her heart froze. Had she been too late? Had Chris been hit?

She tried to push up on her elbow, to see him, and Gunter ordered, "Stay down!"

She lay there helpless, imagining her brother bleeding to death only a few inches away. Her ears began to ring, all but drowning out the frightened screams of the people fleeing the area.

Then everything went black.

Sam sat slumped on the couch in his town house, nursing a scotch and brooding. Or sulking. Or a combination of the two.

His cell had been ringing almost constantly for two hours, but none of the calls were from Anne and he didn't feel like talking to anyone. Not when he was perfectly content to sit here alone and contemplate the fact that he'd had everything a man could hope for and he had callously thrown it away.

The divorce papers lay on the coffee table in front of him, still unsigned. He just couldn't seem to make himself pick up a pen. He didn't want a divorce. Didn't want to lose Anne.

But she wanted to lose him and hadn't he put her through enough grief? Didn't he owe it to her to set her free? Even though the idea of her falling in love with someone else and some other man raising his children made him physically ill. But he knew Anne well enough to realize that refusing a divorce wouldn't stop her from getting on with her life. She was so stubborn, it would probably make her that much more determined to forget him.

He sat up and grabbed the document. He hadn't read it, but his lawyer assured him it was pretty cut-and-dry. They would both leave the marriage with exactly what they had brought to it. It would almost be as if it had never happened.

He flipped to the page that was flagged for him to sign. He could *do* this. He grabbed the pen off the table, took a deep breath, raised the pen to the paper…and his damned phone started ringing again.

"Bloody hell!" He snatched the phone up off the table, flipped it open and barked, "What do you want?"

"Sam?" his brother, Adam, asked, clearly taken aback.

"Yes, it's me. It's my phone you called."

"Where have you been? We've been trying to reach you for an hour."

"I'm home. And the fact that I haven't answered should tell you that I don't feel like talking to anyone."

"I thought you would have been at the hospital by now."

"Why would I be at the hospital?" Did his brother think he was so depressed that he would be suicidal?

"You haven't heard the news?"

"What news?"

"There was a shooting. The king and Anne were outside the hospital for some ceremony and there was an assassination attempt."

Oh Jesus. He grabbed the remote and switched the television on. "Is Chris okay?"

"It was confirmed he wasn't hit. Anne shoved him out of the way at the last minute. She saved his life. But, Sam…"

Adam's words faded into the background as the banner announcing a "breaking story" flashed across the screen, and he saw the headline, *Assassination Attempt. Princess Anne Rushed to Hospital.* The remote slipped from his fingers and clattered to the floor and his heart slammed the wall of his chest so hard he couldn't draw in a full breath.

This was not happening.

He listened numbly as the newscaster relayed the events of the shooting. Then they ran a clip of the shooting taken by one of the television cameras in the crowd. Sam watched in disbelief as one minute Anne and Chris were just standing there listening to the hospital administrator, then Anne glanced up at her brother, and suddenly shoved him hard. Gunter was on her immediately, taking her down and out of the shooter's line of sight, then the camera's view was blocked by the podium. Sam couldn't tell if she'd been hit and when it cut back to the newscaster, she said there was still no word on the extent of the princess's injuries, only that she had been unconscious.

He didn't hear anything after that. What must have been a rush of adrenaline propelled him up off the couch. Only when he was on his feet and heading for the door, grabbing his keys and coat on the way out, did he realize he was still holding his phone and Adam was shouting his name.

"I'll call you back," he said, and disconnected. He needed to get to the hospital now.

This was *his* fault. He should have been there with her, standing by her side on that platform. And he would never forgive himself if she and the babies weren't okay.

Fourteen

If a person had to be shot at, what better place than right outside of a hospital?

Anne sat in bed, in the royal family's private wing, wearing one of those irritating, backless gowns that left her behind exposed. And she had no idea why she required a bare ass when all she had were a few minor bumps and bruises from Gunter pulling her down. They had admitted her only because she'd passed out, which embarrassed her terribly, and, even though she'd landed on Gunter, they worried the fall may have hurt the babies. And though everything was fine, they still insisted she should stay overnight for observation.

It was worth it to know that Chris was safe.

The police told her that if she hadn't pushed Chris aside, he would almost assuredly be dead.

Had she acted an instant later, he would have taken a

bullet to the chest, and if she'd reacted a second sooner, the bullet probably would have hit her head instead. Either Chris would be dead, or she would. The idea still gave her cold chills.

The best part was that the police had *finally* arrested Richard Corrigan. Apparently being on the run, and in hiding, had gotten to him. He hadn't even tried to get away this time. The plan had been to kill Chris and then himself, but the police got to him before he could carry out the second half.

Finally, this terrible nightmare, the harassment and threats, were over. They were free again.

As soon as the doctor would allow visitors, her family had flooded the room, needing to see with their own eyes that she was all right. Even though the doctor assured them she was doing exceptionally well for someone who was just shot at and pregnant with twins to boot.

Chris chastised her for putting her and the twins' lives in jeopardy for him, then he hugged her fiercely. She could swear she even saw the sheen of tears in his eyes.

She wanted to call Sam. The last thing she wanted was for him to see it on the news and think the worst, but her phone had gone missing in all the chaos. Everyone had been trying to reach him. Her family, and Gunter, and even the police, but apparently he wasn't answering his phone.

"I'm sure as soon as he hears he'll be here," her mother assured her. She had been sitting on the edge of the bed holding Anne's hand since they let the family in. Louisa was on the opposite side and both her brothers stood near the foot of the bed. There was nothing like a near-death experience to bring a family closer.

Everyone but Sam.

Maybe Sam had heard about the shooting but she had driven him so far away he just didn't care anymore.

She immediately shook the thought away, writing it off as utterly ridiculous. Even if he didn't care about her anymore, he still loved his children.

Gunter stepped into the room about fifteen minutes later and Anne looked to him hopefully, but he shook his head. "We send car, but he was not home."

"So where the heck *is* he?"

"He'll come," Louisa assured her.

"Could he have gone out of town?" Melissa asked, stepping up beside Chris.

"Or to his parents' house?" Liv suggested.

"We already tried there," Anne said.

As she was combing her mind, trying to imagine where else he could possibly be, the door flew open and Sam was there.

His eyes darted to the bed, and when he saw her sitting there, she could actually see him go weak with relief. She didn't have to ask her family to give them privacy. They were barely out the door before Sam had crossed the room and was holding her. The feel of his body, his familiar scent, nearly brought her to tears. How could she have even thought that letting go of him was a good thing?

"On the news all they said was that you might have been shot." He squeezed her, burying his face in her hair. "I didn't know if you were alive or dead. If I would ever see you again. Then I got here and the stupid people downstairs wouldn't tell me anything."

"Well, I'm not dead," she said, and he held her even tighter.

"You're okay? The babies are okay?"

"We're fine. I'm only in here because I passed out."

"I thought I lost you. For good this time." He cupped her face in his hands and kissed her. Firmly and prickly. Then he pulled away and she realized why. It had been so long since he'd shaved, he'd surpassed stubble and now had a full-fledged beard. His hair was shaggy, too, and in need of a trim. And she was guessing, by the dark smudges under his eyes, that he'd been sleeping as poorly as she had. And to top the look off, under his cashmere coat he wore a T-shirt and cartoon-emblazoned cotton pants.

He looked terrible. And wonderful.

"Nice pants," she said.

He looked down at himself and laughed, as though he'd just realized he'd left the house in his pajamas. And because she could, she reached up and touched his dimple.

"Suffice it to say I left in a hurry." He took her hand in his and kissed it. "Annie, I have been such an ass—"

She put a finger over his lips to shush him. "We *both* acted really stupid. But we're smarter now."

"Definitely." He kissed her fingers, her wrist. "I didn't sign the divorce papers. And I'm not going to. I flat-out refuse. I plan to spend the rest of my life with you."

"Good, because I didn't sign them, either. After you move back to the castle, we'll build a big fire in the study and watch them burn."

His eyes locked on hers. "And then we'll make love all night."

She sighed. That sounded wonderful.

He smiled, touched her face. "I am so proud of you."

"For what?"

"For *what?*" He laughed. "What do you think? You saved your brother's life. You're a hero."

"I wasn't trying to be. Everything happened so fast. I saw the laser sight on his coat and I just pushed him."

His brow furrowed. "I should have been there for you."

"But you're here now."

"I'm not leaving you again, Annie. I love you so much."

"I love you, too, Sam.

"I've said it before, but things will be different this time. I know, because *I'm* different."

"Me, too. There's nothing like a near-death experience to set your priorities straight."

He kissed her again, then said, "Scoot over."

He dropped his coat on the floor and crawled into bed beside her, drawing her close to his side. She had never felt more content, more happy in her life. And it was nice to know that she wasn't the family screwup after all. She could finally just relax and be happy.

"I have a confession to make," he said. "About the night of the charity ball. My friends dared me to ask you to dance. And I was tipsy enough to take the bait."

"And here I just thought you were exceedingly brave," she teased.

"You're not angry?"

"I think it's sort of funny, actually. Considering you got a whole lot more than just a dance."

"But you know what? I'm glad you lied to me that night. If it wasn't for the babies, I never would have had the guts to take a chance on myself." He kissed the tip of her nose. "On us. Because we're supposed to be together."

"I think I figured that out a long time ago."

He grinned. "You're clearly smarter than I am."

"I have a confession, too," she said. "And it's a little... well, *racy,* I guess."

One brow peaked with curiosity. "I'm all ears."

She slipped her hand under his shirt, laid it on his warm stomach. "I've always wondered what it would be like to fool around in a hospital bed."

His smile was a wicked one. "You don't say."

"But until now," she said, sliding her hand upward, to his chest. "I've never had the chance to test it out."

He must have had his hand right by the bed controls, because suddenly the head of the bed was sliding down. "I have an idea, Princess."

"Oh yeah? What's that?"

He lowered his head and kissed her, whispering against her lips, "Let's fool around and find out."

Epilogue

June

The babies were finally asleep.

Anne blew a silent kiss to her slumbering angels, made sure the baby monitor was on, then gathered the skirt of her gown and crept quietly from the nursery.

"I'll be back to check on them later," she told their nanny, Daria.

"Have a good time, Your Highness."

A glance up at the clock said she was already an hour late, but motherhood was her number one priority these days. Still, she didn't want to make him wait *too* long.

She stopped in her room to check her makeup one last time, then rushed down to the ballroom. In honor of her father, they were holding their second annual charity ball. And she could see, as she descended the stairs, that the turnout was even more impressive than last year.

Standing just inside the ballroom, chatting with Chris and Melissa, was Melissa's family, the royals of Morgan Isle. King Phillip and Queen Hannah, Prince Ethan and his wife, Lizzy, and the Duke, Charles Mead, and his wife, Victoria.

Several feet away Louisa and Princess Sophia stood, both pregnant and just beginning to show, comparing baby bumps while their husbands wore amused grins.

But the one person she wanted to see, who was supposedly waiting for her, was nowhere in sight.

Anne nabbed a glass of champagne from a passing waiter—the babies would be getting pumped milk tonight—sipped deeply and scanned the crowd.

"You're looking lovely, Your Highness," someone said from behind her.

The sound of his voice warmed her from the inside out.

She turned to face him. "A pleasure to see you again, Mr. Baldwin."

He bowed in greeting, and as he did a lock of that unruly blond hair fell across his forehead. "Please, call me Sam."

"Would you care to dance, Sam?"

He grinned, his dimples winking. The fire in his eyes still burned bright after a year. "I thought you'd never ask."

He took her hand and led her out to the dance floor, pulling her into his arms and holding her close. She pressed her cheek to his, breathed in the scent of his cologne.

"I'm the envy of every man in the room," he whispered.

She didn't know about that, but no one called her *The Shrew* any longer. That woman had ceased to exist the moment she met this amazing man. He brought out the best in her.

He nuzzled her cheek. "I'm the luckiest man here. And the happiest."

"How soon do you suppose we could sneak upstairs and do some real celebrating?" she asked and he cast her a sizzling smile. It was, after all, their one-year anniversary. And though there had been hard times and sad times, they had so much to celebrate. So much to be thankful for. Two healthy and gorgeous children, a family who loved and supported them.

And better yet, they had each other.

* * * * *

"If you think you can charm your way into my life again, you're even cockier than I thought."

"I'm surprised you'd let your hormones override the biggest business deal either of our firms have ever seen."

In his slow, easy manner, Cole moved across the room. "You're right. But, I just had to know."

"Know what?"

"If the sparks were still there." Cole stood squarely before her, leaned to her ear and whispered, "They are."

Dear Reader,

Falling in love for the first time is not only exciting; it can be a bit scary venturing into unknown territory. I have to say, I've never been on a more rewarding adventure than to have married my first love.

I cannot think of a better way to express my love and celebrate my eleventh wedding anniversary to my high-school sweetheart than the release of *From Boardroom to Wedding Bed?*

In this reunion story, you will soon discover that, like most people, Cole and Tamera never forgot the first time they fell in love. Now fate, and a career in the same field, has given them a second chance at a love so rare, so perfect.

I hope you experience all the emotions with Cole and Tamera as you did the first time you fell head over stilettos. :)

Much love,

Jules

SAVE OVER £31

Subscribe to Desire today to get 4 stories
a month delivered to your door for 12 months,
saving a fantastic £31.80.
Alternatively, subscribe for 6 months and save
£12.72, that's still an impressive 20% off!

FULL PRICE	YOUR PRICE	SAVINGS	MONTHS
£127.20	£95.40	25%	12
£63.60	£50.88	20%	6

As a welcome gift we will also
send you a FREE L'Occitane
gift set worth £10

**PLUS, by becoming a member you
will also receive these additional benefits:**

- 🌹 FREE P&P Your books delivered to your
  door every month at no extra charge

- 🌹 Be the first to receive new titles two
  months ahead of the shops

- 🌹 Exclusive monthly newsletter

- 🌹 Excellent Special offers

- 🌹 Membership to our Special Rewards programme

No Obligation- You can cancel your subscription at any time by writing
to us at Mills & Boon Book Club, PO Box 676, Richmond. TW9 1WU.

To subscribe, visit
www.millsandboon.co.uk/subscriptions

MILLS & BOON

D1HF1

FROM
BOARDROOM TO
WEDDING BED?

BY
JULES BENNETT

All the characters in this book have no existence outside the imagination of the author, and have no relation whatsoever to anyone bearing the same name or names. They are not even distantly inspired by any individual known or unknown to the author, and all the incidents are pure invention.

Published in Great Britain 2011
by Mills & Boon, an imprint of Harlequin (UK) Limited,
Eton House, 18-24 Paradise Road, Richmond, Surrey TW9 1SR

ISBN: 978 0 263 88313 8

51-0811

Harlequin (UK) policy is to use papers that are natural, renewable and recyclable products and made from wood grown in sustainable forests. The logging and manufacturing processes conform to the legal environmental regulations of the country of origin.

Printed and bound in Spain
by Blackprint CPI, Barcelona

Jules Bennett's love of storytelling started when she would get in trouble as a child and would tell her parents her imaginary friend Mimi did it. Since then her vivid imagination has taken her down a path she'd only dreamed of. When Jules isn't spending time with her wonderful supportive husband and two daughters, you will find her reading her favorite authors, though she calls that time "research." She loves to hear from readers! Contact her at julesbennett@falcon1.net, visit her website at www.julesbennett.com or send her a letter at PO Box 396, Minford, OH 45653, USA.

For my first, my only, my love…Michael. *Ti Amo*

One

"I'm offering the contract to…both of you."

Panic surged through Tamera Stevens as she jerked upright in her plush, leather seat at the same time Cole Marcum exclaimed, "You're serious?"

"I settle for nothing less than the best." Victor Lawson, world-renowned hotelier, spread his hands wide and tilted back in his leather chair. "Having my first hotel in the U.S. designed by the top architects in the country is what I want. If this is a problem, I need to know before anything is signed. I hope we can all work together to make this the biggest, grandest hotel not only to come to Miami, but to the entire country."

Problem? Oh, no. No problem at all, Tamera thought as she fought the urge to cry, scream or just race from the boardroom. Could they hear the rapid thump, thump, thump of her heart beating against her chest? Had perspiration already broken out along her top lip or forehead? God, if she didn't breathe she was going to pass out.

So, aside from the fact that Cole Marcum, her once fiancé, had broken her heart back in college and this was the first time she'd seen him in over a decade, no, there was no problem.

Oh, and now they were going to be forced to work together because no one, absolutely no one would turn down the chance to work with Victor Lawson.

Dandy, just dandy. Yup, this would be a problem-free work zone.

She wanted to throw up on her trendy silver pumps. If she and Cole agreed to this once-in-a-lifetime opportunity, they would be spending every waking moment together for months.

A lifetime had passed since they'd spent every waking, and several sleeping, moments together. Being together in such a tight-knit environment would certainly test her strength in taking over The Stevens Group and proving she was just as powerful and capable as her father of running the family's multimillion-dollar company.

But, did she really have to spend so much time with Cole? Couldn't she work with someone else in his firm? She was having a hard enough time being in this meeting that had only lasted ten minutes.

"I've never worked with another agency on a design," Cole spoke up, causing every nerve ending in Tamera's body to shiver. "A Marcum design is priceless and unique."

So, he still had a high opinion of himself? Obviously his ego had grown through the years since his abrupt departure.

Tamera couldn't deny the fact Cole had gotten even sexier as he'd aged, but his curl-your-toes, exotic good looks were merely a facade covering up the ugly persona beneath a billion-dollar smile and expensive, Italian suits.

She wished she could go into this amazing, once-in-a-lifetime opportunity with the excitement that came along with new projects, but how could she when the devil himself sat next to her?

Victor nodded, leaning forward to rest his elbows on the gleaming mahogany table. The billionaire was only in his late thirties, but he'd done more in his young years with his European businesses than many people do in a lifetime. With his blond hair, tanned skin, and blue eyes, he looked like the all-American playboy. And from the rumors and tabloids, he was known worldwide for breaking women's hearts.

"I understand your concern and confusion, Mr. Marcum, but I assure you, both of you, that this will be beneficial for all of us."

Beneficial? Business-wise, sure. On a personal level, this could be detrimental to her health and her heart. She'd had to put it back together piece by shattered piece. Was fate offering up the ultimate test to see how she would measure up?

Dammit. Why did he have to look even better than what she'd remembered? Those broad shoulders beneath his charcoal suit, coal black hair and chiseled facial features were only more of a distraction.

Yes, he looked every bit the professional, but he also looked a bit rugged with those hard, dark-as-night eyes that held you in your place.

Did he smile anymore? Was his demeanor just as cool as his stare? As a businessman, Cole and his twin brother Zach were sharks, but on a personal level, what was Cole like now?

No. She would not be swept into his world again. She would not sit and wonder what he did in his spare time. She would not think about the women who'd come through his life since he'd left her hurt and confused. She was a professional and she would remain as one, especially during the duration of this development.

Cole was extremely sexy, but sexy men were everywhere, especially in Miami. This man was no big deal. Really. Just because he'd taken her virginity, offered her the world and promised to love her forever, she wasn't about to sit around and pine over a dream that died long ago.

She was stronger now and had much more pressing matters to worry about than being slapped in the face with her past.

Like the fact that her father was nearing the end of his life.

Which was just one more reason why she had to get this project. Now that the CEO position had been turned over to her, she couldn't disappoint anyone in the company, especially her father. She wanted to prove to him, before he passed, that she would take care of the company that had been in their family for three generations.

Other than the caregivers she'd hired, no one knew of his illness. No one could. Stocks would fall and clients would pull projects if word spread about her father's sudden diagnosis with stage four lung cancer.

Walter Stevens *was* The Stevens Group. He'd worked at that firm before he went to college. He'd started at the lowest level and worked his way up and there wasn't a contractor in the business who didn't know him on a first-name basis. Which meant she had to be on her game with Victor Lawson. Errors, even of the smallest proportions, were unacceptable.

And Cole could never find out why her father was not in charge. He would use the untimely hardship to his advantage and she refused to allow him the upper hand in her life ever again. Or any man for that matter.

She supposed she should thank Cole. Because of his heartless act, she was stronger, more independent.

"I want this to be extravagant," Victor went on to say. "I want Miami and the entire world to see the passion behind this structure, the sexiness behind the elegance. People come to Miami to get away. I want them to be swept away to another time. I want lovers to feel like they are fulfilling a fantasy."

With any other project, the word "lover" wouldn't set her nerve endings on edge. This wasn't like any other project, though.

Tamera summoned all her will to fight and all of the B.S. she could handle to the surface. "Mr. Lawson, I can't speak for my associate, but I can speak on behalf of The Stevens Group when I say we would be delighted to work on this design with any firm of your choosing. We are anxious to get started."

Take that, Cole, Mr. I'm-Calling-Off-the-Engagement-and-I-Don't-Need-to-Provide-a-Reason.

Great, now she was turning juvenile. Poking jabs at her colleagues this early in the game would only cause problems…something she definitely didn't need right now. Especially with Victor's talk of "passion" and "sexiness."

Victor offered a triumphant smile and she nearly applauded her performance.

"I'm happy to hear that. I expected no less. Even though your father has started his retirement on such short notice, I knew any child of his would come through for me."

"Mr. Marcum?" Victor turned his attention to Cole. "You have nothing to lose here. You will not be splitting the money. You will each get the agreed amount when you put in your bids. That is only fair. Keep in mind I've never done that before, but I budgeted in the extra amount and with the design you two come up with, I'm sure I will still turn a nice profit from my investment in your companies."

His high hopes in her abilities only made the quivering in her stomach that much more erratic. And, she couldn't correct Victor's assumption of her father's "retirement." To anyone other than herself and the doctors and nurses, her father *was* in retirement. If only that could be the simple truth.

She'd been in her father's company since graduating college, working from the ground up just like he had. And now she was the CEO, though she would give the prestigious position up in a heartbeat if that meant her father could be well and come back to work.

Tamera inwardly sighed and steeled herself against the bubbling of past feelings as she, too, turned her attention to wait for Cole's answer. Past or no past, Tamera found herself intrigued by his powerful, sexy presence. If she were meeting him for the first time, she'd be interested in seeing him on a personal level. And that was saying quite a bit considering she hadn't found herself wanting to ask any man out lately. Not in years, in fact.

Where had the time gone? Obviously by the wayside with her nonexistent sex life.

Had she really turned into that thirtysomething

woman who had given up on happiness and relationships all because of one bad experience?

"If this is the only way we can work a deal, then I'm in, too."

Tamera breathed a sigh of relief, yet cringed at the thought of working with Cole. Yes, she wanted this job more than anything, but she really thought he'd put up more of a fight about working with her.

Could they actually pretend there was nothing between them? Their past was the proverbial elephant in the room and the darn thing had plopped down right between them, though Cole's cold stare and demeanor left her feeling foolish. Seems he wasn't as affected by her presence as she was by his.

Had Victor picked up on the tension or was he too caught up in his latest venture?

Working with Cole would be fine, she assured herself. Seriously, what choice did she really have here?

Professional. She would remain professional no matter what and the past would just have to stay where she'd left it eleven years ago…along with her heart.

"Excellent." Victor came to his feet. Tamera and Cole followed. "I'll have the contracts drawn up and sent to your offices. I hope to have them to you by the end of the week so we can get started. I will also send over a more detailed list of all my requirements and some of my own ideas. Questions or concerns should be addressed directly to me. Also, please feel free to step outside the box, literally. Get out of your offices and work where your creativity can flow without the interruptions of faxes, phones or assistants. Let yourself get carried away with this fantasy as you design."

Get carried away with the fantasy? No thanks. Been there, done that, got the broken heart as a souvenir.

Tamera shook Victor's hand, grabbed her designer handbag and headed out the door. Meeting over, no need to stick around and torture herself one more second than necessary with the crisp scent of Cole's cologne. Though she may as well get used to the agony. Working on this project would take months and she had a feeling this was just a small portion of what was in store for her.

Tamping down on the hurt of past memories, Tamera took the glass elevator down to the lobby of Victor Lawson's newest office building.

She was a professional now, not the twenty-two-year-old-girl who was young and in love with the man who'd promised her the world and then left her for no good reason. Oh, he'd mumbled something about being too young and getting engaged too fast, but she didn't believe that. Something happened to make him change his mind.

Whatever it was, if he wasn't strong enough to fight for her and what they had, she didn't want him. She was just surprised that someone like Cole, who'd seemed so in charge of his life and had a good grasp of where he was going, would take the easy way out when it came to love.

And if Cole Marcum was expecting her to be that same innocent girl, he would be sorely disappointed. She didn't have time to stroll down the broken path that led to memory lane. She had a company to run and a father to care for.

No, she didn't have time to even give Cole a second thought.

So why, from the moment the meeting started, was he the only topic in the forefront of her mind?

"Get in my office."

Cole slid his iPhone back into his pocket and paced

in what he liked to call the "pace space"—the area between his oversized chrome and glass desk and the large windows overlooking Miami's harbor and the countless yachts lining the dock.

Tamera Stevens.

Could the tightness in his chest be more bothersome? Hadn't enough years gone by to erase that band of guilt squeezing his heart? How could he have time to feel guilty for hurting Tamera, though, when he was running a multimillion-dollar company? Yes, he'd moved on and hadn't looked back. That didn't mean he was happy with the way he'd treated someone he'd deeply cared for.

But Victor Lawson merely piled on more guilt when he dropped the bomb that the two architectural firms would be working together. And not just the firms, but he'd specifically asked for Tamera and Cole to design the resort themselves. No assistants needed. No structural engineers to step in. Just the heads of the companies.

Fate was a fickle woman.

"What's up?"

Cole didn't stop pacing even when his twin, Zach, came to stand on the other side of the desk.

"We got the Lawson project," Cole told him as he stopped to look at the harbor, wishing he could be out on his own yacht.

"And your chipper tone is due to the fact that you hate signing multimillion-dollar deals with the biggest business mogul in the world?"

Cole threw a glance over his shoulder. "Sarcasm is not appreciated right now. We have to work with another firm on this."

That got Zach's attention. "Who?"

Turning back to the beauty of the water, Cole clenched his teeth. "The Stevens Group."

"Walter Stevens? You hate that bastard."

Wasn't that an understatement? Who wouldn't hate the man who'd threatened to ruin his future all because he fell in love with the man's daughter?

"It's a bit more complicated." Cole sighed, spun around and sat on the edge of the windowsill. "Walter isn't working on this for some reason."

"Tamera is."

Even though it wasn't a question, Cole nodded, prompting a low whistle from Zach.

"Want me to handle the design?" Zach asked. "I don't mind working with her. It actually may be best, considering."

The thought was tempting, but Cole refused to back down now. "No. I want to work with her."

"You can't be serious." Zach said. "It's been, what, eleven years? She's not going to be the same person you fell in love with, Cole. Trust me, love dies."

Cole couldn't argue the truth. And his twin knew firsthand. Zach had a marriage that didn't get much past the "I do's" before the bride took off with another man. But Cole didn't want love. He wanted Walter Stevens to see he was strong enough to be paired with his precious company and daughter. The merging of companies on this project was priceless. In fact, it was just the opportunity he'd been waiting for to show Walter Stevens he was just as powerful, if not more so, than the old man.

"What are you going to do?" Zach asked, leaning against the corner of the desk. "Are you finally going to tell her you were threatened by the old man?"

"No. She wouldn't believe me and that was so long ago, we've both moved on." So many thoughts and ideas bounced around inside his head. "Granted, I can't avoid the fact she's still the sexiest woman I've ever seen. Who knows? Maybe that sexual chemistry is still there. It would sure make for an interesting few months."

Zach let out a chuckle. "What if she's just a typical spoiled little rich girl who's stepping into shoes she can't even possibly fill?"

Cole considered the possibility. "That may be, but I don't want anything from Tamera other than a good partner on this project. Besides, she still seems sweet and innocent. Nothing like Walter."

"Sweet and innocent was probably shot straight to hell when you trampled her heart without giving her cause," Zach said, as if Cole needed the reminder. "I don't know about you, but I think a multimillion-dollar deal is far more important than lust. Will you be able to concentrate?"

The Stevens Group was one of the top design firms in the country, which made her a complete professional. They could do the job, and hopefully if that sexual attraction still existed…well…

Not that he wanted anything remotely like what they'd had. Hell no. He only wanted to see if she tasted the same, if her skin still shivered beneath his touch. What hot-blooded male wouldn't want to explore that body again?

Tamera Stevens was a typical Miami bombshell with long blonde hair, blue eyes and a body that was centerfold material. He'd be interested in her even if they'd just met. The fact that they shared a past only made the situation more intriguing.

As for love? No thanks. Any feelings remotely resembling love had died along with their dreams of a life together. Love didn't have a place in his world…not when his life consisted of nothing but his scale, butter paper and the art of design. Love was a lost emotion that Walter Stevens had personally sucked right out of him.

"I'm concentrating," Cole said with a grin. "Believe me, I'm concentrating. Tamera has no idea of the man I've become."

Zach raised a brow. "This competition isn't between you and Tamera. It's between you and her father."

Walter Stevens had never liked Cole, but when Cole proposed to Tamera the summer between their senior year of college and right before graduate school, Walter pulled out the threats.

If Cole didn't let Tam go, Walter would get Cole's scholarship taken away. Walter Stevens had connections everywhere and Cole knew the man wasn't just blowing hot air.

And because Cole, Zach and their baby sister Kayla were raised by their grandmother and basically had to scrape to get by, Cole had to give in. He had no connections and his only ticket out of near poverty was his scholarship.

Choosing between the future of his career and the future of his heart was the hardest decision he'd ever had to make…and one he'd questioned every day for a long time after the breakup. But he firmly believed everything happened for a reason and Cole was just fine with how his life had turned out.

The next few months would certainly be a challenge. But Cole was up for anything. Especially if it meant making millions—and exploring Tamera's seductive curves once again.

Two

The contracts were signed. There was no turning back.

She could do this. Working with Cole would be just like back in college at the University of Florida when they'd worked on designs together in her off-campus apartment or his dorm room.

Except now they were dealing with millions of dollars and not grades…or feelings.

Okay, so they were dealing with feelings, at least, she was. But any emotions she had were just remnants from what they had before.

What they had before? Tam rolled her eyes and shut down her computer, thankful to be going home. Anything they'd had before had been strictly one-sided or Cole wouldn't have been able to walk away without looking back. She'd gotten over the fact that he'd walked away, but what she hadn't recovered from was his reasoning…or lack thereof.

When he'd called their engagement off, Tamera was sick. She'd taken her father's advice and transferred schools so she could break ties with Cole and start new. But even though she'd moved on, she never forgot the man she'd loved with her whole heart.

The man who currently stood filling her office doorway.

"Cole." Erratic heartbeats and instant jellylike knees made her thankful she was seated behind her desk instead of standing. "What are you doing here?"

"We need to talk."

He made his way across the plush, white carpet. Even at the end of a long business day, the man still looked amazing. He'd shed his tie and jacket, leaving him in black pants and a baby blue dress shirt with the sleeves rolled up onto his tanned forearms. A bit of dark shadow around his jawline made her catch her breath.

Past or no past, this man was sexy as all get-out and she couldn't deny the fact. Why couldn't he at least have gotten an unsightly beer gut after all these years?

"I was just heading home," she told him, trying to ignore his pantherlike eyes. "If you'd like to call tomorrow, I'd be happy to discuss the initial planning of the design."

Instead of taking a seat across from her desk, like most visitors, Cole came around the side and propped a hip on the corner, mere inches from her. That same masculine cologne he'd had on during their meeting with Victor tickled and teased her senses. His broad shoulders filled his dress shirt and his lips were just as full and kissable as they were the day he'd asked her to marry him.

Mercy. Day one of…how quick could they finish this project?

"I'm not here to discuss the design."

Did the man blink? Why was he staring? Was he really that unaffected by their reunion? Surely the crackle of tension in the air wasn't only vibrating around her.

Tamera cleared her throat and scooted back a bit in her chair. She didn't pretend to misunderstand the topic he was approaching. Did he honestly believe he could barge into her office and pick up where he dropped her?

"Cole, this isn't professional. Rehashing the past won't do a thing toward getting these designs done, so why go there?"

His gaze traveled over her, making her feel even more heated than before. When his eyes roamed back to her face, he seemed to study her. Tamera hated being under a microscope.

"Are you really okay working with me?" he asked in a low, steady voice. "That's the real reason I'm here. We should discuss this arrangement without Victor or our staff present."

Damn the man for being so cool and controlled. And how dare he think she'd be withering at the thought of working with him? If the only reason he came was to make sure she was "man" enough for the job, she'd show him who would dominate this situation.

Tamera came to her feet, causing Cole to look up from his half-seated position. "This is a dream job, Cole. Brainstorming with the devil won't make me back down, so there's no need to coddle me and pretend you care about my feelings."

He smiled, but remained perched on the corner of her

desk. "Zach offered to take my place, but he's normally the on-site guy."

Even though the ache hadn't moved from her chest since she'd seen Cole a week ago at the initial meeting with Victor, she pasted on a smile and moved toward her fourth-story window and looked out onto the city lights of sultry, sexy South Beach.

"So, you two have discussed my well-being? How thoughtful. I assure you, I'll be fine. The question is, will you?"

She turned back to see his reaction and was surprised when the muscle in his jaw ticked. Cole came to his feet, closing the space between them.

Didn't the man know how to read body language? Hadn't she given him the not-so-subtle hint that she wanted space? And why did her body have to betray her by reacting to this enticing man?

"To be honest," he said, looming over her, backing her against the cool glass, "I may not be."

How did she lose control over this situation and in her own office, for crying out loud?

She moistened her lips and cursed herself when his eyes darted to her mouth. Now he chooses to read body language. Surely he wasn't going to kiss her.

"Why is that?" she asked, thankful her voice didn't crack.

"Because you're even more alluring and vivacious than you were in college. I'm intrigued."

"Good for you."

She tried to be nonchalant, but God help her, she wanted to kiss him. She wanted to feel his lips on hers again. She wasn't even going to try to lie to herself.

When they'd been together, they'd been good. For nearly two years, they'd been inseparable. Nothing and no one had come close to filling her heart the way Cole had back then. Kissing Cole would only catapult her back in time and ruin any hopes of being professional on this project.

Sanity prevailed as she shoved him back.

"No." She moved around him and went to her door, gesturing for him to leave. "If you think you can charm your way into my life again, you're even cockier than I thought. I'm surprised you'd let your hormones override the biggest business deal either of our firms has ever seen."

In his slow, easy manner, Cole moved across the room, hands shoved into his pants pockets. "You're right. But, I just had to know."

She hated to be predictable and ask, but she had to. "Know what?"

"If the sparks were still there." Cole stood squarely before her, leaned to her ear and whispered. "They are."

Without another word, he walked from her office. Whistling.

Tamera resisted the urge to slam the door. Could he be more maddening?

Whistling? Ugh! If he thought for one minute he could play around with her emotions, business, personal or otherwise, she'd show him. Nothing, absolutely nothing would come between her and this project.

Especially not an ex-fiancé who looked even sexier now than he had when she'd been head over heels. Too bad he had a cocky attitude and an overinflated ego.

Tamera was still seething that evening when she drove her silver BMW through the wrought-iron gates of her father's Coral Gables home. But by the time she'd pulled up in front and walked up the concrete steps, she'd forced herself to calm down.

Her father didn't need to know she was working with another firm right now. He especially didn't need to know it was Cole's firm. All he needed to do was concentrate on having pain-free days…if such a thing existed at this point.

She was certainly glad she'd calmed herself when her father's nurse came from his room with a grim face.

Panic coursed through her. "Danita, what is it?"

The elderly lady gripped Tamera's arm and led her to the living room. "I'm afraid it's time, Miss Stevens."

Tamera knew this day was coming. The day when remaining at home would no longer be a possibility for her father. Hospice was, of course, her next step.

She nodded. "I'll do what needs to be done, then. I just want him as comfortable as possible."

Danita offered a sad smile and squeezed Tamera's arm. "I'll talk to the doctor and see if there's any way we can keep him sedated here until the time comes."

For him to die. The sentence wasn't completed, but the words hung in the air just the same.

"I'd rather he be home," Tamera thought aloud. "But, if the hospice center can take him now, I will make those arrangements myself. I just signed on with a huge project at work, so I won't be able to take time off, but I will get him whatever he needs. I want him to be as comfortable as possible."

Two months ago her father was running one of the top architectural firms in the country and now he was struggling just to hang on. For her.

Tamera knew he had no reason to go on other than to make sure she was happy. And knowing how stubborn he was, he was probably hanging on to make sure she didn't screw up his company.

The idea made her smile through the pain. She wouldn't put it past him.

Seriously, though, she had to get this project drawn up. She had to contact Cole and make this happen sooner rather than later so she could give her father one last gift.

He could go in peace knowing she'd carry the torch that was passed down to her. He could rest assured she would go on to build amazing structures, and live up to the reputation her grandfather had fought hard to achieve for the company.

Tamera eased the door open to her father's room, careful to be quiet in case he was sleeping. No such luck.

She pushed the door open and stepped into the sunlit room. "I thought I'd find you asleep."

Walter Stevens turned his attention from the floor-to-ceiling window overlooking the bay toward her. "I didn't expect you today."

They went through this at every visit and every time she just laughed. The doctors said his mind would slip with this disease, but she didn't believe so. He was still just as sharp as he ever was. He was only testing her because he felt she should live in her office...as he had.

"What can I get you?" she asked, coming to stand beside the high-backed headboard of his bed, which was full of plump pillows. "More water or a snack? Danita is making dinner, but it won't be ready for another hour or so."

He waved a frail hand in the air. "You two worry too

much about me. Tell me about what's going on with the firm."

"We're moving forward and so far, so good. No one has asked too much about your absence because they're satisfied with the explanation that you're not fully retired, just practicing to see if it fits."

Once upon a time, he would've picked up on the fact that she'd danced around the question and eased into another topic. But that was when he was on his game and not fighting for every day he had left to live.

There was no way she was going to talk to him about the deal with Victor Lawson. He would only worry about details she had under control instead of his own health. She didn't want him to worry about anything.

Added to that, if she went into the details of the Lawson project with him, she'd have to add that they were paired with Cole's firm. She didn't want to have to explain that. Considering Tamera had cried herself to sleep for months and her father held her hand most of those nights, she doubted Walter would want to hear anything about Cole Marcum.

The project was best left out of the discussion. At least for now.

"I'm sorry all this is on your shoulders, Tamera. Work must be stressful," he told her, studying her face. "You have dark circles under your eyes. You're not taking care of yourself."

Offering her father a smile, she patted his arm. "No worries. I've got it all under control. I'm just getting used to filling the big shoes you left me."

He didn't chuckle at her half-hearted attempt to lighten the moment. "What aren't you telling me?"

She shook her head. "Nothing you need to worry about right now."

"I'm going to worry as long as I'm drawing breath," he assured her. "We haven't lost any clients, have we?"

"Of course not. All the clients, old and new, are pleased with the work we are providing. Now, quit worrying and just concentrate on yourself. I'm in charge now."

Finally, he smiled. "I bet you've waited a long time to say that to me."

"I have." She grinned back, though she hated that he was more like the child now and she the parent. "I'm going to go so you can rest before dinner. I'll call or come back later."

She kissed her father good-bye and let herself out of his Coral Gables estate to head toward her condo in South Beach.

SoBe was such a beautiful, tranquil setting. Maybe one day she'd get to enjoy the fashion shops and nightlife like she used to. She missed dancing, having fun with friends. But priorities came first, and going out mingling in celebratory style seemed inappropriate these days. No wonder she didn't have a love life or someone to support her during tough times. She hadn't been anywhere in what seemed like forever.

A stab of envy jabbed her as she passed the people milling about in and out of the specialty shops, strolling along the beach, laughing. Their lives seemed so carefree, so full of joy.

Tamera allowed the tears to fall, considering she was alone. She figured she was more than entitled. Her emotions had taken hit after hit today.

With the beginning of this project and the ending of her father's life, Tamera didn't know if she could take on an attack from Cole. But, if she could get her crying jags out in private, maybe she could put up a steelier front in public. Vulnerability and weakness had no place in her professional life.

When she pulled into her garage, Tamera pulled her cell from her purse. She dialed Cole's office line, fully expecting to get voice mail, but his strong voice came through the receiver.

"Cole Marcum."

She closed her eyes, rested her head against the leather headrest and swallowed the tears. "I didn't expect to get you this late."

"Tamera." His surprise, and smile, came through the phone. "Then why did you call?"

"To leave a message. I'd like to meet first thing in the morning to start on this design."

"Wonderful. My yacht is at Bal Harbor."

Her eyes flew open as she jerked upright in her seat. "Your *yacht?*"

"Yes, that's where I do my work. It's a place I can clear my thoughts and stay focused without interruptions. I will inform the staff they have the day off."

Tamera massaged her forehead, easing away the start of a tension headache. "I'm not having a meeting on your yacht. This isn't a social call, Cole. We're architects. We meet in boardrooms."

He chuckled, which only added to her already frazzled nerves.

"Tamera, that's how I work at the start of a project. I'll have a lunch prepared so we can just keep working. Besides, didn't Victor say to step outside the box? We can't go against our client's wishes, now can we?"

She resisted the urge to hang up on him. Clearly he was hell-bent on proving this was the only way to go.

"Trust me," he continued in that condescending tone. "You'll like the fact there will be nothing to worry about except how fast your Sharpie can keep up with that creative side I know you have."

Now Tamera laughed, shaking her head. "I'll overlook the fact that you just asked me to trust you and simply warn you that if you even attempt to charm me or toy with me the way you did earlier, I'll walk off that boat and we'll continue every meeting *inside* the box of my office. Now, which yacht is yours?"

He gave her specific directions and by the time she hung up, Tamera felt like she'd let control of this whole situation slip through her grasp. But if Cole did indeed work this way and Victor thought it would aid in the design process, she had to accommodate these men in order to get the blueprints done before…

Tamera stepped from her car and attempted to quickly resurrect some walls around her heavy heart. She couldn't take another beating. Not now when so much was on the line.

Three

Cole hadn't lied when he'd told Tamera he did his best work on his yacht, though if he'd been asked to work with any other firm, he certainly wouldn't have invited them on board.

He needed her to see more of who he was today. Not only that, he wanted to get this seduction plan rolling right off the bat. This was the perfect opportunity to kill three birds with one stone.

In their recent meetings, he hadn't missed the way her pulse leapt beneath that smooth, creamy skin on her neck, nor had he missed the way she moistened her lips as if she were nervous, aroused, or both. She wanted him as much as he wanted her and that angered her more than she cared to admit.

She wanted distance from him, which was understandable considering how he left things so long ago, but that wasn't the main reason she was moving away.

If her voice hadn't shaken, he may have just believed the flames shooting from her glare were directed in a negative way. But as he'd closed the distance between them, her words trembled.

Point for him for getting back under her skin in such a short time.

Reading a woman's body language was second nature to him and he'd had plenty of experience reading Tamera's. He knew her on every level a man and a woman could know each other. True, eleven years may have passed, but she hadn't changed that much. She was torn between wanting to see if their chemistry still existed and wanting to rip his eyes out.

Cole couldn't wait to see which power prevailed.

He was certain of one thing, though. When he wanted her, he'd have her. Seducing her would be no problem.

Tamera still had heat and desire, even if both were fueled by anger and rage. Her passionate side still existed and he was going to take full advantage.

"Hello?"

Tamera's voice echoed down through the galley. Cole put on his game face and stepped up onto the gleaming cherry finish of the deck. He briefly stopped in his tracks, forcing himself to act like a professional and let this physical attraction play out.

She was wearing a white skirt, simple white tennis shoes and a blue-and-white-striped sleeveless top. With her pale hair in loose waves around her shoulders, she looked so innocent. If only she knew where his thoughts had traveled.

"Come on down," he motioned for her to join him below. "I had the staff prepare some pastries and fruit. There's also a variety of juices."

He moved over to the kitchen and helped himself to a grape.

"Nice yacht."

Her sarcastic tone had him looking back over his shoulder. "Thanks."

"I never expected to see my name on the side of it."

Cole shrugged, refusing to rise to her challenge or mocking attitude. "Not your name. I named my boat "TAM" after the first stock I invested in that turned over a nice profit and allowed me to purchase such a luxury."

She eyed him as if she didn't believe a word he said.

"Oh, you thought I named it after you?" he laughed. "How awkward. But, seriously, I'd have a whole fleet if I named boats after all my exes."

He turned back to the fruit, ignoring the hurt in her eyes, not caring what she thought. He wasn't lying. Though he didn't tell her he invested in that stock because of her.

He was over what they had. Too much time had passed for him to still be harboring feelings for someone he'd cared about over a decade ago and he had too much on his plate these days anyway to keep someone like Tamera entertained in a relationship-type setting.

All he wanted from her was two things: design and sex.

He readied a plate for her and watched from the corner of his eye while Tamera stood in the entryway taking in her surroundings. His pride swelled. He knew how his cruiser yacht appeared—expensive and elegant.

"This is nice, Cole." Her tone had softened.

The surprise in her voice both irritated and pleased him. Growing up with nothing and working your way to the top did have advantages, but hadn't he told her he'd never have to scrape by again? Hadn't he said those very same words to her father? Hadn't he promised Walter Stevens that Tamera would never want for anything if Cole could marry her? Did she not think he could do it?

Obviously he had been the only one with faith in himself. Now he was even more irritated that he was second-guessing the past and replaying it over and over in his head.

"Yes, it is."

Reining in these emotions was the best approach right now. He had to keep the past out of their conversations and simply do what he told Zach—work on the design, and make Victor Lawson the happiest client and hotelier in the world. If anything happened with Tamera on an intimate level, well, he would consider this project a smashing success.

She placed her black briefcase on the table in front of the sofa. "I was running late and didn't get a chance to grab breakfast. That fruit is calling my name." She took a strawberry from the plate Cole offered her.

Cole reached for another grape, popped it in his mouth and stared. Was she really going to go on like there was no history? Like there was no sexual tension? Like they were just colleagues meeting for the first time?

Fine. That was just fine. He could work with this. The fact that she hadn't looked him in the eye since she'd stepped on board was just another positive in his favor. Her nerves were getting to her and he'd most definitely use that to his advantage…in business and pleasure.

"Do you want to sit on the sofa or at the dinette?"

She looked around the cozy living area. "The sofa will be fine for now since we're not actually drawing anything out. I think we need to brainstorm and then I can draw up some rough sketches."

Cole took a seat near her on the sofa.

She pulled papers from her briefcase and moved the case to the floor at her feet. He couldn't help when his eyes tracked her movements and he locked in on her small, tanned ankles against the stark white shoes. Nor did he feel guilty about reacquainting himself with her body all over again.

She was so delicate he wanted to run his hands up her petite legs to see if she still trembled beneath his touch. He wasn't delusional, though. Cole knew when he got his hands on her again, she wouldn't be the only one trembling. But this time, Cole wouldn't get his heart tangled in such a mess as love…or anything that remotely resembled that useless emotion.

"I assume you've had a chance to glance over everything," she said, reaching for another strawberry and biting into it.

Cole nodded and focused on the Lawson project instead of her full, pink lips making an O shape around the fruit. "Yes. It'll be an exciting ride, but well worth it, not only to our companies, but to the economy in Miami as well."

"I agree." She swallowed and pulled a paper from the folder. "I went through and categorized Victor's ideas."

Cole laughed, easing back into the corner of the beige leather sofa. "I remember you used to group everything. That was one of the things I lo—"

He shook his head at the major slip-up, and before he could backpedal, Tamera spoke up.

"We share a past, Cole. It's bound to come up at some point." She pointed to the sheet. "But as I was saying, I broke this down into groups. Necessities are marked in yellow, structure is in green, safety features are in red, décor is in pink. I saw Kayla's name on the contract. Is she working with you and Zach?"

Cole nodded. "She usually does all the décor for our projects. Actually, my sister is really anxious to get started on this. She's finishing up a project in L.A. right now."

Tamera tilted her head, causing her soft blond hair to swing over her shoulder. "Does she do independent work as well, though?"

"Yes, but the project she's doing now is for an office building Zach and I designed. She should be home in a couple of days."

Tamera's blue eyes sparkled. "I can't wait to see her again."

Not only had the Cole/Tamera tie been broken, so had the Tamera/Kayla bond. All because Walter Stevens had a chip on his shoulder and wanted better for his little girl than "trailer trash."

Tamera's soft, soothing voice slid over him as she talked about various groups she'd outlined. Cole listened, but only halfway. Her voice always did have that hypnotic effect on him.

Back at the University of Florida, Cole always found himself trying to study with her in her studio apartment and the next thing he knew they were naked and tangled in each others arms on the couch, floor, wherever.

When they stayed at his dorm, they always had to deal with Zach and his revolving door of women. That made evenings awkward for all parties involved, so they tended to stay at her apartment. It was amazing either of them made the good grades they did.

"Did you zone out on me?"

He shook aside the pleasant memories from what seemed like a lifetime ago and saw that she was smiling. "Just thinking ahead to the finished design."

She reached for another strawberry. "Tell me what you've been thinking as far as the theme for the hotel."

This was a no-brainer for him. "Classic. Timeless. Something from an era when life was simpler, women were elegant and men were gentlemen."

Her smile widened. "We're on the same page, then, because that's exactly the vibe I was getting from Victor's requirements and ideas."

"He knew we'd make a good team."

Damn. Admitting that in his head was one downfall he didn't appreciate. Having it out in the open was even more fatal to his position. He'd never let a woman have control over his emotions since Tamera and he'd be damned if he'd let her have that privilege ever again. Though the breakup was no fault of hers, the whole situation left a bitter taste in his mouth.

Tamera's baby blues stared as her smile faltered. Cole didn't say another word, but he could practically see the wheels spinning inside her head and those thoughts bumping into each other in her mind had nothing to do with business.

"This is going to be harder than I thought." She came to her feet, tossing the folder onto her vacated seat on the sofa. "I knew the past would come up in conversation, I just didn't expect it to be this uncomfortable."

Her declaration surprised him and he got up, too, standing almost toe-to-toe with her. "Look, if you can't handle this, you should've told Victor before you signed."

She shoved her shoulders back. "I can handle this just fine. I said it was uncomfortable. That's all."

"Really."

"Yes. Really. I mean to see you after all this time and then to act like this is a typical job. Not to mention the fact this is my first project as CEO."

"Congratulations, by the way," Cole offered, in an attempt to lighten the mood. "Didn't know your father retired."

He hated thinking of her father, but he hated even more when all color drained from her face at the mention of the man.

What the hell?

"Tamera?" Cole reached out to take her arm. "What's wrong now?"

She shook her head. "I'm fine. I don't want to disappoint my father and I don't want to let the firm down. I just have a lot riding on this."

No, there was something much more than that. Cole knew this woman well enough to know when she was holding something back, and she definitely was. Now he just had to figure out what was going on with Walter Stevens. She'd been fine until the mention of her father's absence. Odd that Cole hadn't heard of his retirement before. Was the man indeed retired or was something wrong?

She went on to say, "I'd actually like to work on this as much as we can to finish up the drawing as soon as possible."

"Not a problem." Why was she so rushed, he wondered, releasing her arm. "The sooner we get this done, the sooner we can start construction and hopefully get done before the projected date."

"That would be amazing."

"If you're so nervous about letting people down, why don't you just ask your father for advice? I'm sure he'd be more than willing to help you, especially since he just turned over the reins to you. He may even consider coming back for such an important project."

Walter would do anything for his baby girl, Cole thought, including threaten her fiancé and not give a damn he was hurting his precious daughter in the process.

Oh, but the thought of going toe-to-toe with Walter again got Cole's blood pumping. The image of the two of them being paired on this project was laughable and Cole found himself actually wanting the opportunity to present itself so he could show the old bastard what he was made of.

Tamera turned her back to Cole, her head drooping between her shoulders. "I really can't talk about my father, Cole."

Seriously? Something was definitely wrong.

Had something happened? Had he threatened Tam about this project? Surely not. But what had her so upset?

"Tam."

To hell with their past, present, future. To hell with the designs and his promise not to charm her. He needed to at least appear concerned. How else would he get her where he wanted her? He needed her to trust him, especially now, so he could get to the truth about Walter's real reason for being a no-show on the biggest project his firm had ever seen.

Cole placed his hands on her slender shoulders, squeezing gently when she only tensed.

"Whatever it is, push it aside. We can't allow personal emotions to interfere with this project."

When she turned back around, her eyes were misty, but that defiant chin was tilted. And because he didn't want her to mistake his touch for anything intimate, Cole removed his hand.

"It's just personal," she said, looking up. "Nothing I can't handle. I've just got more riding on this deal than you will ever know."

As if he didn't have a great deal riding on this project himself? The reputation of his firm was on the line.

"But I am begging you," she added. "Please don't make me stroll down memory lane with you. I just can't. I don't have the energy to fight you about it, either. Not now."

Cole nodded. "You have my word."

A mocking laugh escaped her. "That means nothing to me. Just concentrate on business."

More and more intrigued at what plagued her, he let her go, but knew without a doubt that whatever was hurting Tamera this much had to be something major. For her to give in to her emotions and nearly break down in tears in front of him told him that this strong woman was teetering on the edge.

Four

"Sleek, yet bold and elegant."

Tamera nodded, adding, "Old World elegance."

"Perfect."

Working in Cole's million-dollar yacht, earning high praise and approval from him shouldn't make her feel warm and tingly like a schoolgirl, but it did just the same.

Between her father's illness and the stress of trying to perfect the one design that could be the biggest career move she'd ever taken, she'd gladly embrace all the warm feelings she could muster…even if they came from the only man who'd taken her heart, squashed it and handed it back without even so much as an apology.

Cole eased back into the leather club chair and crossed his ankle over his knee. "Tell me more of your vision."

Tamera pulled out her black Sharpie and a sheet of

butter paper and laid it across his long, glossy dinette table. "Since this is Miami, we need to continue with the white stone, column and arched look, but keep it in the massive size." She drew some quick sketches, then stopped with her marker hovering over the sheet and closed her eyes. The finished product floated through her mind. "We want this to be grand like in *Casablanca*. Refined. Maybe not so much glitz, but all of the glamour. Polished."

"There should be two wide sets of stairs facing opposite directions, coming together as one and then leading up to the arched, open doorway of the resort entrance. Large pillars, maybe covered with greenery or flowers trailing over them at the base of the staircases with oversize, lantern-type lights."

"Stunning."

Tamera jerked upright, opening her eyes. Cole stood directly beside her, mere inches away. His heavy-lidded gaze roamed over her face, pausing on her mouth.

"All of it."

Tamera licked her lips and cursed herself when the innocent gesture sent the muscle in Cole's jaw ticking. The last thing they needed was more sexual tension. Hadn't he given his word *not* to rehash the past? Granted he wasn't saying anything, but his actions were purposely throwing her back to a time she couldn't settle into.

"Tell me your visions." She'd force him to be professional. But if he didn't step back, she was in danger of getting swept away by that intense gaze, by his amazing masculine cologne.

"Clean, crisp. Flawless."

"We're on the same page then. I'll draw up some more rough sketches in the morning and get with you in a couple of days. I'll call your assistant and set up another time to meet."

Placing her lid back on the marker, Tamera turned fully in an attempt to gather her things, but ended up bumping Cole in the process. He hadn't offered her room to maneuver, so now he was within inches of her face.

Wonderful. Not only did he have that sexy stubble on his face, those wide shoulders blocked her view of anything behind him. That darn cologne of his surrounded her just as if he'd wrapped his arms around her and pulled her against his broad chest. And, heaven help her, she knew precisely how those strong arms felt.

"I have everything on board to do rough sketches. My scale is in the desk." Though he didn't offer to move to get it. "No need to leave."

She looked him dead in his navy-rimmed eyes. "We both know there is."

"If you're uncomfortable—"

"Uncomfortable?" Tamera raised a brow and propped her hands on her hips. "I'm not uncomfortable. What I am is a professional."

A corner of his mouth kicked up, mocking her. "And you're implying I'm not."

She merely shrugged, moved around him and went to pick up her bag. But before she could make it back to the sofa, Cole's hand closed around her bare arm.

"Let's just get this out of the way." He spun her around to face him, his grip tight. "The Marcum Agency has an impeccable reputation, which is what landed us this job. I have never been, nor will I ever be anything less than professional. I'll admit working with you is difficult— I'm human and I'm male and you're still damn sexy. I can't help the fact I'm still attracted to you.

"Now, do I plan to act on my ill-timed feelings?" he continued, still holding her arm. "No. But I won't try to pussyfoot around the topic either."

Tamera refused to lick her lips, swallow or allow her gaze to travel from his eyes. She would not give him anymore ammunition to add to this awkward moment or his power over the situation.

She knew she needed to regain control, but nearly laughed at the irony. This was all they'd ever fought about before…control. Some things, bad as she hated to admit it, never changed.

"If you think I'm still attractive, that's an issue you'll have to deal with." Even if the idea made her tingle, he was still a cold-hearted, selfish jerk. "I'm not here to do anything other than work. I have too much going on in my life, even if we didn't share a past breakup, to pursue anything with anyone."

Again, he studied her face. Why did he feel the need to do that so much?

She jerked her arm free. "I'll have my assistant call yours."

Before he could call her back or get hold of her again, Tamera grabbed her bag, raced up the short stairs to the deck and onto the dock. Any more of those long, not-so-innocent looks or touches would send her up in flames. Because, like it or not, Cole Marcum was sexier now than she'd ever dreamed possible—and she had dreamt of him over the years. His professional status and standings only added to that sexy, exotic allure he had.

Why did fate have to mock her? Why did this person have to come back into her life at this point in time when she was most vulnerable? If he kept insisting on touching her, she might just give in to her desires and let him. Would he act so cocky then? If she surprised him and told him to take what he wanted, would he?

Just once she'd like to feel strong arms around her. Arms that would embrace her and lift all her heavy baggage and burdens. Arms that belonged to a man who loved her and cared whether she was happy or miserable.

But those were dreams she'd given up on long ago. If Cole offered her anything, it would be nothing beyond lust and she just didn't have the time or the energy to deal with uncomfortable emotions.

Since they were inevitably going to be spending time together, why couldn't she take what she wanted? Yes, she and Cole shared a past and were two different people now, but there was still that sexual pull. Even she couldn't deny that.

Tamera flew through the streets toward her condo and plotted. Yes, if Cole kept insinuating they should explore this passion that still lingered, she'd call his bluff.

Then they would see who held all the power.

"I'll come by and sign the papers tomorrow."

Cole stood in Tamera's office doorway and waited for her to acknowledge he was here. He leaned against the door frame, listening as she chatted away on the phone.

Beauty personified. Her head was tilted back against her leather office chair, the gesture exposing her creamy skin from her chin to the deep V in her silk blouse. Her silky blond hair was piled on top of her head in a sexy, messy way that only added to her appeal.

She held the phone to her ear, rubbed her forehead and sighed. "I want this to be as painless for him as possible."

Who? Obviously this was a personal call. All the more intriguing and all the more reason he should continue his ill-mannered eavesdropping.

Could this be the secret he'd wanted to discover about Walter or was there another man in her life? Too bad. He wanted this woman back in his bed. Now. Another man would just have to back down because he sure as hell wasn't going to.

"I appreciate all your help. Yes, I'll be fine. We knew this was going to happen, but knowing it and following through are two separate things. See you first thing in the morning."

Cole cleared his throat and righted himself as Tamera eased forward in her chair to hang up the phone. Had she known he'd listened in on much of a personal conversation, she'd blast him for his rudeness and expect an apology. Something he wouldn't dream of.

"Still believe in working overtime, I see."

He stepped into her office, and though he wasn't sorry he'd snuck up on her and listened when he really had no right, he was sorry for the shadows under her eyes and the turmoil broiling behind those beautiful baby blues.

"How did you get in?" she asked, coming to her feet.

"Your assistant let me in on her way out." He crossed the plush, white carpeting to stand on the opposite side of her glass-topped desk. "I told her we had a meeting scheduled late."

Tamera crossed her arms over her silky green shirt. The innocent gesture did absolutely amazing things to her chest, but that was definitely a thought he'd have to keep to himself.

"We don't have a meeting," she countered with a lift of one perfectly arched brow.

"We can," he said with a smile, hoping to take her mind off the intense phone conversation. "Let's go grab something to eat."

"We're not dating."

No, he didn't want anything that complex. "It's dinnertime and we can do some more brainstorming and combine our plans."

She searched the length of his body and back up. Again, the innocent gesture thing was killing him.

"I don't see your plans."

"They're in the car." He offered her another smile. "You coming or not?"

With a sigh, Tamera held her hands up in surrender. "All right. I have a few sample designs on my laptop. Tell me where we're going and I'll meet you there."

"I'll drive."

She eyed him, but Cole held her stare. No way was he going to let her get behind the wheel. She looked stressed, exhausted and ready to drop.

Seducing her into his bed would be so easy.

His body literally ached for that close contact again. But how could he take advantage of her in her condition?

Damn, why did he have to be such a gentleman at times? Especially when she obviously didn't even appreciate the fact.

"Fine, but don't think this is anything other than business." Tam came around her desk, crossed to a small closet tucked in the corner of her office and pulled out her bag. "Pull your car around front. I'll meet you there."

She followed him to the double glass front doors,

unlocked them and let him out. Even though she had no clue about his ulterior motive of getting her into his bed, Cole knew she wasn't stupid. She had to know that a chemistry as strong as what they had never fully disappeared, no matter how much you want it to.

God knows he'd thought she'd evaporated from his mind. But since the moment she'd breezed into the boardroom at Victor's office, then froze in her tracks at the site of him, she'd occupied more space than he cared to admit.

Liquor, women, fast cars, power and money had gone a long way in helping him recover from the damage Walter Stevens had done, the hurt he'd caused.

Granted, Tamera's father gave him an ultimatum of losing his scholarship or losing Tam. Had Cole had the funding to continue college on his own, he would've told the old man where to stick it, but since Cole, Zach and Kayla were all going to school on scholarships, he couldn't risk it. Not when they had absolutely nothing to fall back on but the old, run-down house their grandmother had raised them in after their parents' untimely death in a car accident.

Cole tapped the remote and his luxury SUV chirped as he unlocked it. As he slid behind the wheel he thought back to the days immediately following their breakup. He'd been purposely cruel so she wouldn't try to come after him or beg, because God knew if she'd begged he would've said to hell with school and the scholarship. Though there were countless times he'd wondered if he should've done just that.

But, in the end, how could he complain? He'd built, from the ground up, a multimillion-dollar business with Zach and Kayla. Without Walter's brash actions, he may not have been as successful and powerful.

And now that he held the power, he could hold the woman.

Cole pulled in front of The Stevens Group where Tamera stood in her classy emerald green, button-down shirt and slim gray skirt stopping at her knees. The soft Miami breeze sent loose strands of her hair dancing around her shoulders.

He swallowed. Hard.

Bombshell or not, he'd still made the right decision in giving her up.

Five

She should've known he'd choose the flashiest, most expensive restaurant in South Beach. Not to mention one that needed reservations at least a month in advance. Of course, once he flaunted his billion-dollar smile, the cute perky hostess, who may have been all of twenty, promptly seated them.

Cocky jerk always got what he wanted.

"We could've done this in my office," Tamera stated as she slid into the semi-circle booth in the back corner of the restaurant.

"We could've, but I'm hungry and if your habits are like they used to be, you skipped lunch."

Tamera froze, clutching her slim laptop case. "Stop trying to reminisce. You bring up the past every time we're together. We dated, you broke up. I've moved on."

Cole reached across the table, took her left hand,

examined her bare finger. "Doesn't seem like you have."

Fury bubbled through her as she jerked her hand away. "My personal life has no place in our conversation. You left me. Remember?"

She set the laptop on the edge of the table and unzipped the case. This had to remain a business meeting because if she even stopped to think about how his strong, smooth touch felt, she'd ask him to take her home.

How pathetic was that? The man had completely destroyed her happily-ever-after fantasy and her body still betrayed her. Whose side were her hormones on? His obviously.

Before he could comment, the waitress came and took their drink orders and offered fresh-baked rolls. Tamera booted up her laptop and tried to ignore the fact that Cole sat so close.

"Here."

She glanced up at a buttery roll all spread open and ready to devour. Cole smiled as he placed it on her saucer. Where exactly did he think his charms were going to take him?

"I can't concentrate on business if your stomach is growling," he commented, buttering his own steamy roll.

Once again he was seeing to her needs in small, subtle ways that made her want to ask what the hell happened to him all those years ago? Didn't she deserve some kind of detailed explanation? Didn't devoting nearly two years of her life to someone require some type of courtesy on his part when he made his exit?

"I hope that scowl isn't in regards to the design you're

about to show me," Cole said, drawing her thoughts back to the present.

She smiled sweetly. "My examples are flawless. My scowl is due to present company."

To Cole's credit, he kept his smirking mouth shut.

"Good evening."

Tamera glanced up to see Cole's twin, Zach, standing on the other side of the table with a leggy, busty blonde draped over his arm. The man was just as exotic-looking and handsome as Cole with dark eyes, dark skin and black hair. But Zach had always had a rougher, edgier side.

"Business meeting?" Zach asked, eyeing Tamera's computer.

"Yes."

Tamera thought it best to let Cole speak. There was no need to get back into that family any more than necessary. Though seeing Zach did bring back a flood of memories of a time when they all double dated with whoever Zach's love of the day was.

God, they were such different people then.

"The Lawson project?" Zach asked.

"It's the only project I'm concentrating on right now," Cole replied.

Zach's eyes roamed back to Tamera. "Good to see you again, Tam. How have you been?"

"Good, thanks."

She couldn't help but smile. Zach had been like a brother to her, though she could easily see why women wanted to be with him. The Marcum men were irresistible.

"I'll let you two get back to work." He turned and whispered something to his date, which prompted a high school-like giggle. "See you in the office, Cole. Tam, it was a pleasure."

Zach led his date to an intimate table across the restaurant and Tamera couldn't help but wonder what it would be like to be a woman who didn't allow her emotions to get all tangled up in a man. What would it be like to just let the moment take you away?

"That wistful look is much more pleasant than the scowl," Cole whispered in her ear. His warm breath tickled her shoulder through the thin silk blouse.

"Just taking a moment to daydream."

Cole rested his elbow on the table, not bothering to back away. "About my brother."

Tamera sighed and shifted to look Cole dead in his bedroom eyes. "Jealous? Fine. Since you're so hell-bent on rehashing this past between us, let's lay out all the cards."

The flash of surprise in his heated gaze gave her a brief moment of satisfaction.

"*You* ended our engagement," she began, refusing to allow the hurt or the anger to rise to the surface. "*You* wanted to move on for reasons you never explained to me."

Cole held up a hand, opened his mouth.

"No." She couldn't allow him to break her concentration with smooth words or useless excuses. "Your reasons don't matter to me now, they mattered then. If you are so concerned with what is going on in my personal life, just ask me. Granted, if I choose to answer you, you probably won't like what you hear. I've dated since you, Cole. I've even slept with some of the men I dated."

Okay, so she'd only been intimate a couple of times

since Cole, but he didn't need to know she was so pathetic she'd seldom had sex in eleven years.

"I'm sure you've been with women since me. It's life and it's the life you chose. So I'm done with your not-so-subtle stroll down memory lane. Can we please move forward now and work only on this project? I'm sure Mr. Lawson would appreciate that."

Cole smiled. He actually…smiled. "Your eyes still go ice blue when you get really angry. And it's just as sexy as ever."

"Did you not hear a word I just said?" God, the man could be so infuriating. Nobody else ever had the audacity to smirk at her after she'd confronted them. Then again, no one pushed her buttons quite the way Cole did.

"I heard you. But I should tell you something as well." He brushed a strand of her hair over her shoulder, leaned in and whispered, "I still want you. Business and past aside, you know you want me, too. I can see the desire in your eyes and don't think I haven't noticed how you bite your lip. You only do that when you're nervous or aroused."

Tamera jerked as if he'd hit her and the waitress chose that moment to come back to take their order.

"I'm not staying," Tamera informed the girl. "Cole, I'll call your assistant to set up another meeting. In my office."

Before he could say anything else, before Tamera's heated face gave away her true feelings, she snatched her laptop, case and purse and fled the restaurant. Zach and his date didn't even notice her abrupt departure because they were too busy forming one body in the corner of their booth.

Thankfully she'd driven here in her own car. There

was no way she could be in close quarters with Cole and his ego…there simply wasn't enough room.

Why did she have to find that confidence attractive? Had she not learned her lesson the first time? She did not need this added pressure right now, not with her father's health hanging by the proverbial thread.

Tamera slid into her silver BMW, set her belongings on the passenger seat and rested her head on the steering wheel. If she thought, for even a minute, that Cole had changed, that he could comfort her in the way she needed right now, whether in bed or out, she'd jump at the chance. To have strong arms envelop her, to rest her head on a set of shoulders that could carry her burdens, would be more of a turn-on than any charm he could throw her way.

But Cole wasn't offering anything that personal or intimate. Their versions of intimate were polar opposites and she just couldn't commit to his.

A sterile, stark white environment was not what Tamera wanted for her father's last days. Thankfully, the hospice nurse wasn't lying when she said the hospice facility was comfortable, less like a hospital and more like a home.

The private quarters were carpeted, and had small kitchens, beds and sitting chairs. Small chests of drawers and coffee tables with televisions completed the décor. Patients were free to bring personal items to feel more comfortable.

Regardless of the coziness, signing the papers to have her father put into strangers' care was one of the hardest things Tamera had ever done. Removing him from the home he'd made with her mother at the start of their marriage and placing him into hospice seemed like giving up.

But Tamera had to face reality. He wasn't going to get better so she may as well make his last days as comfortable as possible.

His cancer had spread throughout his body and there was no more the doctors could do. Some days his mind wasn't working as well as other days. He still knew who everyone was, but he would forget simple things like if the nurse had drawn his blood that morning or why he wasn't at home.

Nothing about this situation was easy and she had a dreadful feeling it was only going to get worse from here.

Tamera went from the nurses' station to her father's room to check on him one last time before she left for the night. Exhaustion had long since set in since she'd been back and forth all day bringing things from the house and making sure his room was set up to his liking. She'd do everything in her power to make him happy.

Thankfully he was asleep. Tamera clicked off the television and stood in the silence staring at the man who'd once made billionaire tycoons quake with fear. Now a pale, frail man, Tamera had a hard time believing this was her father.

Her throat clogged with tears. She'd give up all the money, houses, cars, yachts, everything in the Stevens dynasty if the cancer would just disappear.

After covering her father with his brown throw from his own bed at home, Tamera smoothed his thin hair from his forehead, kissed him and shut off the lamp.

This would be a good night. His medicine was strong enough to allow him the much-needed rest he deserved. These were the nights when Tamera caught up on her sleep as well. God knew she needed it now that she was dealing with Cole and Victor. She honestly didn't know which man scared her more.

Oh, who was she kidding? There was no contest.

With her hospice folder loaded with all her copies of the paperwork and her purse, Tamera waved goodbye to the nurses and stepped out into the unusual chill of the April evening. The somewhat crisp breeze seeped through her silky blouse, sending shivers all over.

She hated these odd Miami days. They were few and far between, but she'd stick with the days that were either hot or hotter. The folks up north could have this chill.

Tamera settled in her car, giving her body a moment to recover from the bitter wind she hadn't expected from Miami in April. As soon as she got home, she vowed, she'd change into her favorite lounge pants and long-sleeved T-shirt.

Driving through the streets toward her condo, she longed for home and a good book. All she needed was a steamy romance and a corner of her sofa where she could hopefully sweep her mind into a fictional life and leave the troubles of hers behind for a few minutes.

Unfortunately, as she pulled up, she saw one of her main issues sitting in his flashy, luxury car in her driveway. How many cars did the man have?

The sleek, black Lincoln could either belong to an FBI agent or a powerful CEO. She'd rather face the FBI.

Cole exited when she raised her garage door and pulled in. This was not what she wanted or needed. The last thing she could think about right now was the Lawson project or the fact that Cole had blatantly stated he wanted to sleep with her.

Tonight was *not* the night for her to give in and call

him on his threats. She didn't have the energy or the will to fight right now.

When Cole opened her door, Tamera gave in to the inevitable and gathered her folder and purse. He wouldn't leave until he came to say whatever was on his mind, so she may as well get this over with.

Tamera was shocked when she stepped from her car. Cole at least had a gentleman's knowledge to move back and allow her to ease out without brushing against him. Minor kudos to him.

He closed the door. "I called the office and they said you took the day off."

"Yes." Tamera stepped into her house through the door attached to her garage and slapped the button to close the garage door. She punched the six digit code to turn off the alarm. "I tend to do that at times."

Cole followed her inside, obviously intending to stay. "At a crucial time like this? I don't know about you, but I intend to work around the clock until this is perfected and turned in before Victor wants it. We need to put up a united front—"

"I had personal business," Tamera yelled, slapping her folder onto the central stone island in her kitchen. "Did you come here to criticize my work ethic or did you have a point you needed to make?"

Cole's eyes darted down to the folder and Tamera rushed to cover it with her purse. Too late.

"Who's in hospice?"

An exhausted sigh escaped her. "What do you want, Cole?"

His eyes darted back to hers. "Your father's in hospice."

Of course he'd guess. Cole wasn't stupid and her silence only validated what he'd surmised.

"I suspected something was wrong, but I had no idea." He took a step closer. "Why didn't you tell me?"

"And I should've told you why? You care? Or so you could use it against my company in the future?"

Too disgusted to look him in the eye, Tamera turned and marched through the open living space into her den. Habit had her settling into her wide window seat, grabbing a beaded throw and holding it to her chest, as if to hold in the pain, the hurt so Cole couldn't see.

She didn't want him here. Why couldn't he see that?

"You'd be surprised what I care about." Cole followed her into the cozy room and stood in front of her. "No matter how things ended between us, I don't want to see you hurt."

Bitterness over his soft words had her jerking her gaze up to his. "Then you better leave."

Six

If her bottom lip had quivered, if she had unshed tears, Cole would've left her to her emotional breakdown. But the fact that she tilted her chin in a defiant manner and the shadows under her eyes confirmed how exhausted she was, he couldn't leave her. Not like this. Not when she was on the verge of breaking and barely holding herself together.

Damn, he was always a sucker for distressed damsels, especially sexy, vulnerable ones. And as much as Cole hated Walter, he didn't want Tam this upset…about anything.

Cole eased down beside her on the window seat and fisted his hands in his lap when she turned to look out onto the lush, floral gardens.

When he'd called the office to get together to collaborate again on the rough sketches, he'd nearly gone into shock when her assistant said Tamera had taken a personal day.

But now he didn't know what he was more shocked at—the fact that her father was dying or that she'd done such a stellar job of hiding his condition from the world around him. Even Cole's assistant hadn't been able to uncover the reasoning behind Walter's untimely absence.

"How much longer does he have?"

"Not long."

At least she answered him, even if she wouldn't look at him. "And you're taking care of everything yourself, right? Including keeping his terminal illness a secret from associates and staff? Pulling long hours just to make sure the clientele doesn't catch on and to keep everything at the firm running smoothly?"

She swallowed and shook her head, sending a lone tear sliding down her cheek. He reached up and swiped her damp skin with the pad of his thumb, cupping her jaw with his palm.

Much to his surprise, she leaned into him.

How long had she been keeping this secret? How long had this burden been wearing her down and did her father ask her to go to all this trouble? Did he want her to bear the weight of such a large dynasty on top of the secrecy of his illness?

Walter Stevens' condition changed everything. Miami society in general would not be the same. This was news Zach and Kayla needed to know about as soon as possible. If any other bids came through the office, he needed them to keep an eye out. No way would he allow The Stevens Group to get ahead of him. Not now. Not when he could so easily take them over during this weak period.

If other contractors knew Walter Stevens was no longer running The Stevens Group, they would certainly think twice before submitting bids, no matter how formidable Tamera and her crew were.

Which begged another question: Just how long had Tamera been running the company? Obviously, she'd been doing a fine job, or there would've already been talk, but people in this business didn't like change and they didn't like being kept in the dark.

But once Walter died, how long would Tamera be able to keep this going? Perhaps buying The Stevens Group should be next on Cole's priority list.

Yes. Most definitely. Zach and Kayla would surely be on board with that plan.

"I hate this," she whispered, pulling back from his hand. "I hate my father being so fragile. I hate being in charge of his final days. And I hate that you came by tonight."

"I'm glad I did."

And he was. This useful piece of information would go a long way in boosting Cole and his firm beyond anything Tam's father could've fathomed.

"Is it so bad to lean on me for a bit?" He rubbed the tips of his fingers against his palm.

"I learned long ago not to lean on people."

The steel behind her emotions came through her tear-clogged voice. He didn't ask what time period she referred to. He'd let her down once and she wasn't so trusting anymore. He not only understood her point of view, he respected it. She was on her guard, which was probably safest for her in this case.

If she really knew that everything he was doing was because of the project and he was using that advantage to get her into his bed, she'd kick him so far from her home, he'd never see her in a personal setting again.

And now that he'd made the discovery about Walter, well, he needed to remain extra close to be ready to take over The Stevens Group when opportunity struck.

She needed to believe that selling was the only way... and that it was her own idea.

Speaking of what she needed, she needed to get out and enjoy all that Miami had to offer. A club near her condo in South Beach would be perfect. Perhaps a few drinks would relax her a bit and she could concentrate on herself and her needs.

She swiped her cheeks and Cole didn't hesitate to reach out, pulling her back against his chest.

"Relax," he crooned when she stiffened. "Don't read anything more into this than a friend helping you through a rough day."

"You're not my friend."

She may have protested with words, but her body slowly relaxed against his. Cole actually felt the tension leave her, starting with her shoulders, her back.

"Why are you doing this?" she whispered into the dimly lit room.

"You're hurting, Tam. Do you think I'm that cold-hearted?"

Silence stretched through the room for several minutes, but Cole didn't care, not when Tam felt so good against him. Her warm body only heated his that much more.

Her head tilted to the side, resting firmly against his heart. Her breathing slowed. She'd fallen asleep.

Cole smiled, settled his arms firmly around hers, which were wrapped around her abdomen. Having Tamera sleeping in his arms was sweeter than anything he could've planned. Dying or not, if old man Stevens could see them now, well, that would definitely do him in.

Eleven years ago he'd purposely hurt her to make her keep her distance. She'd cried then, too, but in that steely, I-hate-you way.

But, seriously, what did he expect when he'd delivered the "it's not you, it's me" speech? In reality, though, it *had* been him. If he'd come from money he wouldn't have had to worry about those blasted scholarships. Not only that, he'd had to worry about Zach's and Kayla's as well. He couldn't disrupt his whole family because of her father.

A moment which plagued every day of his life since. Not only did he not stand up for the woman he loved and what they shared, he didn't stand up for himself.

Pathetic. Cole hated thinking about how weak and powerless he'd been.

Now, there was no reason for Tam not to see him for the man he'd become. Holding her like this only made him want her more. He wanted to explore that sexual pull he knew still existed between them. Granted, her father may have sucked the romance and love right out of anything Cole knew, but the man couldn't change the fact that Tamera was sexier now than ever and Cole intended to have her.

Tamera stirred against his chest and sighed. When she woke, he'd discuss her needs and subtly force his way into her personal life. He needed to gain her trust once again if he was going to persuade her to sell the company. But he knew this plan teetered on a fine line. Tamera was a strong, confident businesswoman. Convincing her to sell would be quite a challenge.

Cole's eyes scanned her den. The spacious room

with all its little accessories and knickknacks was so Tamera, but Cole also got a sense for the woman she'd become.

The beaded lampshades and Persian rug were no surprise, but the small certificate hanging behind her desk did catch him off guard. She was a member of the "Make-A-Wish Foundation." Hanging next to the certificate was a card, obviously made by a child's creative hand. It depicted a smiley face at the end of a rainbow. Drawn on pink construction paper, the word "thanks" was written in all caps with a backward k.

His eyes scanned over to her selection of CDs, again giving him a glimpse as to the woman Tam was today. Back in the day she enjoyed country music and was ready to let her hair down. He only saw one country CD, Faith Hill. The others were a mix of jazz and light rock.

What had she done in those eleven years they'd been apart? Had she fallen in and out of love again? Had her father meddled in her personal affairs? All questions he wanted answers to, but knew he wouldn't get and didn't deserve. And, he asked himself, why did he care at this point?

Tamera stirred once again and started to sit up. "Cole?" she asked, her voice groggy. "What time is it?"

He glanced at her desk clock illuminated by a small Tiffany lamp. "Midnight."

She eased up, brushing her hair from her face. "I didn't mean to fall asleep on you."

"You needed the rest." When she tried to ease away, Cole tightened his hold around her waist. "Are you okay now?"

She nodded, looking him in the eye. "Why didn't you

leave? You could've left me lying in the window. I have taken quite a few naps here."

He smiled. "Wishing on stars?"

Tamera's gaze moved to the window. "Something like that."

"Sneaking out is for cowards. I face complications head-on."

She looked back at him, questions, hurt swirling in her eyes. "This isn't right, Cole. You really shouldn't be here."

"Because of what we're feeling? What isn't right about it?"

Her delicate hand came up to her forehead as she closed her eyes. "We're business associates, nothing more. I can't concentrate on my father, this project and you all at the same time."

"Then don't." He took her hand from her face and held it. "Concentrate on this."

In a possessive manner he took her mouth. Every fiber of his being wanted to claim her, take her in a fast, frenzied manner, but she needed to ease into this. She needed comfort and he would be the one to offer it.

Her lips parted beneath his and Cole knew everything they'd shared before was nothing compared to the intensity of this moment. In her den, her own territory, Cole knew Tamera could relax. The dim light, the hour, all worked together in his favor. No phone would ring, no one would disturb them.

This moment was all about giving in to the inevitable.

Cole released her hand and brought his up to frame her face as he changed the angle of the kiss. Tamera twisted her body so they were more in line, then slid her arms around his neck.

Tamera's need must've taken over because Cole's control slipped from his grasp and easily into hers. A controlling woman in an intimate setting was sexy personified.

The familiar taste and touch only added to the need swelling inside him. Tamera was the only woman who'd ever been able to pull that desire he'd kept so hidden to the surface.

Cole had to tamp a portion of that desire back down. All he had to give Tamera was here, now. He had nothing else to offer, and even if he did, their souls were too battered from the first encounter. Lust was all this was, all it could be. And he was fine with that. Actually, right now, he was feeling pretty damn good.

"No." Tamera eased back shaking her head.

"What's wrong?" Cole asked, though he knew that was a dumb question.

"This," she gestured between their faces. "I won't do this with you again."

"Tam, I'm not taking anything you aren't offering. Anything beyond this moment doesn't matter."

She looked him dead in the eye. "*Everything* beyond this point matters. You crushed me once. It won't happen again."

When she sprang to her feet, turning her back on him, Cole didn't stop her.

"Why can't you just go with what you're feeling?" Cole came to stand behind her, but didn't invade her personal space by touching her again. "I'm not looking for anything beyond right now."

A small, sarcastic laugh escaped her. "That almost makes it worse," she whispered. "Just go."

Those were the two words he'd been both waiting for

and dreading to hear. Cole was torn between wanting to stay to comfort her and giving in to her request.

"I don't want you to be alone when you're hurting."

She turned to face him, tears shimmering in her eyes. "Seeing you, touching you, that's making the hurt worse. This is too familiar, Cole and I just can't get involved with you on a personal level again."

"Too late."

"Cole, please. Don't."

Despite her plea, Cole reached for her, taking her by her shoulders. "This attraction won't go away, Tam, no matter how hard you push me away. Our past had nothing to do with that kiss."

She grasped his forearms, her fingers biting into his cotton shirt. "Do you enjoy pressuring me? You say you don't like to see me hurting, yet you're still here, still bullying your way into my life when I've tried to keep you out. If you're regretting the decision you made all those years ago, that's something you're going to have to deal with. But leave me alone."

Shoving him aside, Tamera walked back to her window seat and curled up with her throw pillow. Her rigid back, her gaze out onto the starry night, was all he needed.

She'd begged, she'd nearly cried, but her silence and stiffness told him he'd reached her breaking point. Tamera had her pride, something he could appreciate. He wouldn't make her break even more tonight. He'd pushed, she'd given what she could, which was more than he'd expected. But he would get nothing else from her right now. Soon, he vowed.

With a heavy heart for Tamera's hurt, and the

knowledge of her father's terminal illness, Cole let her be, retreating to plan his next course of attack on both business and personal levels.

Seven

"Yes, Mr. Lawson, Cole and I are moving quicker than we'd anticipated with the designs."

Tamera leaned back in her leather office chair and rolled her eyes. No need to add that Cole was moving faster than she'd expected with the personal side of things as well. Her lips still tingled, her heart still ached.

"I'm glad to hear it, Tamera," Victor said. "And please, call me Victor. I'd like to set up something with the three of us later in the week so I can see where we stand. I prefer to be very hands-on when it comes to my properties."

Already? God, now she would have to put in extra hours with Cole to get this design more definite. Wonderful. Just what they needed. Working together after hours with no one else around but the two of them. Perfect.

"I'll have my assistant set up the appointment," Tamera offered. "I will let Cole know. We are very eager to show you what we've come up with."

Yeah, so far they'd managed to have a meeting aboard Cole's yacht where they shared some ideas and a very rough design, a botched dinner where she'd barely managed to get her laptop out of the case and an impromptu meeting at her house which only led to a course of events she didn't want to think about.

"Thanks, Tamera. I'm anxious to see the initial design."

"See you next week."

Tamera hung up her phone and laid her head on her desk. Her plans were nearly completed, so perhaps she could just e-mail them to Cole. They'd pretty much collaborated together that first day at his yacht and decided on the main architectural design for the exterior. The interior was still questionable, but perhaps with a couple meetings this week they could decipher the exact layout.

But first a phone call needed to be made. Tamera picked up her phone and dialed.

"The Marcum Agency," Cole's cheery assistant answered.

"This is Tamera Stevens for Cole Marcum, please."

"Hold one moment, Ms. Stevens."

Not five seconds passed before Cole's low, rich tone came over the phone. "Tamera, what can I do for you?"

She shoved aside the bubble of arousal at his voice and gripped the receiver. "We need to have a business meeting tonight after work. We can meet here in my office. I will have my caterer bring in some food."

"I had plans tonight," Cole countered.

Tamera leaned back into her buttery leather chair and gritted her teeth. "Call her and cancel. We have work to do."

"Jealous, darling?" Mocking laughter reverberated back through the receiver. "I'm flattered."

The urge to throw the phone against the wall was strong, but she refrained from acting like a child. "I didn't call to stroke your ego, Cole. I'm sure your entourage of women do that for you. I called on a professional matter, not a personal one. So, call your… date and tell her you have other plans."

"Will you make it worth my while?" he laughed. "Just kidding, don't get all worked up again. I'll be at your office at six."

Without another word Cole hung up and Tamera cursed herself for sounding like a jealous teenager…and cursed him for mocking her. Why was it her business if he was spending the evening with someone else merely because he'd heated her up in her home last night? Hadn't she come to her senses and kicked him out?

There was no time for anything but work, not only on this project, but in her life. She just couldn't let her mind wander to Cole and what he did in his free time. She already had enough to keep her mind and heart occupied every waking minute.

Heart?

Great, now she was delusional enough to think her heart was getting tangled around this project just because she was working with Cole. Just what she needed.

Tamera asked her assistant to hold all her calls and show Cole in when he arrived. She also had her call the caterer they always used and order enough food that the two of them wouldn't need to leave the confines of her office for a very long time.

Closing all the documents on her laptop, Tamera then pulled up her design on the screen. She twisted her hair up into a clip and slid her reading glasses from her desk and plopped them on the end of her nose. Not the sexiest look—she was only thirty-three and needed cheaters—but work came before beauty.

She tweaked the exterior just a tad to showcase the expansive, arched entryways. Six ran along the front of the resort, separated only by wide marble columns. Yes, marble. Why hadn't she thought of that before for the entryway? A Mediterranean flare with Old World elegance…it would be breathtaking and well-received.

Because her mind had been on other things, that's why she hadn't thought of the obvious.

There needed to be large, trickling fountains both inside and out as well. The soothing effect would only add to the fantasy getaway.

Tamera slipped off her Gucci shoes and left them beneath her desk. Padding over to her easel, she pulled out the rough sketches she'd made before she'd received the contracts and was just wishing she'd get the bid.

The lighting wasn't quite right in her initial draft on her computer, but what she'd originally drawn seemed like a better fit. The tall tapered lights weren't too overbearing to take away from the scrolling wrought-iron stair railings and the carved marble trim above the columns, surrounding the sculptured ceiling.

Encased lights needed to be set above each arch to shine down on every opening as well. This resort needed to appear to be glowing from the water's edge, rising from the ocean like a dream come to life.

She hovered over her board, looking at all the other initial ideas she'd taken to paper. Sometimes your first instinct was the best decision.

"I left early."

Tamera spun to her doorway to see Cole striding across her office.

Okay, there was that exception to the rule about your first instincts. Sometimes they were way off base, especially where this man was concerned.

"What time is it?" she asked, straightening from her tilted board.

"Four, but I didn't have any meetings left today."

Tamera rubbed the soreness in her back and twisted from side to side.

"Kayla wanted me to tell you 'hi' and she hopes to see you soon."

Smiling at the image of Cole's younger, quiet sister, Tamera said, "Tell her to call or stop by. I'd love to see her."

Cole closed the space between them, spun her around, making her face away from him. Next thing she knew, his fist was rubbing at just the right spot in her back where the cramp was.

"I was having dinner with her tonight." His touch continued to scorch her through her thin, silk blouse. "That's who I had plans with."

"Oh."

Nothing else came to mind to say, not with his warm breath on her neck, his magic hand doing wonders for her achy back and certainly not with the memory so fresh of their kiss.

"Do you know what a picture image you made when I came in?" he whispered next to her ear. "Bare feet, all that golden hair piled on top your head, those sexy glasses perched on the end of your nose?"

Sexy glasses? The ones she continually referred to as her "cheaters"?

"You're lucky it was me and no one else." Cole turned her back around. "I've never seen a sexier sight."

His mouth came down so fast, so hard on hers, she didn't have time to think or to react in any other way than to wrap her arms around him and let him in.

God help her. She didn't think she could've stopped him if she'd even wanted to. And that really, really should be a red flag. Their level of intimacy was growing with each and every encounter.

Cole's hands covered her back as he wrapped her in his embrace and arched her body. The heat from his chest did amazing things to her sensitive breasts through her thin top.

He lifted his head, still keeping her dipped beneath him. "Don't ever tell me again that there's no attraction between us."

Abruptly Cole released her, causing her to nearly stumble back before she regained her footing.

Damn that man for heating her up twice in one day and making her forget her priorities. And what the hell was that little stunt? Was he mocking her? Making her doubly aware that, yes, she was turned on by him and, yes, he could probably still have her in his bed?

Tamera straightened her blouse back into place, smoothed a hand across her forehead to remove stray hairs and crossed to her desk.

From here on out, this meeting was going to be hands-off. The desk or a blueprint would remain between them at all times.

Or God help her, she'd probably give in to her desires and say to hell with it and let Cole have what they both wanted.

Eight

If she wanted an apology for his actions, she would be waiting a very long time. He hadn't had a choice in the matter. Not when he'd stepped into her office and seen her barefoot with bare legs stretching up beneath a slim skirt as she bent over her easel.

And, if that hadn't been enough to get his testosterone pumping, she'd spun around with those sexy gold-rimmed glasses and her hair pulled into some strange, yet ultra sexy mess atop her head.

Technically, she should be apologizing to him. Since the start, she'd tortured him with her sultry style, her innocent looks and her demanding persona.

In a fruitless attempt to let them both regain their bearings after that scorching kiss, Cole stepped over to her sketches she'd been studying.

"Looks good," he said as his trained eye ran over nearly the exact same design he'd constructed in his mind.

"I didn't ask for your approval," she snapped.

Her clipped tone had him glancing over his shoulder, but he wasn't foolish enough to grin. He'd gotten under her skin. Good, because she sure as hell had been under his since the second they'd been in the boardroom two weeks ago with Victor.

"I wasn't giving it. I don't know why, but I'm surprised at how much your drawing resembles my own."

She glanced around. "And where, precisely, is your design? You came here for a business meeting, not to paw me again."

This time, foolish or not, he did smirk as he turned to give this vivacious woman his full attention. "Paw you? Honey, I haven't even begun to paw. Just say when."

The growl that came from her throat as she spun toward her desk only made him laugh. "That wasn't very ladylike."

Tamera dropped into her seat. Back ramrod straight, she glared out of the corner of her eyes. "I'm not feeling ladylike where you're concerned."

Taking his time, he crossed the spacious office and leaned a hip on her desk. "Your drawings by hand are way better than anything I have on my computer. You always were the really artistic one."

She wiggled her mouse and clicked on her computer. "I have a more updated version on here. I actually find the drawing and plotting on paper relaxing and lately, I need that."

He understood all too well, though he wouldn't admit that to anybody but himself. And certainly not to Tamera.

Cole moved to look over her shoulder at the exterior she'd pulled up on her screen. "Perfect. That's exactly what we'd discussed. You've certainly captured Victor's visions."

She smiled, glancing up at him. "Thank you."

Cole swallowed a bitter lump as Tamera looked back at her screen, pulling up yet another new design. She'd genuinely smiled at him and all he did was compliment her work.

Obviously they were more alike than he'd wanted to admit. When a client or fellow associate complimented his work, nothing pleased him more. The bond with their work was something he hadn't considered.

Perhaps he'd been taking his approach with Tamera in the wrong direction. He needed to get to her through her business. Talking about designs could be sexy... couldn't it?

They were in Miami, for pity's sake. Miami was the sexiest city, as far as he was concerned. Wealthy, powerful people simply added to the allure. Besides, hadn't Victor himself required a sexy theme for his hotel? The client's needs always came first.

"The entryway?" he asked over her shoulder, getting back to the task.

Cole also had a feeling that staying focused would not only throw her off and make her want more, but she'd also find him more attractive. Now if he could just keep his hands to himself.

The things he did for the goals he wanted to achieve.

"Yes." She pointed to the blueprint on the screen. "High intricate ceilings with large chandeliers. I'm thinking three, but we'll leave that final call up to Kayla."

"Good idea," he laughed. "She hates when I try to move in on her territory."

Tamera clicked her mouse again and pulled up the first floor layout. "Here's where the offices, meeting rooms, sauna, gym and maintenance rooms will be."

"What about the ballrooms?" Cole asked, studying the draft.

She clicked again. "I've put them on the top floor to have access to the rooftop where I'm hoping Kayla will put a botanical garden of sorts. She does all the interior, but she's so great with gardening, I'd like her to take this on as well. I also added the courtyard, but, yet again, will leave those main details to Kayla and Victor. I'm sure she'd love to handle this aspect of the project as well."

Cole was amazed at all the detailed work Tamera had already done since they'd first met aboard his yacht... especially in light of her father's condition. Though he knew Walter's condition was precisely the reason she'd worked herself to death.

"I'll run that by her," Cole said. "Though I'm sure she's already thought about every single aspect of this project. She's just as eager as the rest of us to please Victor, though she's a little intimidated."

"There's no need for that. She's amazing." Tamera pulled up another screen. "Here is the first floor. I'm keeping this layout simple seeing as how Victor wants each room to feel more like a loft than a hotel suite. I've factored in twelve guest rooms on the first six floors and the eight middle floors will have larger suites with full kitchens. I've also placed the honeymoon suites on the top, three floors to give couples privacy and a wonderful view from higher up."

Cole eased back and stood straight up. "I'm impressed, Tam."

Swiveling around in her seat, Tamera smiled that

bright smile that had never failed to clutch his heart years ago. He'd better keep a tight hold this time. No way did he want anything that resembled a relationship or commitment.

But, seriously, how had someone not captured Tamera's heart in eleven years? Was she that caught up in the firm? That he could understand, but he still couldn't believe some man didn't make her take the time to enjoy life.

"Thanks. I was hoping you'd like what I did. I tried to follow Victor's instructions and add a few of my own ideas as well."

Cole nodded. "Now we just need to do some more detailed planning as far as structure setup."

A knock on Tamera's office door pulled him from his thoughts. Tam came to her feet, still bare, and crossed over the plush, white carpeting.

As she swung the door open, her assistant came in, wheeling a cart. Silver-domed plates on a three-tiered cart came to rest in front of Tam's desk.

"Thanks, Mariah," Tamera said. "You can go now. Mr. Marcum and I will be working late tonight. I'll see you in the morning."

Mariah smiled and nodded to Tamera and Cole. "Good night."

Once the assistant closed the door behind her, Cole's gut tightened. They would be alone for the rest of the night and he was supposed to concentrate on designs?

"This smells so good," Tamera commented, lifting off the lids. "I'm starving."

Cole nearly laughed. Starving, yeah, so was he.

He wished Tamera would just give in to the sexual pull she was fighting so he could focus on the biggest business deal The Marcum Agency had ever dealt with.

He'd hate to screw this project up for his brother and sister all because he couldn't control his adolescent hormones.

Tamera picked up a piece of fresh pineapple and sank her teeth in, groaning. Wonderful. Just wonderful. Groaning was certainly not going to help him concentrate or keep his lust levels under control.

God, had she just groaned? That was so not meant to slip out.

Tamera swallowed the bite of succulent pineapple and turned to Cole, who was eyeing her beneath heavy-lidded eyes. Damn, so he had noticed the groan.

"Help yourself," she gestured toward the spread. "We can set all the plates over there if you'd like."

She picked up the tray of fresh fruit and went over to her long, granite-topped table by the floor-to-ceiling windows in the corner.

Cole just wheeled the cart over and began arranging the plates. "Were you really hungry when you ordered or do you plan on keeping me here until the hotel is built and open for business?"

Eyeing all the food, she laughed. "Sorry, it all sounded so good at the time, but now that I'm looking at it, it is an awful lot."

Fresh fruits, peeled shrimp, her favorite veggie wraps, some bread with raspberry dipping sauce, wine.

Okay, so maybe she did want to keep Cole here, so what. She wanted the man on a purely physical level and there wasn't a thing wrong with that. Was there a woman alive who didn't appreciate broad shoulders, tailored suits, dark, exotic looks and an edge of cockiness?

Was it her fault her memory was good and she recalled all their nights together so many years ago? No.

She was a woman with needs. That didn't mean she had to act on them.

End of story.

"I had no idea you were a member of the Make-A-Wish Foundation."

Tamera glanced up as Cole reached for a wrap, handing it to her on a small square napkin embossed with the restaurant's logo.

"How did you know?"

"I saw the small card a child had made you hanging next to your certificate in your den."

Tamera's throat closed up. "Emily made that card for me two weeks before she died."

Cole eased down in a leather chair across from her. "I apologize for bringing up bad memories."

"It's okay. She was the sweetest little girl, though." Tamera recalled the frail six-year-old with bouncy blond curls and bright blue eyes. "She also called me Tam because my name was hard for her. She's the only person, other than you, who's ever called me that."

Cole reached across and placed his hand over hers. "You don't have to tell me. I was just caught off guard when I saw that picture."

"We met when the foundation called and asked for monetary donations. I never can resist helping children, so I took the check personally to the office and there was this little girl and her mother. The little girl looked so full of hope with her big blue eyes. Her mother, on the other hand, looked lost, sad.

"I immediately took to Emily and she to me, so I became more and more involved. She made me that card because the foundation sent her to Disneyland and I went with them. All she wanted was to meet Minnie Mouse." Tamera looked over at Cole, tears clogging her throat.

"Do you know what it's like to give someone such a simple gift, knowing there's nothing else they want? I could've bought Disneyland for her, but it wouldn't have changed the fact that she was going to die."

When a tear escaped, Tamera pulled her hand from beneath Cole's and swiped angrily at her face. "Sorry. I just get so worked up thinking how unfair it is that people have to suffer such a horrible disease while I go about my life making more money than I could possibly spend and living any way I desire."

"She had cancer, didn't she?" Cole asked, his voice low.

Tamera closed her eyes. "How did you know?"

"I assumed since you're still so torn up that it was hitting close to home for you right now."

Yes, it was. But rehashing the past and dwelling on the inevitable with her father was not going to get Victor Lawson's hotel designed and built.

And it certainly wasn't helping her situation with Cole. That chip on his shoulder seemed to disappear and make room for her when she needed to lean on him.

Tamera shook aside the glum thoughts. "Let's talk about the design, okay?"

Cole eyed her as if he wanted to say or ask something else, but in the end he nodded. "Okay."

But instead of approaching another topic, they ate in silence, for which Tamera was grateful. Cole obviously still could read her well enough to know when she needed space. He also probably still knew how much she hated being seen as vulnerable or weak.

Tamera feared, though, if he kept offering subtle support, she'd take him up on it…and then some. Thank God he hadn't. If she landed in his arms again, especially under emotional circumstances, who knows what would happen.

Oh, who was she kidding? She knew exactly what would happen and she was nearly to the point she didn't care.

Nine

"What about carrying out the columns throughout the hotel, even in the suites? That way the weight-bearing walls won't take up so much space and we can keep the rooms open for that airy feeling." Tamera's Sharpie moved in a quick, swift manner as she refigured some very rough sketches and glanced up to get Cole's reaction. "What?"

He'd shed his Italian jacket and silk tie just after they'd eaten and loosened the top two buttons of his cobalt blue dress shirt. And every moment since he'd done so, that golden skin peeking through the V of his open collar taunted her.

"I think you need to call it a night," he told her, his thick, dark brows drawn together in worry.

Tamera glanced to her glass desk clock. "It's only ten, Cole. We used to work well into the night when we were in college."

As soon as the words were out of her mouth, hovering in the air between them, she wished to snatch them back. She'd been getting on him about rehashing their past, and that was certainly a place she couldn't keep revisiting, but the statement just slipped through her lips.

"Maybe I'm getting too old for all-nighters," he commented.

Those deep brown, heavy-lidded bedroom eyes told her different. A determined man, a *powerful* man like Cole didn't think twice about pulling all-nighters… whether it be the bedroom or the boardroom.

Tamera rolled her eyes. "Please, you're not too old. That implies I'm old and I'm not."

He stepped forward, placing his hands on her shoulders and massaging the tension away stroke by delicious stroke. Mercy, the man did know exactly what to do when she needed something. She didn't even have to ask.

"You're still just as beautiful as you were, Tam," he told her in a low, sexy tone. "Age only improves you. But I do think you've reached your limit today. We can work more tomorrow."

Eyes closed, she leaned into his hands and enjoyed, just for a moment, what he was so graciously offering. His smooth words settled over her, giving her a brief sense of calm she so desperately needed, craved.

Why couldn't they be meeting for the first time? Why did all of her memories of this man come with an ache in her chest that she could never ease?

"Do you have plans this Friday night?" she asked.

His soft laughter filtered through her quiet office, making her even more aware of the fact they were in this massive building all alone. Even the janitor had left at eight.

His hands stilled on her shoulders as he leaned down to whisper in her ear. "You're the only plan I have."

Why did that threat sound so thrilling?

"Fine. We can meet here when you get off."

He began massaging once again. "No, we need a change of scenery to keep our creative juices flowing. Let's go back to my yacht. It's private, it's supposed to be a nice evening, maybe we can work topside under the stars."

Seduction. He was trying to seduce her. She was just intrigued enough to see his course of action. And, she had to admit, she enjoyed being on his yacht. It was quiet, and if the staff was off that day, there should be no interruptions.

"Would you offer this deal to just anyone that you'd be working with on a project like this?"

"What deal?"

Tamera turned in her chair, causing his talented hands to fall away from her shoulders. "Meeting, once again, on your yacht."

Cole shrugged, placing his hands in his pant pockets. "I'm not working with just anybody, Tamera, I'm working with you."

And that was the problem, she was starting to like working with Cole…a little too much for her comfort level. What was worse, she had a feeling he knew where her emotions were headed…straight to him no matter where he led her.

"I'll provide the food," he continued as if she'd already agreed to step into his web of deceit. "Just e-mail me all those files we worked on."

She studied him, seeing him for the young man she'd

fallen in love with. He'd shown so much potential to be a powerful CEO then. Of course, the man Cole was today was not exactly the man she'd envisioned.

She hadn't expected the cocky demeanor or the take-charge attitude where everything was his way or no way. But in the back of her mind, she still kept that vision of him as a husband, a father. He'd be just as powerful in running a family as he was running a multimillion-dollar company. What happened to make him so hard and brash the majority of the time? Every now and then, though, she appreciated, and was attracted to, those moments when he slipped back into the man she used to know.

"I'll make sure I'm at the yacht by five," he told her, moving around her desk to the club chair where his jacket and tie lay. "If there's any problem, just text or call me."

That was it? He was just going to leave without attempting to kiss her? After the whirlwind way he swept into the room he was going to exit without any fanfare?

Mixed signals, anyone? What game was he playing with her?

Tamera gestured over to the table where the spread of half-empty plates and silver platters full of fruit and wraps lay. "Do you want to take any of this food?"

"No. Why don't you save it for your lunch tomorrow? There's enough for your assistant, too."

Tamera smiled. "You make millions of dollars each year and you are worried about leftovers?"

His face sobered as his eyes captured hers. "No matter the amount of money I make, I still remember where I came from."

As if she needed another piece of her heart to melt

at this man with whom fate had mockingly reunited her. She couldn't get swept into another entanglement with him. Seduction was one thing. Sleeping with each other, if that's where this was headed, was one thing. Keeping her heart intact and to herself was a whole other matter.

"I'll make sure it doesn't go to waste," she promised. "See you tomorrow."

He walked back and leaned down so they were eye to eye. "Go home and get some sleep."

The way he loomed over her as she sat in her office chair made her feel uneasy, and even though he demanded instead of asking, she knew he was concerned.

"I'll be leaving in a few minutes."

"I'll wait to walk you out."

Crap. She'd wanted to do just a couple more things before she called it a night. But more than likely he knew she was lying, so that's why he called her on it.

"All right."

There wasn't a woman, no matter who she was and what she'd been through, who didn't want to be looked after, cared for, in some regard. If Cole wanted to make sure she didn't overwork herself and see that she got to her car safely, then who was she to put up a fight? A little white knight routine every now and then would go a long way in helping her get through this ordeal with her father.

"Let me get all the lights and my purse."

"I'll wrap up the food and put it away."

Tamera gestured. "The refrigerator is through those doors over there in my makeshift apartment."

Cole laughed as he dropped his jacket and tie back in the chair they'd just vacated and went over to the food.

"Why am I not surprised you have an apartment in your office?"

"Because I'm sure you do, too."

He turned around, still smiling. "You know I do."

Her heart lurched just a bit because she did know. They'd always joked that when they were big in the corporate world they'd need an apartment in their office because they'd never want to leave. Making money was all that had mattered to Cole back in the day, while being powerful enough to fill her father's shoes had been her main objective.

Guess they both got their wish. But as she looked back, the old saying came back to bite her in the butt... "Be careful what you wish for."

5:15. Tamera pulled her BMW into the marina and cringed. She hated being late, but today was the day from hell and there was nothing she could do about it. TGIF at least.

She glanced down at her clothes and groaned. Still wearing her running shorts, sports bra and racer-back tank, she knew Cole would wonder what on earth she'd been doing.

Tamera grabbed her purse and her sketches that they'd worked on at the office and made a mad dash down the dock toward Cole's million-dollar yacht. The palm trees overhead rustled in the breeze, mocking her. The sun beat down, making her already break into a sweat. Unfortunately, she didn't have time to appreciate the swaying palms, the pristine white boats docked here or even the sultry heat.

No, her day had been spent inside, talking with health care workers about her father and then administering to his needs. She didn't have time to focus on the simple things…not when her father's life was slowly drawing to a close and his entire empire hinged on her making this deal a success.

It was the least she could do for a legacy he'd handed down with the utmost faith in her abilities.

Tamera held her hand over her brows to block the sun as she stared ahead to Cole's yacht. He stood on the dock watching for her. The sun illuminated his broad shoulders, making him seem even more dominating, more powerful.

"I know, I'm late," Tamera said in a rush as she reached him. "I'll apologize for both that and my less-than-professional appearance."

After he assisted her on board, he climbed on himself. "Just get back from a workout?"

"I wish." She followed him down into the galley and laid her sketches on the table and her purse on the sofa. "I was leaving for my morning run when the hospice nurse called and said they needed to see me right away. Needless to say, I didn't take time to change."

"Everything okay?" Cole grabbed a bottle of water from the bar and passed it to her.

Tamera unscrewed the cap and took a cool, refreshing drink. "Nothing that we hadn't expected. His blood counts are off and his medications needed to be adjusted."

Cole leaned a hip on the edge of a barstool. "So why did they call you so early?"

"Because he had a bad night and was asking for me." Guilt crept up and nearly suffocated her. "I hate that he's in an unfamiliar place with strangers. I wasn't there when he needed me."

Cole closed the small gap between them and took her by the shoulders. "Go back to your father."

Shaking her head, she clutched the water bottle. "No, I need to do this. He was resting when I left, so he's fine. The nurses have my number and will call if they need to. I'll swing by there when I leave here anyway."

The muscle in Cole's jaw ticked. "You run yourself too thin. The nurses have everything under control. You need someone to look out for you for a change."

She brushed him aside and bent to get her sketches. "I don't have time to be spoiled or pampered, Cole. I have to work."

Besides, she thought, there was no one else to take care of her. Her father was all she had left. Oh, she had friends and business associates, but if something were to really happen to her, who would she turn to?

Cole? What would he do? He was nothing more than a business associate at this point. Right?

"If you insist on stressing yourself over this, then at least have a seat." He gestured to the small work area he'd set up with leather club chairs and a glass table. "The offer remains, though, I can work on this tonight and we can go over it sometime over the weekend if you want to leave."

"Cole, I'm fine. Can we just work?"

Obviously he was concerned about her. The way he kept staring at her as if he were waiting for her to pass out or break down and cry was disconcerting. But she'd be damned if she'd show weakness. It was bad enough that she'd fallen asleep in his arms the other night, no way could she appear to be anything less than on top of her game now.

Cole nodded. "Whenever you want to eat, I had my chef prepare some food and we can dine out on the deck."

"I'm not hungry right now. I'll let you know."

Cole booted up his laptop while Tamera spread out her sketches. As they worked in harmony, it was really hard not to recall another place and time when they'd worked without speaking a word and their ideas just melded together into one glorious plan.

They'd had such high hopes of being partners in a firm one day. Now here they were, working together, but to gain prestige in their own individual companies.

After about an hour, Tamera's cell rang, jarring her from her groove of design.

She rushed forward to her purse and pulled out her BlackBerry. "Hello."

"Mrs. Stevens? This is Camille from the hospice center."

Tamera turned back to Cole, who gestured for her to take her call in the bedroom.

"Is something wrong?" she asked, stepping into the captain's quarters, closing the door. "Is my father okay?"

"Yes, yes dear," the elderly lady assured her. "That's why I'm calling. The day nurse told me you'd been here all day. I was off last night, but I heard he had a bad evening. Anyway, I wanted to let you know that I'm pulling a long shift and I'll be here 'til morning. Right now your father is eating a bit and he seems content. I just wanted to keep your mind at ease."

Tamera sagged on the king-sized bed with relief. "Thank you, Camille. You don't know how much I appreciate all you guys are doing to keep him satisfied."

"Oh, dear, that's our job. We're here for Mr. Stevens and his family. Have a good night."

Tamera disconnected the call and rested her elbows on her knees, head and cell in her hands.

"Tamera," Cole said, coming into the room. "Everything okay?"

She looked up and nodded. "Yes. The nightshift nurse just wanted to let me know my father was doing okay and eating."

"Which is what you should be doing," he told her.

Tamera shook her head. "I don't need anything. We need to get this outline completed so we can present a flawless plan to Victor on Monday afternoon."

Cole stepped forward. "You need to rest."

"Why do you keep insisting on what I should be doing? I'm fine."

"You have circles under your eyes and you're looking pale." He squatted down before her. "Take thirty minutes and rest here. I can get the food set out and make sure everything's ready while you take a breather. No is not an option."

Tamera looked down at this man who insisted on doing for her what she should be doing for herself. Without notice or warning, tears sprang to her eyes. She laid her cell beside her on the bed and covered her face with her hands.

"Hey. Come now, Tamera." Cole grabbed her wrists and pulled her forward, looping her arms around his neck. "Don't do this to yourself."

"It's just, when my c-cell rings, I get so scared."

She hadn't even admitted that until now. But she knew the day was coming when the nurse would call and tell her that her father had passed.

"I know," he whispered. "Let me care for you. Just for a few minutes."

Tamera nodded, unable to fight any more tonight. "Only thirty minutes. Get the food ready and I'll be out."

Cole kissed her on the forehead and urged her down onto the bed. He pulled off her tennis shoes and tugged the navy throw from the end of the bed over her legs.

"I'll yell when it's all set up. Just rest."

Tamera smiled, closed her eyes, giving in to the fatigue that overwhelmed her.

Ten

One hour turned into two and Cole didn't care. He could've stood in the doorway to his master suite and watched the rise and fall of Tamera's chest for two more hours.

He wasn't denying himself the opportunity to watch her. No, this wasn't professional, but they had long since passed professionalism. They'd teetered on a fine line and damn if he wasn't less than an inch from crossing over.

Between checking on Tam while she rested, he'd tweaked the design more and had pretty much gotten it to where he and Tamera had wanted. Hopefully, that would be where Victor wanted as well.

His eyes traveled down the dip in Tam's waist and up over the swell of her hip. When he'd seen her rushing down the dock in nothing more than skimpy workout shorts and a tank, he nearly dropped to his knees and thanked God.

He'd ached to see her smooth, creamy skin once again. But, on the other hand, if he wasn't touching her, he felt cheated. There wasn't a man alive who wouldn't want to run his hands over those well-toned curves. Cole wanted nothing more than to reacquaint himself with everything Tamera had hidden beneath her vulnerable exterior.

She hadn't moved. Since the moment he'd covered her with the navy throw, she'd slept peacefully. He didn't want to wake her, not only because he knew she'd be furious that he'd let her sleep this long, but because she needed the rest. She was running herself ragged and if she didn't want to take care of herself, then he damn well would.

But he wouldn't let his heart get into this mix. No, he was strictly looking out for her because they were working on the biggest project of their careers.

Cole crossed the room, gave her shoulder a gentle shake and waited on her lids to flutter, waited to see those vibrant eyes shine with irritation. They didn't.

Damn. She was in a deep sleep which required him to do more than a subtle approach. Wonderful.

He eased onto the edge of the bed, running his finger along the satiny softness of her bare arm. Her skin instantly reacted by popping out in goose bumps. Always so responsive. That was one thing he'd remembered, and loved, about her.

"Tamera."

He didn't raise his voice. To be honest he wanted her to sleep, but he didn't want her to regret waking up in his bed in the morning. If she was going to sleep here, he wanted her to be fully aware of why she was there and what she was doing…and he wanted the benefits of having her in his bed.

"Tam."

Running his palm down her arm and back up over the curve of her shoulder, he watched as she started to come to. She rolled over onto her back, her arm went above her head, doing amazing things to the pull of her tight, white tank over her breasts.

Desire stirred even more in his gut. This woman was really testing his control. Of course, he could get up, walk away and let her wake on her own. He could, but he wouldn't.

"Wake up, Tam, before you hate me even more."

She let out a little moan, her lids slowly lifting, blinking against the subtle light filtering in through the doorway from the galley.

The awakening was just as beautiful as the rest. Her eyes focused on his face, as if she were struggling to figure out where she was. But her gaze never left his and that irritation he'd expected to see was absent. In its place…pure desire.

The silence aboard his yacht enveloped them, as did the darkened room. With just the glimpse of light, Cole could barely make out her face, but the slant of the glowing lamp from the galley made her eyes sparkle.

Instinct had Cole not thinking of his actions. He leaned down slowly, giving her ample time to resist or to stop this moment from happening. It was inevitable, though. They were meant to be here, right now. The project had nothing whatsoever to do with what was about to take place.

And he knew precisely once he started kissing her in his bed, neither of them were going to get back to work tonight.

Her eyes shifted to his mouth as her tongue darted out, moistening her plump lips. The invitation was clear, all he had to do was accept.

"Be sure," he warned, a split second before he closed the gap and captured her mouth beneath his.

The sudden intake of breath from Tamera was quickly followed by total abandonment. He knew she wouldn't fight him, not on this. Not when everything that had transpired before this moment had led them here.

This is where he'd wanted her since being reunited in that boardroom weeks ago. The familiarity of her kiss, her touch, rushed back to him and he had to clamp down those long-ago buried memories of love and foolishness and concentrate on the now. This was nothing more than physical attraction. Absolutely. Nothing. More.

Cole rested his hands on either side of her face, the feather pillow giving beneath his weight. Nothing could be sweeter than getting Tamera back in his bed.

Not only did he want her for purely selfish reasons, he wanted that instant gratification he'd receive knowing he'd won. He'd not only bettered himself to a level Tam's father never would've believed, but he also got Tamera right where he wanted her. In bed.

Love was definitely not something he wanted at this point in life. Why would anyone need love when there were contracts to be won, designs and structures to be created?

No, what he wanted was right here beneath him. Tamera's warm, willing body moving in a familiar rhythm with his. She was more than accepting, more than giving.

Her hands came up, wrapped around his neck and toyed with his hair. Subtle touches were one of the things he remembered most about Tamera. The woman was potent, but in an easy, nonaggressive way. But she made her point just the same and she continued to give as much into the kiss as he took.

Cole kept his body weight on one hand and allowed the other hand to move freely down the side of her curvy yet trim body. He wanted her out of these clothes five minutes ago, but he couldn't rush, not when he was so close to getting what he wanted.

Still in a dreamlike state, Tam arched her body beneath Cole's, silently begging him to rip her clothes off and take what they both had been denying themselves for weeks.

The weight of his body felt so familiar, so good pressing against hers. Consequences would come soon enough, as would regrets, but right now she needed, wanted, Cole to possess her. She wanted him to take control. She didn't want to think about what she was doing or where this would lead.

Nothing mattered but what she was feeling now and how much she'd missed the touch of a man. The touch of Cole.

Sensations she'd only experienced long ago tingled down through her body as Cole's hand slid behind her bare thigh, lifting her leg.

"Cole."

So much for silent begging. Her body had far surpassed the longing and craving of normal sexual desires. The need to feel his skin against hers consumed her and she didn't care if she did beg...so long as it got her closer to what she needed.

His hand moved to the elastic waistband of her running shorts. He lifted his body slightly and tugged the shorts down. Tamera scissor kicked her legs to move the unwanted garment on down the line.

Cole trailed kisses down her neck. "You feel so good," he murmured.

She could feel better if he'd finish this undressing process instead of chitchat. Obviously she was going to have to take control here for a bit. She tugged at his Polo shirt until it flew across the cabin to parts unknown.

Before he could settle back down against her, though, she placed both hands on his chiseled chest.

"Wait." Her fingertips explored every dip of smooth, hard muscle beneath bronzed skin. "Just…let me…"

Words were lost as Cole crushed her mouth beneath his, still keeping his chest levered off hers. As she continued to run her fingers over his pecs, his hips tilted into her.

Perhaps his desire *was* as urgent as hers.

Cole broke the kiss, sat up and pulled her up with him. Sitting on their knees, they made quick work discarding the rest of their clothing.

Then they froze.

Tamera's eyes traveled over Cole's as his did the same over hers. The gentle light streaming through the doorway beamed just enough glow across the bed to provide a romantic ambiance. Though romance was the last thing either of them were looking for…at least she wasn't and she highly doubted Cole was.

"Amazing," he whispered. "I didn't think you could get more stunning."

Tamera smiled. "Cole, I'm already naked, there's no need for compliments."

Fingertips trailed over her collarbone, down the slope of her bare breasts. "Perfect."

Cole's mouth dropped to her nipple as his hands

wrapped around her waist. Tamera's head dropped back as sensation after sensation of arousal coursed through her.

The force of his affection on her chest had her falling backward again. Cole followed her down, hands roaming up and down her sides as he turned his attention to the other breast.

Tamera wrapped her legs around his waist, urging him to hurry.

He lifted his head, quirked a smile and fumbled with the bedside table until he revealed a condom. Once he was ready, he glanced down to the part in her legs and guided himself in.

Tamera watched his face, hoping he'd look at her, but he kept his eyes closed. Distance. He was still keeping distance.

Perhaps she should do the same. After all, she didn't want more than tonight…did she?

No, no way could she put herself on the line any more than that where this Casanova was concerned. She would take this moment and revel in it, but then she would get back to business and hopefully get Cole out of her system and her life. Maybe she could finally have closure. Maybe.

Their bodies moved in an urgent need. Tamera locked her ankles, keeping Cole right where she wanted him.

As her climax slammed into her, Cole's body arched above hers, the muscles in his biceps straining as he held himself still.

Once the tremors ceased, Tamera waited to see what he would do, say. She didn't know what she expected, a little term of endearment, a little kissing, snuggling maybe, but him levering himself up off her and immediately getting dressed? No, that was not what she'd expected at all.

But this colder side of Cole was no match for the iciness she'd encountered years ago. She should be used to his reaction toward her. Still, she pulled the soft sheet up over her chest, suddenly feeling the chill.

"I'll be in the galley when you want to come in and finish working," he told her before disappearing into the living area.

Ahh, the romance. Not that she was looking for it, but seriously? Couldn't he have just thrown a bucket of cold water on her? The freezing effect would be just the same.

Eleven

Cole pulled a beer from the mini fridge beneath his bar and twisted the lid off. Well, he'd gotten what he'd wanted, now what? Tamera certainly wasn't out of his system. If anything, she was deeper under his skin.

How the hell had his perfect plan backfired? He'd gotten her in his bed by purposely having them meet aboard his yacht, yet her vulnerability made him feel like a complete ass for taking advantage.

God, he was even contradicting himself. Did he or did he not want to seduce her just because he still could? Did he not just get what he wanted, on his own turf? And was he not still just as frustrated as he'd been before?

To top the icing on the proverbial cake, he'd treated her like a cheap hooker when he'd all but jumped out of bed, discarded the condom and basically ordered her back to work.

Smooth, really smooth.

Good thing he wasn't looking for romance or love, because those qualities were obviously long gone.

He heard her shuffle across the carpeted galley, but didn't turn. He wasn't ready to see the regret or hurt that would no doubt be in her eyes.

She opened the larger refrigerator, moved some things around and finally closed the door. Cole moved over to the work area he'd set up on his long, rectangular table before she'd arrived.

While she'd been asleep, he'd spread out her sketches and worked off them. Now, he returned to the work he'd done mere moments ago.

Yet so much had changed since he'd stood here last time.

Tamera came around to the table. From the corner of his eye, he noted she'd dressed in her running wear again, right down to the tennis shoes. She stood sipping a bottle of water, glancing down at her designs, which he'd altered.

"You need something to eat," he told her, keeping his gaze on the table.

"I don't like what you did here." She ignored his remark and pointed to the entryway of the hotel. "This wall cuts off that airy feeling we were going for."

He followed her perfectly manicured finger across the sketch to the area of the lobby they'd set aside for the registration desk. "There's no way to avoid it. They will need a safe and counter space to work and columns can only offer so much support. Especially on the ground floor."

"I don't like it," she insisted.

"I don't think it matters what you like or don't like," he snapped, turning to look at her. "Victor makes the final judgment calls and we have to be professionals about this and realize that the wall has to remain where it is."

She jerked her body around, slamming her bottle on the table...thankfully the lid was on it.

"Professional?" Her hands went to her hips. "Don't you dare question my professionalism. How professional was that?"

She pointed toward his cabin.

"That had nothing to do with business," he told her.

Tamera let out a clipped laugh. "No, you're warmer to business associates than you were to me. You're absolutely right."

Guilt wrapped around his chest and squeezed. "We both knew going into that that we were just acting on physical attraction."

Tamera held up a hand. "Forget it. Just forget it. I don't know why I expected more from you. Obviously I didn't learn from my previous experience."

She crossed to the couch, grabbed her purse and marched up the steps onto the deck.

Cole didn't have to go topside to know she was gone. She wasn't just up there getting air. She was pissed and had every right to be.

She'd be fine once she cooled off. They had to meet with Victor in two days. This design had to be completed by then. So, whenever Tamera was done with her tantrum, he'd be waiting. If nothing else, she was a professional. She wouldn't let this project fall behind simply because of what had happened in his bedroom.

Tamera knew Cole, at least the business side of him. Even though it was Saturday, the man would be in his office. There was no need to call to confirm, she didn't want to give him a heads up so he could plot and scheme more ways to make her feel inadequate.

The only way she'd call is if the front doors to his building were locked, but even then, he'd only have minutes to come up with some way to mistreat her.

After storming off his yacht last night, she'd calmed down enough to know they had a project that needed their attention. Surely they could put hormones, their past and whatever else was crackling between them on hold for the duration of this design phase.

Once Zach took over on-site for the actual construction, which would take months, she wouldn't have to see Cole nearly as much, if at all.

Tamera pulled her BMW in front of The Marcum Agency's three-story glass structure and took a deep, calming breath. Okay, so maybe it wasn't calm, but she was trying here.

She grabbed her tote bag and locked her car. The sun was shining bright today, the glare bouncing off all that shiny glass, making Tamera even more annoyed. Even the sun shone down upon the high and mighty Cole Marcum.

One tug on the door and, praise God, it opened. She took the elevator to the top floor and marched down the hall toward his office.

She heard laughter. Female laughter.

Two-timing jerk.

Wait. Two-timing? No. That would imply that she and Cole had a relationship. They'd had sex. Big difference.

Tamera shifted her white designer bag on her shoulder, smoothed a hand down her pale yellow sheath. Taking another deep breath, she entered Cole's office where she encountered the body behind the female voice.

Kayla.

"Tamera," Cole's sister exclaimed, rushing across the room. "What are you doing here?"

Tamera accepted her old friend's hug. No matter what had transpired between her and Cole, Tamera had always held a special place in her heart for Kayla. She was most definitely the sister she'd never had…too bad they'd lost touch.

"I came to work," Tamera replied, easing back to look at Kayla. "You're still stunning."

Kayla, being a shy woman, simply smiled. "I didn't know you and Cole had a meeting set for today."

Tamera eyed the man in question, who seemed perfectly content to lean against the corner of his desk and smirk. Okay, he may not have been two-timing, but he was still a jerk.

"We didn't. We do have a meeting with Victor Lawson on Monday and we need to finalize some plans. I just assumed Cole would be in his office today."

"No rest for the weary," Zach chimed in.

Tamera turned and smiled as Cole's twin strode across the office with a folder.

"Here's the construction company I'm looking at." Zach handed the folder to Cole. "If you want to run this by Victor and see if he knows anything about them. We haven't used them before, but they do specialize in resorts all over the country, some in Mexico. I've seen their work and haven't heard one complaint or negative remark."

Cole nodded. "Thanks. You heading home?"

Zach glanced to his watch. "Probably should. I have to pick up Sasha at three."

"Sasha?" Kayla threw a questioning look at Tamera. "I've never heard of her."

"We just met."

"And no further explanation will be given," Kayla finished.

Zach laughed and pecked his sister's cheek. "Good to see you again, Tamera. I suppose I have you to thank for getting my brother in a sour mood today. It's good to see him knocked off that high horse every now and again."

Zach strode out whistling.

"I have to leave as well." Kayla went over to the boardroom-style table across the room and grabbed her purse. "I'm meeting some friends for a late lunch."

She hugged Tamera once again. "I hope we can get together for something other than business."

Tamera's heart squeezed. She knew she'd missed the female companionship of Kayla, but she hadn't realized how much. "I'd like that."

"Cole," Kayla called over her shoulder as she headed toward the door. "Call me after the meeting and let me know how it goes."

Cole nodded, still not saying a word. He really was in a mood. Oh well, if he was, it was of his own doing. He'd initiated things last night, and he was the one who'd left her behind in the bed. She'd felt just as cheap as if he'd thrown money onto the nightstand.

Tamera glanced at the boardroom table and noticed her sketches spread out, much like they had been at his yacht last night. She moved over to them, shifting the large, three-ring binders out of the way.

"I'm glad you came to your senses."

Tamera ignored Cole's jab at her work ethic. She would not start this day with him with an argument. That would do nothing but waste time and make her feel worse than she already did. And if he was in a bad mood, then by all means who was she to help him out of it? He deserved to live in a bit of misery after all he'd done to her…and not just last night.

Her eyes scanned the papers, but one particular area caught her eyes and tugged at her heart.

"You changed the registration area," she murmured, tracing her finger over the new design.

Tamera threw a glance over her shoulder as Cole moved like a predator across the room. He filled out his crisp white, button-down shirt and dark, designer jeans. Did the man have to look handsome every moment of every blasted day?

"Zach and I worked on this last night and this morning."

"Last night?"

Cole nodded, coming to stand directly beside her. "He met me here and we worked until about two and then I came back in about nine. I caught a few hours in my bed," he gestured toward the makeshift apartment.

Well, lack of sleep would certainly put a damper on anyone's mood, but Cole didn't look sleep deprived… he looked torn.

Was he regretting last night? Was he sorry they'd been intimate or was he sorry about his actions afterward? Tamera knew in her heart, that even if he was remorseful for what he'd done, he wouldn't admit it. Cole Marcum would never admit to weakness or being wrong.

Damn prideful man. Just like her father.

She drew her attention back to the drawing. "This is exactly how I wanted it."

Cole reached across the table, picked up the binder and slammed it shut. He took it and placed it back on the floor-to-ceiling shelves stacked with numerous other black binders containing designs and sample materials for the firm's projects.

"Did Zach think this was a good idea?" Tamera asked, trying to get a sense of what exactly Cole was mad about.

Cole turned, settled his hands on his hips and shrugged. "He said it would work either way."

"Then why did you remove a good portion of the wall?"

"I just did." He pulled out another sheet, this one for the top floor, and laid it over the one she'd been studying. "We need to work on the details for the ballrooms."

Okay, so that topic was closed.

Had Cole done the redesigning out of guilt because they'd had sex? Tamera felt absurd even thinking such a thing, but why else would he have worked so late into the night? And why else would he have called Zach in?

Perhaps Cole wasn't the jerk she'd deemed him to be. Perhaps he did have a heart after all.

Or perhaps he just thought he could get into her good graces again and get her back into bed.

Twelve

"I don't know why we need to have a meeting without Tamera," Kayla stated as she took a seat on the black leather sofa in Cole's makeshift apartment adjacent to his office.

Cole poured himself a shot of whiskey. "Because we've run into a glitch."

Zach breezed through the door. "What the hell is the big emergency? I need to finish these calls I have out to this construction company before I take off for the day."

"Have a seat." Cole motioned to the vacant cushion beside their sister.

Zach stopped in his tracks. "Oh, no. What have you done?"

Cole eased a hip onto the barstool, rested an elbow against the bar and swirled his drink. "I didn't do anything. I have something I need to run by you two."

"Why isn't Tamera here?" Kayla repeated, crossing her legs and quirking a brow.

"Have a seat, Zach." Cole eyed his brother until his twin propped himself on the arm of the sofa next to Kayla. "Walter Stevens is dying. He's in hospice care right now."

"Oh, poor Tamera." Kayla put a hand up to her mouth, tears already forming in her eyes. "How is she holding up?"

"Just like you'd expect her to," Cole confirmed. "She's stubborn, won't accept help from anyone and is insistent she can run things herself."

Zach and Kayla shared a look, like they had some private joke between them.

"What?" Cole asked.

"Sounds like you," Kayla told him. "She's not going to show her weakness, Cole. You of all people should appreciate that."

Appreciate it? The woman was damn near driving him insane with her stubbornness.

He waved with his drink. "We're getting off track here. With Walter dying, the fate of The Stevens Group hinges on Tamera and her ability to run the company as well as her father and grandfather did."

Zach shrugged. "Okay, so?"

"There's no reason we can't make her an offer." Cole set his glass on the bar and came to his feet. "Tamera is vulnerable right now and will be even more so after Walter's death. I don't see why we can't approach her about joining forces."

The look was exchanged once again between his siblings.

"Has Tamera hinted that she's uncomfortable with running the company?" Kayla asked.

"No."

"Then what makes you think this is even a good idea?" Zach piped in.

Cole paced to the windows where he looked out onto the bay. "Because…this merger would benefit our firm…if we combine forces, just think of all we could accomplish."

"This has nothing to do with what's going on between the two of you personally?" Zach questioned.

Cole glanced back to his twin, who sat with a knowing smirk. "No, this is strictly business."

He turned his attention back to the crystal blue water, lined with tall, sturdy palm trees.

"I don't think it's a good idea," Kayla said. "I think it's low to dive in and attack while she's down. And it's even worse you're planning the attack for when she'll be the lowest."

Cole shoved his hands in his pockets, turned and leaned against the warm glass. "It's not an attack, Kayla. It's a good business move for both of us."

"Says who?" Zach demanded. "The Stevens Group has been around longer than we have. Why would they suddenly merge with us?"

"Because Tamera isn't stupid. She's seen what we can accomplish and with both our names on Victor's hotel, clients will want us as a package deal in the future."

"So, you're just going to ask Tamera to sell her father's legacy, the only substantial thing she has left of him, and come to work with us?" Zach shook his head, laughed. "Yeah. That'll go over well."

"She'll think this was all her idea," Cole countered. "All I will do is encourage her. I need to know what you two think."

Kayla ran a hand down her black, glossy hair and

shoved it past her shoulders. "I think it would be a fantastic business move for us, but on a personal level, I don't think it's wise. You and Tamera share a past. Should you keep this entanglement going?"

Should he? Was he just asking for more trouble down the road? Perhaps, but in his life, business came first. No matter what.

Kayla came to her feet, smoothed her hands down her red sheath and smiled. "Cole, when you find out what Tamera really wants, then we'll talk. Until then, I think this is a premature conversation."

With her quiet, easy manner, Kayla left the room, leaving Zach behind.

"Go ahead," Cole said to his twin. "I know you want to say something."

Zach stood and crossed to the window to stand beside Cole. "Have you lost your mind?"

"Not yet."

Zach rubbed his stubbled jaw. "Who are you trying to prove something to, Cole? Tamera, her father, or yourself? Walter is dying. He doesn't care what you do anymore. This competition is completely one-sided."

Cole fisted his hands. "I'm not proving anything. I'm trying to move us into a better direction."

"I didn't know we were going in the wrong direction," Zach mocked. "If this is about your guilt over a decision you made years ago, move on."

Thankfully Zach hadn't mentioned that aspect while Kayla had been in the room. Kayla had never been told the real reason for the breakup. She would've no doubt gone and told Tamera which, in turn, would've caused a rift between Tamera and her only living family member.

"I've moved on." Cole gritted his teeth, narrowing

his gaze at his brother. "We both know this is a good move."

"Maybe it is, but at what cost?"

Zach crossed the room and left the office. Cole hated that Zach was always so easygoing, yet to the point. The man knew just how to pinpoint the heart of a problem. He was a man of few words, but when he spoke, they were important.

Zach was right, though. At what, or should he say whose, cost would this merger be carried out?

Running a hand through his hair, Cole moved from the living area back out into his office. He was already thinking in terms of this merger being a done deal. There was no way, no way Tamera would give in to this business arrangement. But she had to think reasonably. The pressure would be too great for her to run a multimillion-dollar company and deal with the grief of losing her father, when that time came.

Cole took a seat behind his desk and wiggled his mouse to bring his computer back to life. Who was he kidding? Tamera was more than capable of running— successfully he might add—Walter's company. Hadn't she done so already without anyone's knowledge as to where her father was?

The truth ate at Cole. He hated admitting it even to himself.

He wanted Tamera working with him. Period. She was intelligent, resourceful and determined. If she weren't so stunning, those qualities in themselves would have him attracted to her.

But she was stunning. Just the thought of her had him catching his breath. He could admit, only because he was alone, that he wanted her on his team so he could keep an eye on her. He wanted to know what she was doing in business and her personal life at all times. Call it overbearing, he didn't care. He didn't want to let Tamera out of his life again.

No, he didn't want love. No, he didn't want a relationship. He was simply incapable of those two things. But he wasn't immune to caring.

So, Tamera would have to see his side of things. He'd make sure of it. And, in the end, she'd come to work for The Marcum Agency thinking everything was her idea.

Thirteen

"Amazing."

Tamera crossed her legs and watched as Victor scanned through the first draft of his first American hotel. He sat across from her and Cole at the long boardroom table in Cole's office.

Trying to appear calm, Tamera resisted looking over at her co-designer sitting directly to her right.

"The exterior is absolutely perfect," he said, his eyes still riveted to the drawing. "Breathtaking."

Tamera couldn't stop the grin from spreading across her face. "We wanted to give guests a feel of another time and place. Something extravagant, classic and timeless."

He lifted his gaze, looking between her and Cole. "You two make a great team. I knew I'd made the right choice hiring both agencies. Have you ever thought of joining forces? You'd monopolize the architectural world."

Okay, that comment made her a bit squeamish. She didn't want to be a "great team" with Cole any more than she wanted to "join forces." Those days were long gone…and the other night aboard his yacht didn't count.

She'd thought that using him, just as he'd done her, would make her feel better, powerful. Quite the opposite. She felt even worse about herself and this entire pairing.

A boardroom union was fine for now, but this was not something she wanted in the long run. Her emotional state had already taken a beating and she'd only worked with Cole for a few weeks.

"We have enjoyed working on this project," Tamera piped up.

Victor glanced down to the spread of drawings. "It shows."

"Shall we go on to look at materials for the exterior?" Cole asked.

"I actually had my assistant e-mail you both as I was on my way here," Victor said. "In her message is everything I want to see as far as textures, lighting, metals, in both the exterior and interior. I have another meeting in South Beach in thirty minutes. I appreciate the use of your office seeing as how I had several places to be today and this was on my way."

"Not a problem," Cole said. "Anywhere that's convenient for you to meet is fine with us. We're here for you."

When Victor came to his feet, looking at his watch, Tamera and Cole rose as well.

"If you have any questions, please feel free to

contact me or my assistant and she can get ahold of me," he continued as he walked to the door. "Zach and I have a meeting scheduled later in the week to discuss contractors. I'm pleased with how quickly this project is moving."

"The Marcum Agency is efficient," Cole beamed.

Victor nodded. "I will be in touch."

As soon as he was out the door, Tamera resisted the urge to slam it, simply shutting it with a louder than average click.

"What the hell was that?" she demanded, whirling around on Cole.

"What?"

She clutched the door handle behind her with both hands so she wouldn't be tempted to strangle him. "You implied your agency is more efficient than mine. We are in this together as a team, which means we're equals."

"I never said otherwise." Cole turned his back on her, walked over to the table and began straightening the papers.

Tamera tried counting to ten, but only made it to three. "Don't brush me off like some child."

"Then quit acting like one," he said, still with his broad back to her.

She marched around to stand in front of him. "You are being deliberately rude and hateful."

His hands froze on the papers he was holding as he shifted to face her completely. "Am I? Perhaps you're just too sensitive because you're overworked lately. Why don't you take the rest of the day off and rest?"

Fury that had been rising to the surface for the past minute finally bubbled over. "You may be used to bossing your staff around, but I do not work for you. I work for myself and, at the moment, Victor. And I don't have time to rest, not with all that is going on."

The muscle in Cole's jaw ticked. "You've been to see your father today?"

"Yes."

"Going back?"

Tamera shook her head. "I will probably go after dinner and see that he's settled in for the night."

"When are you going to tell people about him? They're going to find out soon enough."

Tamera didn't want to think about what would happen "soon enough." "I'm not worried about that right now, Cole. Hospice is caring for him."

"Is he at Mercy Hospice Center?"

"Yes."

Cole brushed the pads of his thumbs beneath her eyes, his hands came to rest on her shoulders. "You're not taking care of yourself."

Uneasy with the fact he knew her so well, Tamera took a step back, forcing Cole's hands away. "I don't have a choice. You know that."

"If you're not going to relax, at least do something for just you that isn't work."

Tam laughed. "Yeah. When would I have time for that?"

He studied her face, his eyes lingering on her lips a bit longer than she was comfortable with. "Let's celebrate tonight after you go see your father."

She jerked back, stunned. "Celebrate? What?"

"Victor's stamp of approval." Cole moved closer. "We need to concentrate on nothing but having a good time. It'll do wonders for you."

Tamera thought of the possibilities that could come from spending an evening with Cole "having a good time." She deserved as much, though, didn't she? She could more than handle his charms and she'd throw a few of her own his way if he got out of hand.

What could going out hurt? She'd have her cell if the nurses needed to get ahold of her. A night without cares was exactly what she needed.

"Maybe." She smiled, already looking forward to the endless possibilities. "Where do you want to go?"

"We'll stay in South Beach. Find a nice club, some dinner."

Tamera nodded, wondering exactly what his motives were. Cole didn't do anything, she'd noticed, without gaining something to his benefit.

"Fine."

Cole gestured toward the designs and the piles of black binders. "When do you want to meet again to work on the final draft and intricate details before passing them on to Zach?"

Tamera's week of events rolled through her head. "I probably can't do anything until Friday. I have late meetings and I have dinner with Dad two nights."

"Do you want to come here or do you want to meet somewhere after work?"

Memories of him waking her, his hands undressing her, his mouth on her body consumed her. "I think it's best we meet in the office. Mine."

A cocky smirk tilted the corner of his mouth. "If I want you, Tamera, the location won't matter."

"You bastard," she whispered. "If you think you can have me on a whim and discard me whenever you feel like it, you're insane. I may have been foolish once the other night, but it won't happen again."

Cole snatched her around her waist and tugged her flush with his body at the same time his mouth came down on hers. She struggled for about two seconds before kissing him back.

If nothing else, the man knew how to kiss.

She didn't give him the satisfaction of touching him back, though. She kept her hands dangling at her sides. No, she was taking this kiss and giving nothing back.

His lips were rough, demanding and Tamera's body betrayed her by letting out a soft moan.

Cole pulled back. "Don't lie to me or to yourself. It will happen again."

The heat in his eyes combined with his promissory tone had Tamera pulling from his hold, grabbing her purse and all but running from the room.

"Pick you up at eight," he yelled just before she slammed the door.

Cole cursed himself for allowing Tamera to get the best of him, making him lose his control. He wasn't lying, though, when he told her he could have her whenever he wanted. He wasn't oblivious to the fact she melted every time he touched her. She was not lost to the fact they were still attracted to each other.

"Everything okay?"

Cole turned from the conference table to see Zach standing in his doorway. "Fine."

"Then why do you look like you just ate a sack of nails?"

Cole did not want to deal with his twin right now. "Busy here, Zach. What do you need?"

His brother crossed the room to the long table and picked up a sheet of paper, studied it. "First, let's start with why Tamera stormed out of here, nearly knocking me over in the hallway, then acting as if she didn't even see me."

Cole snatched the sketch from Zach's hand. "Ask her."

"I'm asking you," he said, leaning against the table, crossing his arms over his chest. "You didn't mention the notion of her coming to work here, did you?"

"No. She's got a lot on her plate right now, that's all." Cole wasn't about to elaborate further, not even with his twin. "We're going out tonight to celebrate. She'll be fine."

He'd make sure of it. Because at the end of the night, she was going to be back in his bed. And, unlike last time, she'd be more than satisfied with his performance afterward.

"Going out?" Zach asked. "I thought you weren't going to get entangled with her again. And don't tell me this is another business meeting."

"Not business. I don't plan on doing any business tonight."

Zach let out a low whistle. "Doesn't sound like you're trying to avoid the entanglement, Cole. Sounds like you're weaving the web."

Cole shrugged. "Perhaps I am, but I'm still in control of where I lay the threads."

"Just get this design done, make Victor happy and let me step in and do what I do best. Build. And don't screw with Tamera's head again. She's in a fragile state right now. You of all people should understand that."

Cole gave a mock salute. "If you're done harassing me, I need to get back to work so I can get ready for my evening."

"Don't screw this up."

Zach walked out, closing the door behind him.

Screw this up? What exactly was he referring to?

Didn't matter, really. Cole didn't intend on screwing

anything up. Not the agreement they had going with Victor Lawson and certainly not this evening he had planned with Tamera.

He intended to take Tamera to the hottest nightclub and dance so close to her, she'd be begging him to take her home. He wanted to feel her body close to his again. He wanted to make her blue eyes go icy with desire.

But most of all, he wanted her to know he was much better now than he'd been years ago.

A curl of excitement swirled deep in her belly. Cole knew her inside and out. He knew when she needed a break, knew how hard to push to make her cave.

She didn't want to give, didn't want to acknowledge that he had so much power over her personal life.

But there you have it. Cole Marcum still held a piece of her. Sometimes she just wished it wasn't the piece that controlled her heart.

Tamera hit the button to drop the top of her sporty car. She wanted to feel a bit reckless, a bit of freedom if only for a few minutes.

The air whipped her hair around. Tam smiled as she glanced up to the clear blue sky stamped with the amazingly tall green palms lining the highway.

For once in her life she was going to forget her troubles, enjoy this opportunity fate had handed her.

If Cole was determined to show her a good time, she'd show him just exactly what she was made of.

Fourteen

Did someone order sexy?

Tamera turned from side to side, checking herself out in the floor-length mirror. Her short, red halter dress showed off her curves. The loose curls she'd put at the ends of her blond hair were bouncy, perfect for dancing. She applied a subtle gloss to make her lips appear even fuller, luscious.

If Cole wanted a hot night, he would be one extremely happy man when he knocked on her door. She wasn't letting him forget, even for a minute, what he'd let go of so long ago. Was it so wrong to rub it in every chance she got?

Why did she have to find Cole's cocky, take-charge attitude irresistible?

And even though she was still infuriated with him for those actions earlier in his office, not to mention the way he always told her how to live her life as if he knew what she was going through, she was looking forward to having a night of fun. Cole had always been a good time and she had no doubt tonight would be no exception.

Besides, she needed something positive in her life. For an hour, maybe two, she wanted to pretend her world wasn't crumbling, her emotional state wasn't so fragile.

She couldn't remember when she'd last had a night out. Not only that, she couldn't recall when she'd actually been on a date.

Date?

Tamera groaned, turning from the mirror to grab her small, silver handbag, dropping her lip gloss into the pouch.

This was most certainly *not* a date. Just because they were going out to dance, eat, and possibly end up in bed…okay, that was more probable than possible. None of that meant this was a date.

They were simply celebrating a milestone in both of their careers. Besides, Cole was right. She did need to relax, take a few moments for herself and have a good time.

So why did she feel guilty for needing this reprieve while her father lay in a hospice center living out his last days?

She jerked when her doorbell chimed. She smoothed a hand down her dress as she rushed to the door.

Cole's eyes widened as he raked his gaze over her.

Tamera was more than pleased with Cole's reaction. The flirty, saucy dress was certainly not her normal, everyday wear, but she'd been waiting for the perfect opportunity to wear it. Showing Cole what he'd missed out on was the best occasion she could think of.

But, the surprise was on her, too, when she slid her eyes down his body.

Cole wore faded jeans paired with a black T-shirt that made him look like the devil she knew him to be.

She swallowed, stepped out onto her porch and closed the door behind her.

The visual lick he gave her body from her head to her French-manicured toes made her shiver. "I'm ready."

"Yes, you are."

"Where are we going?" she asked, trying to avoid the way her body reacted to this delectable, yet infuriating man.

"Just a little club owned by a friend of mine. Great food, even better dance floor and live band."

Tamera offered a smile. "Can't wait."

He closed the gap between them, his eyes settling on the plunging V of her dress. "We'd better get going before I change my mind and we stay in to celebrate."

Yes, they'd better go because the way he kept those heavy-lidded eyes roaming over her only made her want to give in. Even though their last bedroom encounter left her feeling cold, lonely, she was feeling anything but chilly right now.

Could her feelings for this man be more all over the spectrum? One minute she wanted to throttle him, the next she wanted to strip him.

He escorted her to his sleek, black sports car that probably cost what was for some people a full year's salary. Just how many vehicles did he have? Everything about this man demanded attention and attention was precisely what she wanted to give him tonight.

Though they drove in silence, the sexual tension bouncing around in the car was deafening. In a way, she wished he'd have said to hell with it and had his way with her in her foyer.

But he knew what he was doing…and so did she. He wanted her, she wanted him. They were playing a game centuries old and in the end, they'd both win.

Cole pulled his car into a parking spot behind one of the many clubs South Beach had to offer.

"You're friends with the man who owns Live?" Impressed, Tamera glanced to see Cole's reaction.

"Zach and I redesigned the interior when Matt bought this place."

"Only certain people can get in." She couldn't believe Cole's social status. "I've always heard this place rivals the line and security Studio 54 had."

She stared at the "Live" sign hanging above the back entrance, still in awe that Cole had such connections. How many times had he used this ace in the hole to lure women back to his bed? No, she wouldn't think like that because tonight, she was the woman with him and that's all that mattered. Tonight.

"We'll get in," he assured her as he exited the car.

Cole led Tamera to the back door, his hand on the small of her back. The intimate gesture sent shivers racing through her body even on this humid evening.

With the way her dress scooped in the back, his thumb kept caressing her bare skin. Tamera didn't know if he was doing it on purpose or if it was an innocent gesture while he chatted with the security guard. Either way, the circular motion he made completely wiped her mind free. She had no idea what the two men were discussing, didn't care. Nor did she care about going into such a reputable club.

She wanted to go back home. With Cole. Now.

"Thanks, Enrique."

Tamera offered the Cuban guard a wide smile and stepped into the club when he opened the door to allow them to pass through.

Okay, she could do the club scene for a while, but then she was demanding Cole take her back home. Why was she fighting her most basic of urges?

"So you do know the secret handshake," Tamera joked as the door was closed behind them. "I should've paid attention."

Cole leaned down to her ear. "If you're nice, I'll teach you sometime."

Mercy. The man was good.

The darkened atmosphere, only illuminated by cobalt blue lights suspended from various parts of the ceiling, made this evening more intimate…as if they needed more of that.

The architect in her was impressed as she took in the two sets of wrought-iron stairs on either side of the spacious room. A stage at the far end to her left supported the amazing band belting out some sexy salsa music.

The bar was hopping with people ordering drinks. She appreciated the fact there were no chairs. She always hated maneuvering her way between bar stools to order.

Large, leather couches were dotted around the end to her right. Oversized, low ottomans were also spread about. Nearly every spot was occupied with beautiful people enjoying the renowned South Beach night life.

She turned to Cole. "Thanks for bringing me here."

His dark eyes roamed over her face, while the tip of his finger ran along her jawline. "My pleasure."

O-kay. She needed to keep the upper hand here. Yes, she wanted to relax and have a good time with Cole, but seriously. If she didn't get her emotions under a tight grasp, she'd likely find herself in the very spot she'd been in eleven years ago. And the fact that she wanted him so desperately on a physical level wasn't helping.

"I'll get you a drink," he said, moving toward the bar. "Cosmo?"

Tamera shook her head. She wanted something stronger than a drink. She wanted Cole. She wanted his hands on her, she wanted to feel his body against hers. She wanted that heat she could only get from him…no matter the chill afterward.

"No. Let's dance."

She took his hand, leading him to the crowded dance floor as the band changed their song to something even faster with a frenzied drumbeat.

Now this was what she needed. So long as she stayed in the moment, didn't let her heart get swept away by Cole's charming words, she'd be just fine. Just fine.

Tamera put her arms in the air, tossing her head from side to side as the beat of the music took over. Cole's hands circled her waist as his own hips moved to the beat.

Her flowy skirt tapped against her thighs. Her nipples puckered behind the thin material of her dress. And Cole's eyes may as well be his hands the way he kept looking over her face, her chest. The warmth and strength from his hands permeated through her silky dress.

Yeah. They wouldn't be at this club for very long. Not with the sexual tension mounting second after agonizing second. Add in the sexy atmosphere to their already growing arousal and they had the makings for some major combustion once they got alone. If they made it that long.

Tamera didn't know how long they danced. She stopped counting after three songs. All she knew was the music was awesome, the club was packed and Cole never took his eyes off her. Not once. And for a second, she found herself back in time to a place when nothing mattered but her and Cole. Their level of intimacy, their bond. Their love.

Her mouth went dry. "I'll take that drink now."

With his signature cocky grin, he nodded. Keeping one hand around her waist, Cole led her toward the bar where he ordered a foreign beer and her cosmo.

"Cole."

Tamera turned to the man who'd just come up and slapped Cole on the shoulder.

"Matt." Cole smiled and the two men did the typical male "half hug." "Good to see you," he shouted over the band.

Matt glanced at Tamera. "So you finally brought a lady into my club. About time."

What did that mean? Cole hadn't brought his dates here before? Interesting. Of course, that didn't mean a thing. Perhaps Matt just hadn't seen the women. Tamera couldn't imagine Cole *not* flaunting his abilities to get into this club, through the back door no less.

"This is Tamera Stevens," Cole introduced. "She's an associate."

Tamera reached for her drink on the bar and smiled. "Nice to meet you."

Associate? Even more interesting. Seriously, though, what did she expect him to say? This is the woman I've put through hell, slept with once recently, fought over designs with and will probably hook up with again tonight?

Yeah. Associate was much simpler.

"The pleasure is mine," Matt said, smiling at Cole. "Come on up to the VIP room and have dinner on the house."

Cole glanced at Tamera, the heat in his eyes no less than when they'd been torso to torso on the dance floor. Had someone opened the door and let the Miami heat in? Good Lord, she was sweating.

"We're going to finish our drinks and go."

Matt laughed. The man wasn't stupid. He knew exactly why they were in a hurry.

"I don't blame you," the club owner said, still smiling. "It's an open-ended invitation."

Tamera turned her attention toward the band as Matt walked away. She didn't want to appear anxious, or worse, desperate, but she was ready to yank the tie at her neck and get the night moving in an even better direction.

Cole slid the icy tip of his beer bottle across the slope of her shoulders. "Finish your drink," he bent to whisper in her ear. "We're leaving."

Say no more. Tamera took a few more swallows, knowing the swift intake settling in her empty stomach was not a good combination, especially when she needed to keep some sort of control.

She turned, set her empty glass on the bar and looked up to Cole. "Why the hurry?"

Her sweet tone, combined with a sultry smile she offered had him slamming his longneck onto the metal bar, grabbing her arm and escorting her back to the rear entrance.

Laughter bubbled deep inside her, but she didn't let it out. She'd never seen Cole lose control and if she played her cards right, she'd see it again before the night was through.

When the security guard bid them a good night, Cole merely raised his arm in a silent farewell.

Speechless as well? My, my. This was turning into an even better night than she'd planned.

Fifteen

Cole maneuvered his car, faster than usual, through the streets of South Beach toward Star Island. Tamera may think she had control over tonight, but he was going to his own turf.

He'd never taken a woman to his house. Oh, he'd taken them to his vacation homes, but never his private domain. Ever. Star Island was for invited guests only... or, it was supposed to be. And Tamera was definitely invited.

Damn this woman for getting under his skin. He didn't want this, nor did he have time for anything beyond a sexual interlude.

But he would grant Tamera the full night. They both deserved long hours of intimacy.

He pulled up to the guard, waved and drove over the bridge.

Cole looked over at Tamera. She was all but spilling

from the top of her dress. One jerk of that bow around her neck and his night of fantasies could begin.

This time of the evening was always beautiful with the magnificent homes lining the beach, their lights bouncing off the water. This was what he'd always wanted. The money, the prestige. The woman beside him.

And though his goals weren't that of a twenty-two-year-old boy, they weren't too far off. But he wasn't naïve like he was in the past. He knew whatever was going on between Tamera and him now, would likely end when their association with Victor Lawson came to a close.

But he'd conquered what he'd set out to do. Tamera was willingly coming to his home with the full intention of staying. He didn't believe she was delusional enough to think they would have anything beyond the bedroom. She was an adult and she fully knew where he stood on relationships.

Which just made this night all the more sweet. No misconceptions about what tomorrow would bring or what the next step should be. There was no next step.

The second he pulled into his circular drive he killed the engine. He'd called earlier, before he picked Tamera up, and sent his staff home with a full day's pay. He wanted this night to be completely about him and Tamera.

She was out of the car before he could round the hood and open her door. The way the bright, full moon and the exterior lights from his house lit up the driveway, she looked like an angel with all her glowing blond hair and sun-kissed skin.

Of course, he didn't think angels wore red dresses. Sexy, short, cleavage-enhancing red dresses.

Control snapped. Cole grabbed her shoulders, pushed her back against the car as his mouth descended to hers. The breasts she'd been torturing him with all evening pressed firmly against his T-shirt, making him want to rip both articles of clothing off right here in his driveway. Thank God for the privacy gates surrounding his property.

She wrapped her arms around his neck, rose on her toes to meet him and gave him everything he was demanding and more.

She eased back just enough to whisper, "Touch me."

As her mouth sought his once more, he swept her hair aside, yanked the tie around her neck and tugged on the top of the dress until she was bare and all but trembling in his arms.

"We need to get inside."

Cole picked her up, thankful she'd wrapped her legs around his waist. She buried her face in the crook of his neck and nibbled her way up to his jaw.

"You're killing me, Tam."

Once they were inside, Cole made quick work of resetting the alarm system, and sat her down on the base of the steps.

The glow from the chandelier suspended from the second floor illuminated them. The two scraps that had covered her chest all night now dangled haphazardly down her thighs.

"You'd better do more than look," she threatened with a genuine smile.

"Oh, I plan to."

He tugged his shirt from his waistband and over his head, tossing it without a sound onto the checkered, tiled floor. He stepped up onto the step below hers at the same time she kicked off her stilettos. They fell down the two stairs with a clunk.

"Condom?" she asked, her bright blue eyes heavy with passion.

He pulled one from his pocket, laid it on the newel post. "No more talking."

Once again their mouths fused as one as he lowered her to the steps.

They weren't even going to make it upstairs and that was just fine with him. Why waste time when she was feeling the urgency just as much as he was?

Cole came to his feet, leaving Tamera heaving, lying back against the stairs. He made quick work unfastening his belt, unfastening and unzipping his jeans and discarding them, along with his boxer briefs, in a puddle at his feet. He kicked aside the unwanted clothing and knelt back down, but not before reaching for the condom.

Tamera gave his body a hungry glance, then grabbed his shoulders, pulled him toward her and proceeded to make some demands of her own with that talented mouth.

Without breaking contact, Cole opened the foil packet, covered himself. He eased to the side, so he sat on the wide step and urged Tamera to straddle him.

Hands roamed in a frantic motion as he bunched the dress up at her waist and pulled on the thin scrap of panties until he had total access to what he wanted.

Without a second thought of easing into this, Cole took her. He couldn't be gentle if he tried. He'd left his control back at her house hours ago and he'd been hanging on by a mere thread since.

A quick thought flashed through his mind as to whether or not he was too rough, too demanding, but

Tamera's soft moan was all he needed to continue. She broke the kiss, rested her forehead against his and closed her eyes.

Cole wanted to watch her, though. Now that she wasn't looking, wasn't thinking, he wanted to watch her face as she lost utter and complete control. He wanted to see that moment when she didn't hold back, didn't try to be strong or put up a front. He wanted to see total abandonment.

It didn't take long.

She bit her lip, squeezed her eyes and gripped his shoulders.

So much for holding his own control. He lost his just as Tam did and closed his own eyes in an attempt to hold this feeling, this time, right where it was. To rein in all the emotion they'd formed together. Why, he couldn't say, but he wanted it just the same. How could he not? Everything about this night had been perfect. As if their past didn't exist and they were just two people who found just how compatible they truly were.

He wanted to hold this moment forever. To revel in the bliss and simplicity.

Unfortunately, that was impossible. The moment had ended all too soon. The quiet settled around them, encompassing them in its embrace. Tamera would probably want to leave, want to put him back in that professional pocket she liked to keep him in.

But he had her here all night. She couldn't go anywhere and Cole would make damn sure she'd stay until he was ready to take her home.

But he had to be careful. Anything beyond the bedroom was impossible. They'd traveled that journey before and only ended up with broken hearts.

Cole pushed past thoughts and journeys aside. He had Tamera now and now is what he'd concentrate on.

Once the tremors ceased, Cole kissed her thoroughly, slowly. He picked her up again, carried her up the wide, curved staircase toward his master bath.

His walk-in shower with six shower heads was beckoning them. And he found himself wanting to care for her, wanting to show her how she should be treated, pampered.

"You were right," she murmured in a dreamy voice, her breath warm against his neck. "I needed this."

Cole swallowed. Hard. He didn't want that warm feeling that coursed through him. He didn't want to care for Tamera any further than right now. Sex was what they had, all they could have. And it was great, so why mess with anything else?

No, he shouldn't care. But he did.

He cared what she would have to deal with in the morning, the next day and the day after that with her father and the company. He especially cared about how she was feeling about him, about this path they'd started down. He knew, in reality, there was no turning back.

He'd be lying to himself if he even tried to act like he hadn't developed new feelings for her. The problem was, what did he do with an emotion he didn't want, and had thought died long ago?

The water sluiced over them, making Cole ultra aware of just how perfect her body was. But there was so much more to Tamera than her sexy curves and beautiful nature. She was career driven, she was giving, she was everything he'd ever want in a woman…provided he was looking for one.

Yes, if he were wanting to marry and settle down, he would be a fool not to pick Tamera. Perhaps he was a fool for not choosing her now, but he just didn't have long-term abilities in him anymore.

As his hands glided over her wet skin, backing her against the tiled wall, he knew all he could offer and take in return was exactly this. And the emptiness that he knew would follow after their lovemaking would just have to be his life companion.

He had no other choice.

"Why am I not surprised you live on Star Island?"

Tamera settled deeper into the crook of Cole's arm, content for now.

"Never came up."

With the second-story patio doors open, Tamera enjoyed the moonlight and the sounds of the water rushing to shore and swaying palm trees. She appreciated the romantic ambience. Cole had provided the perfect setting, the perfect night. She wasn't surprised that the weather gods were in Cole's back pocket. Everyone else was. And she was no exception. She didn't want to get hurt again, but she had a sickening feeling that heartache and pain were inevitable where this man was concerned. All she could do was enjoy what he was offering her now.

"You always told me you'd have the best," she recalled, thinking of the dreams they'd shared with each other so long ago. "You do."

"Yes."

O-kay. Not a man of many words.

Tamera eased up onto her elbow and looked down at Cole. "Care to tell me what's wrong?"

He continued to look up to the ceiling. "Not a thing. Just thinking."

"About…"

At her prompting, he turned his gaze to her. "The past. Interesting how some things come back around."

She studied his expression, his serious tone. "You're referring to us?"

"We both know there can't be an 'us', Tamera. There can't be more to this, than, well…this."

She nodded. Though she'd told herself the very same thing, she didn't so much like hearing it come from his mouth. She'd hoped to avoid that slap in the face from reality for as long as possible.

"If you're worried I'll get caught up in the magical world of love once again, don't be." Tamera got out of bed, suddenly chilly as she went in search of…her dress, which was in the bathroom. "I have too much on my plate as well."

She moved into the spacious, tiled bathroom where she found the scrap of red right next to the massive walk-in shower. After sliding into the dress, she recalled her shoes were downstairs. And her car was not here.

This was why she always wanted her car. She hated being stranded. Especially in an awkward position. Had she been thinking beyond the "fun-filled" night he'd promised, she should've known the awkwardness would settle in.

"You're staying," Cole told her as she came back into the bedroom.

"No. I need to get back."

He pushed himself up onto his elbow. "For what?"

She sighed. "My father. I need to be available when they call."

"They have your cell. No need to rush out of here when we can enjoy the rest of our night."

He did have a point, though she wasn't sure anymore if she actually could just enjoy him. Or would she find herself wanting even more than he was willing to offer?

True, she didn't want to turn back the clock to pick up where they left off. They were too different now. But she almost wouldn't mind seeing what would happen if they started over.

Was that even possible? Had she really forgiven him for all the hurt he'd caused her? God, in eleven years if she couldn't let go of a grudge, she shouldn't be here.

Tamera stared at the gloriously naked chest, tanned and partially hidden beneath the stark white sheets. Inky hair, heavy-lidded eyes. And she knew his solid, muscular body would still be warm and welcoming.

Her dress slid back to the ground in a whoosh. He was right. Why not enjoy right now?

She had every intention of doing just that.

Cole stood in his bedroom, staring at the rumpled sheets. Images of Tamera sprawled across them, her silky blond hair spread over the satin, plagued his mind.

He'd driven her back home just an hour ago, but he missed her already. The emptiness in his twenty-thousand-square-foot home was never so prominent, so deafening.

He hadn't expected any more surprises from her, but she certainly had caught him off guard when she'd appeared like a fantasy for their date. He thought for sure she'd still be smoldering hot about that kiss in his office and how he'd called her on basically being a liar where her feelings were concerned.

But she'd taken his insults and turned them into revenge. He'd have suffered more had she not come back to his house last night. Or maybe he was suffering because of her visit.

All he knew, as he walked into the bathroom where more images of her filled his mind from when they'd showered, was that she'd broken through. She'd gotten past that wall of defenses he'd been so careful to construct.

Resting his palms against the granite counter, he leaned in toward the mirror and laughed. Ironic how an architect of his stature could build multimillion-dollar buildings and homes, yet he couldn't keep a petite woman from busting through the ironclad fort he'd built around his heart.

He ran some cool water and splashed his face, trying to make sense of where his thoughts were headed. He wasn't sure if this thing with him and Tamera would go into anything long-term. The thought petrified him, but he had to pave the way just in case.

She deserved to be treated better than the last go-round they had at a relationship. As did he.

There was only one thing to do. A step he'd known all along he needed to take.

A step that was long overdue and the clock was ticking. If he didn't act now, he would never get another chance to speak his peace and draw closure to his past.

Only then could he move forward and see what path he and Tamera would take…together.

The gleaming white tiles of the Mercy Hospice Center were nearly blinding as Cole made his way from the nurses' station toward Walter Stevens' room. He nearly chuckled at the lie he'd told the nurse to get into the room. Pretending to be the son-in-law was laughable.

He knew there wasn't much time left and Cole had something pressing to see to before the old man left this earth. More than likely nothing would come of this talk, but Cole had to stand up for the man he used to be, the man he'd become. He couldn't let his past get the better of him. And he'd regret *not* talking to Tamera's father if he didn't do it now.

He found the room at the end of the hall. The door was closed, but the nurse assured Cole that Mr. Stevens was indeed awake and, like Tamera said, having a good day…whatever that meant to a dying man.

Cole tapped on the door as he slowly opened it. He didn't know what to expect, hadn't really given it a thought, but he certainly was taken aback when a frail, balding Walter Stevens sat in the far corner in a plush rocking chair staring out the window toward the lush gardens.

The door made a slight creak and Walter turned. Cole stepped over the threshold, ready for whatever may come his way.

"What the hell are you doing here?" the old man grumbled.

The room smelled of potpourri, something fruity that no doubt Tamera had set out. Touches of her were everywhere—from the family photos on the small, white dresser to the fresh flowers beside his bed.

"I came for a talk that is eleven years overdue."

Cole crossed the room and came to stand beside the chair, but kept facing Tamera's father. The man had definitely not aged well, but chemo would probably do that to you. His skin was gray and wrinkled, his eyes a bit more sunken in than when Cole had seen him last.

"Never thought I'd see you again," Walter said, looking up to Cole. "Never really wanted to."

"Feeling's mutual," Cole replied, moving to rest against the windowsill, partially blocking the other man's view. "I'm here about Tam."

"I assumed as much." The other's man's eyes narrowed. "What about her?"

"As you know, we're working together on the Victor Lawson project." Cole took such satisfaction in seeing the man utterly speechless. "She didn't tell you? Just as well. You probably would've tried to destroy that working relationship as well."

"She wouldn't work with someone like you," Walter spouted off. "Not only is my company more prestigious in this industry, you broke her heart years ago and she's never forgiven you. I don't believe Victor Lawson would hire two companies, either. So tell me what you really want before I have you thrown out."

Cole steeled himself at the frailness of the man, but dammit, he needed to get this off his chest. He hadn't been able to confront Walter years ago, but he'd certainly do it while he had the chance.

"Ask her if you don't believe me." Cole came to his full height. "Our working relationship is beside the point, though. What you destroyed and tore apart years ago didn't break me. The only person you hurt was Tamera. I just wanted you to take satisfaction in knowing you did nothing but damage your daughter's heart and make me a stronger man. When you're long gone, my agency will far surpass yours because you were too busy trying to run Tamera's life to actually help her build a career and be happy. I also plan on having her work for me. Your company will flounder and fall."

Walter coughed and pointed up to Cole. "You listen to me. You may be wearing a thousand dollar suit, but beneath that tailor-made exterior is a punk who was and never will be suitable for my daughter. She will have no problem running my company."

Cole couldn't resist. The words just came out before he could think twice.

"No, she won't have a problem, because when we marry, the companies will merge. You may have sabotaged our past, but you won't touch our future. You have no way to blackmail me now out of her life. And if you try, you'll only hurt her in the end."

The sharp intake of breath didn't come from Tamera's father, but from the doorway. Both Cole and Walter glanced in that direction to see Tamera, white as a ghost, standing there with one hand over her mouth, the other holding on to the doorframe as if for support.

Cole didn't apologize, he'd be lying if he did, but he did cross the room to Tamera. "I'll let you two talk."

He left the room, letting Tamera and her father rehash the past he still wanted to get away from. No matter what he'd told Walter, Cole had been devastated years ago. Tamera certainly wasn't the only one hurt, but no way in hell would he ever let the old man know how much his actions destroyed Cole.

Cole only wished he'd been able to spare Tamera the pain of hearing the truth. What good would it do now? They weren't going to be in a relationship, they could barely be in the same room without arguing, unless they were having sex, but still, that didn't mean he wanted her to hurt any more than he already had.

Cole exited the building and paused in the late-afternoon sun. Obviously Tamera changed her routine and decided to not wait until after dinner to visit her father. Fate had a funny way of making things happen as they should.

Tamera was strong. If she survived their breakup years ago, she could survive the truth now.

Sixteen

"Is it true?"

Tamera forced herself to move forward and cross the room to her father. She'd decided it was such a pretty day, she'd skip work and come to get him to take him for a ride.

"Yes."

Her heart shattered all over again. How many times would she have to mend it? Would she get to a point where she just left the pieces on the floor and give up? Because even when she put it back together, there were still shards left behind that couldn't be mended.

"How could you?" She sat on the edge of the bed, unable to make her weak legs carry her any farther. "How could you purposely destroy my relationship with the one man I intended to spend the rest of my life with?"

Her father turned toward her. "I was looking out for

your future. I didn't want you to be with someone that was beneath you."

"Beneath me?" Appalled, Tamera waved a hand at him. "Nobody is beneath me. I loved him, Dad. You saw me after he broke up with me. You watched me cry every night for over a year and you still sat by and did nothing."

His eyes misted. "I'm not saying I made a mistake, but I did what I thought was right at the time."

Tamera clutched her purse in her lap. "Shouldn't I have been the one to decide what was right for my life?"

Silence. At least he wasn't going to keep defending himself. The man was stubborn and proud, so Tamera knew he wasn't going to apologize or continue to make excuses.

"So the two of you are working together?"

Tamera nodded. "I wasn't going to tell you. I didn't want you to think I was incapable of doing a project on my own."

"I would've never thought that, but I am curious as to why you didn't tell me about the Lawson project." Her father studied her beneath his sparse brows and hollowed eyes. "I knew you were bidding on it, but that was months ago, so when you didn't say anything, I assumed we didn't get it."

Aside from the fact she'd been blindsided by Cole on the day of the contract approval from Victor, Tamera had also been knocked down from celebrating when she'd come home to discover her father was only getting worse and would need round-the-clock medical care.

Added to all of that, she wanted him to be proud of her and how could he be when she hadn't even landed the project without having to team up with Cole?

"We did," she told him. "Victor has approved the preliminary plans and the final design is being drafted. Cole and I are starting to look at the various building materials to present at our next meeting with Victor."

Her father swallowed. "I'm so proud of you. I know this company is in good hands, so long as Cole Marcum keeps his off what's mine."

Tamera rubbed her forehead to clear the jumbled thoughts bouncing around. So many questions were fighting to come out of her mouth first.

"Why did you betray me?"

"I helped you," he countered. "Did you really want to spend your life with a man who couldn't even provide for his own family?"

"He was twenty years old, Dad," Tamera cried. "He'd done everything he knew to do with no parents and a grandmother who was well into her seventies."

"I wanted a man to take care of my daughter," he argued.

"I don't need to be taken care of," she shouted back. "I needed love and Cole provided that."

And that's what really hurt. He had loved her and now...who knows what he thought of her. Did it really matter at this point? He'd betrayed her just as much as her father. He could've come to her, talked to her. But he didn't.

Okay, so that's the part that hurt the most.

Oh, it all hurt, who was she kidding? Was she really debating herself over what aspect of this entire decade-long nightmare caused the most damage?

But Tamera looked back at her father and knew that their time was limited. His body was shutting down, the nurses told her that's what the yellow around his eyes and the tint to his skin meant. His liver was running on empty.

She couldn't leave this room knowing it could be for the last time and not have peace with the man who'd raised her and cared for her, though his intentions obviously weren't always the best. He was human. He made mistakes and there wasn't enough time left to argue or place blame. What was done was done.

"I forgive you." With a heavy heart, she crossed the room and kissed his forehead. "I love you, Dad."

His wrinkled hand came up to pat the arm she'd draped around his shoulders. "I didn't want you hurt. In the long run I knew it was for the best."

Perhaps he was right. Because if Cole *did* want to be with her all those years ago, he would've been. He would've found a way to fight for what he wanted.

But he hadn't.

Cole assumed Tamera would come to confront him. He was ready to defend his past actions, but he wouldn't apologize. Because he'd anticipated this, he'd told the guard to extend an open invitation to Tamera.

As she got out of her sporty BMW, Cole held the door open to his Star Island mansion. Her heeled sandals clicked on the drive as she marched with precision toward him. So much had changed since she'd been here two nights ago.

Without a word, she brushed past him and into his home as if she'd done so hundreds of times before.

Okay, so she was understandably pissed. Anger he could deal with. Hurt, not so much.

He stepped over the threshold and closed the door. Tamera had already walked through the open foyer and into his sunken living room. She stood with her back ramrod straight as she stared out the floor-to-ceiling windows overlooking the aqua bay.

"I don't know that I've ever loved and hated someone before," she said, without turning. "I didn't even know the two emotions directed at one person were possible."

Cole came to stand in front of her. If they were going to argue, they were going to do it face to face.

But he didn't see anger, or even hurt. All he saw was regret and exhaustion. Great. How could he confront her when she was clearly running on less than fumes?

"Was I supposed to come running to you, Tam? What would you have done had I told you your father just threatened to take not only my scholarships away, but Zach's and Kayla's as well?"

She leveled his gaze. "I don't know what I would've done, but I know I would've fought. I assumed that the love we shared wasn't one-sided."

Instead of grabbing hold of her and shaking her to make her listen like he wanted to, Cole placed his hands on his hips. "You know it wasn't one-sided. I've never loved anyone like you, Tam. You were it for me."

A laugh escaped her lips. The gesture didn't go with the emptiness in her baby blues.

"Was I? Should I consider myself lucky?" She threw her arms wide. "I feel sorry for all the other women you've had in your life if that's how you treat 'the one.'"

He deserved her wrath, he knew it, but he wouldn't stand in his own home and allow his past to be thrown back into his face.

"Your father made it impossible for me to choose," he argued. "My family had to come first. We didn't have everything handed to us."

Like you did.

He didn't have to say the words, they hovered in the air between them anyway. Yes, it was a low jab, but it was also the truth.

She sighed, stepped aside to focus once again on the stunning view. "I don't know why we're arguing. If it was meant to be, we'd have found our way back to each other. I'm just surprised that you let anyone get the best of you."

"I'm not that man anymore." He never would be. "And you're right. Arguing won't change the past and we're different people now."

Well, other than the fact that he still found her impossibly gorgeous and sexier than any woman should have the right to be.

Not to mention she'd burned him up in his bed, even though he was quick to douse any flame that could ignite into something more…at least in her mind. He didn't want to lead her on.

No matter what Tamera said, she was a "happily ever after" girl. Once her father passed, she would have nothing holding her back and she would need someone to lean on for support…even if she didn't want to admit it. Tamera was a strong woman, one of the strongest he knew, but even the sturdiest needed support during a storm.

She turned sideways, facing him once again. Shoulders back, chin tilted, she said, "Once this project is over, I never want to see you again. I won't be made a fool of twice. But we'll give Victor the best design he's ever had because we're both good at our jobs. Don't think for a second, though, that I trust you…with anything."

"I didn't ask for your trust, Tamera." He clenched his fist in his pocket as he searched her face for something…

anything, but all he saw was bitterness. "This project is all that matters."

She turned to walk out, but stopped just as her foot hit the bottom step of his living room. She threw a glance over her shoulder.

"You were wrong. You're still the same person. All that matters is money and yourself. I just didn't see that's who you were back then." She bit her lip, her chin quivered. "What a lonely world."

The echoing of her heels died with the final click of his front door. He would not feel guilty about the truth coming out. If anything, relief swept through him.

Once they delivered this design to Victor, and it was officially approved, then Zach would take over and Cole could officially close the book on his past and any present involvement with Tamera Stevens.

But would this ache in his chest linger long after that?

Seventeen

Binders upon binders of building materials cluttered Tamera's desk and her boardroom table. Nothing was just jumping out and screaming "multimillion-dollar fantasy resort."

An idea slammed into her. Tamera picked up her cell and dialed an old friend who would certainly be able to help in this respect.

"Hello."

"Kayla? This is Tamera. You know that lunch date we mentioned?"

Cole's sister laughed. "I certainly do. When do you want to meet?"

"How about now?" She glanced at the clock on her desk. "I can have something delivered."

"Now is perfect. I just got done meeting with Victor and my brain is fried. I'll grab something from the deli next to the office. What do you want?"

Tamera gave Kayla her order and hung up. Cole would be furious that he was not included in this little impromptu meeting, but she wasn't too concerned with what Cole thought of her right now. Kayla was the decorator and Kayla was the one she needed to consult with.

If Cole stepped through her door, Tamera feared she'd unleash her fury on him. She'd definitely gone easy on him considering he'd damaged her heart so long ago. She'd mended it just fine and didn't need a replay.

But what really irked her in ways she couldn't even express was the fact he'd gone and slept with her anyway. Twice. Even after betraying her, giving her up, he still thought he could have her when he wanted. And she'd fallen right for his seduction. She'd practically begged for him to seduce her.

Jerk. Yes, she should take a portion of the blame, but she wasn't. All of this mess was his doing.

Tamera stood up from her desk, dropped her cell back into her purse on the floor at her feet and moved around the room.

What she really needed was some female bonding time. It had been so long since she'd really talked to a woman, and her elderly assistant didn't count.

The topic of Cole couldn't come up. She couldn't talk to Kayla about her older brother. Not right now when her emotions were still so open and hurtful.

Did Kayla know about the reasoning behind Cole's breakup? Had everyone known but her? Not that it mattered at this point in time, but, well, it did.

Tamera walked from her desk to the table she'd made a mess of. She closed a few of the binders with samples and pictures of past projects and moved them onto one of the chairs. She could certainly rule out several samples that just wouldn't fit in the fantasy, sexy role this hotel would play.

A light tap on her office door had Tamera jerk her head. Kayla stood in the doorway holding a plastic bag.

"Lunch," she said with a wide smile holding the bag up. "Looks like I'm just in time to save you from yourself."

Tamera laughed. "And I just cleared a spot for our lunch."

Cole's sister was a knockout. She had that coal black hair and those chocolate brown eyes like her brothers. She also had that bronzed skin that had nothing to do with spending time on the beach and everything to do with an awesome gene pool.

"How was the meeting with Victor?" Tamera asked as Kayla pulled out the two chicken salads. "Are you eager to get started on your part with him?"

Kayla flopped into a vacant chair and sighed. "I'm not sure about that. He's a bit…intimidating."

Tamera took a seat, opened the salads and passed one across the table. "That's because you're so quiet. Don't be afraid of someone with all that power, Kayla. You underestimate your own strength."

Strength that was a family trait.

No, no. She wasn't going to think about Cole right now.

"I know I'm good at what I do," Kayla said, stabbing a cherry tomato. "I just don't know if I can handle the way he was looking at me."

Tamera froze, mid-bite. "Looking at you?"

Kayla closed her eyes. "I know it's my imagination."

"Why don't you tell me and I'll let you know if you're imagining things."

Kayla took a bite, chewed, and Tamera figured the woman was trying to figure out the best way to tell the story without sounding conceited.

"Forget it." Kayla jabbed her fork into her salad. "It's not even worth discussing. Tell me what's happening on your end. How is it working with my brother again?"

So much for not talking about Cole.

Tamera chose her words carefully. "It's been a good thing for this project."

Kayla gave her an "oh, really" look. "Now tell me the truth. What has this been like on a personal level?"

"Honestly? It has been trying at times. Your brother is so...so..."

"I know." Kayla smiled, reached over and patted Tamera's hand. "He's been that way since the two of you broke up. Nothing gets in his way, nothing is ever good enough and he doesn't settle for anything that isn't the absolute best."

Again, Tamera chose her words carefully. "Did he ever tell you why we broke up?"

She really hoped Kayla hadn't known. She didn't know why, but just the thought of everyone being in the know but her really bothered her.

Kayla shook her head as she chewed. "He just said that he realized you needed more than he could offer and we were never allowed to mention you or the breakup again. He wanted to move past it completely. I do believe Zach knows the real reason. Those two are like one being. I've never seen closer siblings."

The knife Cole had jammed into her heart years ago just turned again. She shouldn't have pain every time she thought of or spoke of the man.

Tamera pasted a smile on her face. "Well, it was a

long time ago. I'm sure he's fallen in love numerous times since."

Kayla continued to study her salad as she poked around. "Not really. Sometimes he'd bring a woman around, but nothing serious. He's too busy building our empire and moving on to the next big project."

Well, at least he'd had something to occupy his lonely nights. Bastard.

Not that she was going to remain bitter. Her feelings for Cole had died long ago when he'd turned his back on her with lame excuses. And now that she knew the truth, she wouldn't give him another thought…at least not on a personal level.

Her desk phone rang shrilly, cutting into her thoughts.

"Excuse me," she said, getting up from the table. She crossed to her desk, reached across and hit the speaker button. "Hello."

"I've got the afternoon free. Come down to my office so we can work on the materials."

Tamera threw a look to Kayla and rolled her eyes. "Gee, your manners have me ready to toss aside my current meeting to jump at the chance to get to your office."

Kayla laughed.

"Kayla?" Cole asked. "Is my sister there?"

Tamera smiled. "Yes."

"Why?"

All joking was gone from his tone. Tamera grabbed the receiver. No need to let Kayla know how much they weren't getting along.

"Because I needed another opinion," she told him, keeping her tone chipper.

"I'm your partner on this, Tamera. Calling one of my siblings was not professional or acceptable."

Tamera gripped the phone and turned her back on Kayla. "I'm doing what's best for this project. If you have a problem, then it's your problem. If there's nothing else you need, I have to get back to my meeting."

"I'm on my way."

He hung up and Tamera had to take deep, calming breaths in order to face Kayla again.

"Sorry he's so insufferable."

Kayla's tone was laced with worry, her brows drawn together.

Coming back to the table and the lunch she no longer cared about, Tamera shrugged and took her seat. "It's not your fault he's so overbearing. He's coming over, by the way."

"I could've told you he'd do that. He's also very competitive." Kayla gathered the garbage from their lunch, stuffing it into a sack. "He wants to be in on this project from the beginning to the end, no matter what his part is in this company."

"I can't imagine Zach will put up with Cole hanging around the job site," Tamera commented.

"Oh, he and Zach have had their fair share of arguments. Two Type A personalities like that? It can get pretty ugly. And they tend to save their aggressions for family meals and office meetings."

"How lovely for you."

Tamera laughed, earning a laugh from Kayla. Tamera marveled at how easy and fun it was falling back into a sisterly pattern with Kayla.

"I'm sorry we lost touch," Tamera said, dropping all joking from her tone. "That's my fault. After Cole and I broke up, I just couldn't…"

"I understand." Kayla leaned back in her chair. "It's none of my business what happened with you two, but I have to say, I feel like we broke up as well."

Guilt overwhelmed her. "I'm so sorry, Kayla. I thought about calling you, but I really didn't know what to say."

"It's okay, really. How's your father? Cole says he's sick."

Tamera nodded. "He's not well at all. He's in Mercy Hospice."

Kayla's head tilted. "That's what Cole told us. I can't imagine what all you're going through. Is there anything you need me to do?"

"No. Just being a friend is good enough."

"Is this a Dr. Phil show or a work place?"

Kayla and Tamera both turned their attention toward the door as Cole came gliding right in as if he owned the place.

"Looks like I arrived just in time. Have either of you done anything but reminisce?"

Kayla stood up, crossed to kiss her brother on his cheek. "Don't be such a grouch. Tamera and I haven't really spoken in a long time. We'll get to work."

"How did your meeting with Victor go?" he asked.

"Well," Kayla shrugged with a laugh. "He certainly knows what he wants."

Cole smiled down at his sister. Tamera wondered why he never smiled at her in that genuine, you-matter-to-me sort of way. Granted they had argued most of the time lately, but even when good things happened, he still hadn't looked at her like she meant something to him.

Guess those intimate moments in his bed hadn't even warranted a genuine grin every now and then. Work, work, work. And he thought *she* needed to lighten up?

"We really have to get cracking on this." Cole pulled out a seat, taking it only after his sister had sat back down. "I'm actually glad you're here, Kayla. Since you met with Victor, you have a better idea of what we're striving toward."

So, this was a good idea that Kayla was here? Of course, Cole wouldn't thank Tamera or tell her this was a good move. No, having Kayla here wasn't his idea, so thankfulness would be absent from this meeting.

That was just fine. She didn't need anything from Cole other than his mind for business.

She just hated that, deep down, she really couldn't get their past off her mind. She'd been so in love, she would've given up anything to be with him.

Why was she dwelling on this? Why didn't she just cut her losses and move on? Obviously Cole had.

But Kayla's words came back through her mind.

He's never fallen in love since you. He's had girls, but nothing serious.

In eleven years?

"You with us, Tam?"

She jerked herself from her thoughts and focused on Cole's questioning gaze. "Where else would I be?"

Eighteen

Victor Lawson's party was no less extravagant than his buildings. Tamera exited her chauffeur-driven limo, compliments of Mr. Lawson, and smiled to the young gentleman who'd taken her hand to assist her from the car.

Victor also lived on Star Island, big surprise. Well, lived was probably not the right choice of words. This was just one of his many luxury homes, Tamera was sure.

She'd received her invitation to Victor's party a week ago and didn't think twice about attending. The last time she'd been on Star Island she hadn't needed the invitation to get past the guard and onto the bridge. She'd only needed one man.

Tamera shook off thoughts of Cole and his betrayal. She couldn't think of that now. No way would she allow the hurt to creep up and consume her while she was here. This was too nice of an evening to let it get tainted by past memories.

Instead, she focused on the beauty of the home. Much like Cole's, Victor's house had that cozy, Mediterranean feel. Perhaps that was why he approved their initial design for the hotel so wholeheartedly.

Tamera made her way through the arched entryway from the circular drive and was greeted by none other than Victor himself.

"Stunning as always, Tamera."

Victor took both her hands in his, kissed her cheek and escorted her inside.

"This is a beautiful home, Victor. Thanks for the invitation."

She took in the high ceilings, the two sprawling staircases on either side of the formal entryway and the ginormous chandelier casting a kaleidoscope of colors onto the white marble flooring.

"There's no way I could throw a party and not invite my top architectural firms."

Just what she wanted. Another encounter with Cole.

"Kayla and her brother Zach just arrived. Cole has yet to show, but I'm sure he'll be along shortly."

He led her through the living area and out onto the patio where several people mingled with drinks and staff moved about with small, silver trays full of champagne. There was a spread of food on either side of the immaculate, glowing pool.

"I must tend to some other arrivals," Victor told her. "Please, eat, mingle. We'll talk later, but no shop talk tonight."

She smiled back at this handsome billionaire. "Sounds good."

As he walked away, Tamera wondered why her heart couldn't go pitty-pat at the sight of him instead of Cole. Why did the one man on this earth whose eyes she wanted to gouge out make her knees go weak, make her insides get all squishy like a teenage girl's on prom night?

"Tamera."

She turned at the sound of Zach's voice. "Evening, Zach. No lady attached to your arm this evening?"

Zach's laid-back appearance would only fly on him. No tie, white dress shirt unbuttoned two buttons beneath his black suit. This was as dressed up as Zach would get. Even though the man could afford tailor-made suits, he didn't want them. And she had no doubt he rode here on one of his Harleys.

"Actually, my date for tonight is my lovely sister."

Tamera laughed. "I'm impressed. And where is Kayla?"

"She went to talk to a potential client about redesigning their new home."

Tamera glanced around, finally spotting the exotic, gorgeous Kayla off in the distance talking with a middle-aged lady. As usual, Kayla was smiling and nodding, always eager to please clients.

"I'm not sure how much longer she'll be my date tonight if Victor keeps looking at her like he's been doing."

Tamera jerked back around. "Really? Isn't that interesting. She mentioned something like that to me the other day. Victor is used to beautiful women, and your sister is certainly no exception."

Zach took a long pull of his domestic beer. "I figured you and Cole would come together."

"Why would you assume that?" Tamera took a glass of champagne from one of the wait staff walking by.

"Because you've been awfully close lately."

"We're working on the biggest project either of our companies has ever seen. Besides, I doubt Cole and I will be seeing much of each other once the hotel is completed."

Zach took a long pull of his beer. "That's still a long way off. A lot could happen between now and then."

A lot *had* happened.

"Considering my part with Cole is drawing to a close, I don't foresee us working together in the future."

Zach leaned closer to whisper in her ear. "I don't know what Cole has told you, but trust me, he doesn't give up as easily as he used to."

What was that supposed to mean? Did she even want to know?

Cole's twin eased back, pointed with his longneck bottle toward the open patio doors. "Your partner has arrived."

By the time Tamera looked over her shoulder, cringed and turned back, Zach had walked away in the direction of a leggy blonde.

Tamera took a deep breath. If Cole wanted to approach her, fine. No way was she going to him.

Nursing her drink, Tamera walked around the pool, nodding and say hello to a couple of clients she'd worked with in the past. When she spotted Kayla moving away from her own potential client, Tamera made her way over.

"Well, did she like your ideas?" Tamera asked.

Kayla shrugged with a warm smile. "She seemed very interested in what I had to say, so I certainly hope so. Is this house amazing or what?"

Tamera laughed. "It is very nice."

"I thought Cole's was nice, but this is huge."

Even the mention of his name sent dual emotions racing through her. Anger and passion chased each other to be the one on top.

"Are you okay?" Kayla asked with that sweet, buttery tone she'd always had. "Cole told me about…well, what happened in the past. I honestly didn't know. He finally told me why the tension between the two of you is so much stronger now."

"I've been better," Tamera confessed. "It's hard to deal with something eleven years after the fact. I'm honestly not quite sure how to handle it or what I should be feeling."

Kayla put her arm around Tamera's shoulder and squeezed. "If it means anything, Cole has been in a really, really bad mood lately. That's good for you."

Tamera laughed. "How is that?"

"Because nothing ever bothers him." Kayla's eyes drifted off into the distance toward her brother. "You must matter even more than he cares to admit. Even to himself."

Squeezing the crystal stem of her glass, Tamera allowed her eyes to follow Kayla's. "Maybe so, but I don't like decisions being made for me that affect my entire life. Besides, he made his choice long ago when he didn't come back to me after school."

Kayla's arm dropped as she came to stand directly in front of Tamera. "Be that as it may, don't let the past direct your future."

Tamera looked into the dark eyes that were so much like Cole's. "I just can't concentrate on him and this whole mess. Not right now."

"I'm sorry about your father. Please let me know if there's anything I can do."

Tamera smiled at her longtime friend. "I appreciate that."

"Ladies."

Tamera cringed, then pasted on a smile as Cole came to stand beside them. "Cole."

"I think I landed another client," Kayla chimed in. "She's new to the Miami area, just bought a house in Coral Gables and is looking for a designer. My name was tossed her way."

"That's wonderful, Kayla," Cole said, kissing his sister on the cheek. "One of these days you'll be too big for me and Zach."

"Oh, I doubt that." Kayla's eyes darted from Tamera to Cole and back again. "I do think, though, that you two need to talk and I'm definitely the third wheel to this party."

Tamera's heart sank. The dead last thing she wanted was another confrontation with Cole about something that happened eleven years ago. And at Victor Lawson's home? That would be like career suicide because she knew once she and Cole started arguing again, they may never stop. God knew she had a great deal of anger and hatred right now and she was just waiting to unleash it.

"She never did like confrontation," Cole murmured as he watched his sister walk away.

Tamera narrowed her eyes when he directed his attention back to her. "I wasn't going to confront her with anything. She's never betrayed me."

Never one to back down, Cole held her gaze. "Neither have I."

"Really?" Tamera glanced around. Everyone was still

mingling, paying no attention to the feud in the corner. "And what do you call what you did?"

"Protecting my family."

Tamera sighed. "Forget it. I don't want an explanation. Not now. I'm too far gone to care."

"You care," he countered, leaning in so only she could hear. "You care too much and it's eating at you. You know I did what I had to do at the time. If you want to place blame somewhere, place it with your father."

"How are Miami's top architects doing?" Victor interrupted. "No shop talk, I hope?"

Cole eased back, smiled. "Not at all. Just discussing family. You have siblings, Victor?"

"A brother."

Cole nodded. "I was just telling Ms. Stevens how I'd do anything for my family. I'm sure you feel the same."

"Absolutely," Victor agreed. "My brother is all I have left and we are very close. What about you, Tamera, any family?"

Tamera swallowed. "Just my father."

"Daddy's girl, huh? He must be proud of you to follow in his footsteps and take over the family business. It's a shame I haven't gotten a chance to talk to him during this project. I thought for sure we'd meet up again."

Tamera ignored Cole's hard stare and concentrated on Victor. "Have you met my father?"

"Of course. When I first started making money, I had your father design a home for my parents. I wanted to give them a nice house after all they'd done for me. I was able to do so with the help of your father."

See? She wanted to shout to Cole. Walter Stevens was a good man.

"Now probably isn't the best time to share this news,"

Tamera started. "But, my father actually isn't doing very well at all, that's why you haven't seen him."

"Nothing too serious, I hope."

Tamera's eyes darted to Cole, then back to Victor. Her voice softened. "He's in hospice. I'm sorry I didn't tell you at the start of the project, but you were fine working with me and I hope this won't affect our working relationship."

Victor's eyes widened. "Absolutely not. I'm terribly sorry about Walter. He's a good man, a fighter. Please, give him my regards when you see him again."

Great, now tears were clogging the back of her throat. She took one last sip of champagne and offered a smile to the men.

"I really need to get going. Thanks for having me, Victor. Cole."

Before either man could say anything or, heaven forbid, try to stop her, she moved across the moss-and-stone-covered patio, through the doors and headed to the front of the house to the row of limousines. She needed to get out of here.

If it wasn't one emotion piling up on her, it was another. Her father, her past, her present. When would this nightmare come to an end?

God, was she really praying for an end? How selfish was that?

Tamera stepped back into the limo and tried to relax as the chauffeur took her home. But all she could see when she closed her eyes was Cole. Cole when he made love to her, Cole when he tried to comfort her, Cole when he defended himself to her because of his love for his family.

Why couldn't the man just have stayed in the past?

Nineteen

The shrill phone cut through the darkness, jerking Tamera awake.

This was it. The call she'd been dreading. She knew it before she reached across her bed to the nightstand.

"Hello."

"Tamera, this is Camille, the night nurse at Mercy."

Tamera fell back onto her plush pillow. Her hand shook as she clutched the phone. "He's gone."

She didn't ask—she didn't want to hear her worst fears confirmed.

"I'm sorry. We called the funeral home and they are on their way."

Tamera shoved aside the remorse and hurt. She'd have time to deal with her own feelings later. Right now she had to make sure her father was taken care of.

"I'll be there in just a minute."

Tamera disconnected the call and gathered courage to take the first step from her bed. Putting her body on autopilot was the only way she'd get through these next few hours, days. Years.

She pulled a red cotton sundress over her head and slipped into her brown, beaded flip-flops. No time for grooming or any other maintenance like hair, makeup. None of that truly mattered, not in the grand scheme of things. She wanted to get to the hospice center before they took her father's…body.

God, those words didn't sound right even running through her head. This didn't happen to her. Things like this happened to other people. Other people lost loved ones.

Now she was truly all alone. There was no one else in her family.

Tamera took a deep breath, grabbed her keys and purse and headed out to her garage. She couldn't think about what she was doing in the middle of the night while the rest of Miami slept…or partied. Life went on even though her father's had ended and her world would never be the same.

She'd never hear his voice, never have a proud career moment she could share with him and get his nod of approval. Gone. He was just gone.

Before she knew it, she was pulling into the parking lot. Another deep breath and she killed the engine and tugged on the door handle.

She could do this. She had to. There was no one else.

As soon as she hit the nurses' station, Camille came around the desk and put an arm around her.

"The folks from the funeral home haven't arrived, yet. I'm so sorry, Tamera."

Tamera swallowed the lump of hurt. And while she appreciated the nurse's comfort, Tamera knew if she broke down now, she may never stop. "I knew this moment was coming."

"But it doesn't make it any easier," the nurse said, guiding her down the stark white hallway.

"No, it doesn't."

Camille paused outside the closed door. "I'll let you go in and have a moment to yourself."

Tamera nodded her appreciation, unable to express her thanks aloud for fear of losing it right here in the hallway.

Once the nurse went back down the hall, Tamera opened the door. She didn't know what she expected, but seeing her father lying on his bed didn't bother her as much as she thought it would.

He looked as though he were sleeping. Peacefully.

On shaky legs, Tamera crossed the room and tugged the blanket up around his shoulders.

Peace. He'd finally found it. Something about that fact put Tamera at ease as well. Yes, her life wouldn't be the same without him, but it was selfish of her to want him back when he'd just been living in pain. He'd lived a happy, full life and done all the things he wanted to do.

She knelt over the bed, kissed his forehead. Her lips lingered, not wanting to break any bond.

"I love you, Daddy," she whispered. "I forgive you."

Cole hung up the phone. He'd been calling every day since he and Tamera had their blowup to check on Walter. He knew when the old man passed Tamera wouldn't confide in him, so he'd had to keep himself in the loop on his own.

But now Walter was gone and Cole couldn't bring himself to be remorseful.

But Tamera had to feel all alone…she was alone now with no family left. Who would she turn to? Who would offer her a shoulder to cry on, lean on?

Cole wished she'd come to him, but he wasn't naïve enough to believe she'd trust him with anything, especially her feelings, ever again.

And that was fine. Really. In the grand scheme of things, he didn't have time for a relationship, especially one with so much baggage. They'd have to work doubly hard and he really didn't have time or the patience for that type of commitment.

He would send flowers to the funeral home, and a personal bouquet and message to Tam's house. After that, their dealings would be in business only.

Though he did feel as if he should deliver her flowers in person. If nothing else, to make sure she was okay and to defend himself for the final time. Victor's party hadn't given him the right opportunity.

And there was one more thing. What he needed to do was catch her now, vulnerable and all, and make her see his side. Then perhaps he could persuade her to sell her father's company and work for him.

True, he didn't want the relationship consisting of anything that remotely resembled the "L" word, but she was one hell of a worker and Cole wanted her on his team. So long as the rest of The Stevens Group went by the wayside.

Cole pushed up from his sofa and went to dress. Tamera's father had passed away in the middle of the night, and seeing as how it was now ten in the morning, Tamera should be back home.

He quickly dressed, all the while running through his mind all he would and should say to her to sway her to see his point of view in the dealings so long ago and to get her to come over to his side.

In the mood for something a little less "businesslike," Cole grabbed the keys to his Jeep Wrangler. From his house on Star Island, it didn't take long to drive to Tamera's beachfront condo in South Beach, especially early on a Sunday morning.

He pulled in behind her car along the street and got out. He prepared himself for whatever state she may be in. Angry, depressed, shocked, numb. He was ready to console her no matter the emotions she was dealing with.

Cole rang the doorbell and waited. But when the door opened, he realized there was one emotion he'd overlooked. Emptiness.

He didn't wait for an invitation…not that he expected one. He walked through the door and put his arms around her.

"No." Tamera pulled back and turned away. "I don't want you to console me."

Cole stood rooted in place. Tam's rigid back and the steel in her tone concerned him.

"Don't be afraid to break, Tam." He stepped closer. "Crying and getting angry are perfectly normal emotions."

She spun around, her eyes red and swollen, but dry. "How did you know?"

"Does it matter?"

"I don't want you here."

"I'm sure you don't," he agreed. "But who else would you call to come be with you?"

Her chin tilted. "Who said I was going to call anyone? I'm just fine, Cole."

So be it.

"Good." He crossed his arms because he wanted to pull her against him and assure her everything would be fine. Stupid on his part. He didn't need to get tangled up anymore in this woman. "I assume the funeral will be this week."

She nodded, but her eyes remained fixed over his shoulder. She wasn't listening, wasn't comprehending what he was saying. She was running on little more than fumes and it wouldn't take long for her to collapse on this wall she'd built out of sand.

"If you need anything at all, call me. Don't shut me out because of your pride."

"I'm shutting you out because of *your* pride," she amended in a low, sad tone.

"I've put my pride aside. Can you say the same?"

"Put your pride aside?" She stood stone still. "You think by barging in here, hoping to catch me in an emotional meltdown, I'll collapse into your arms and we'll get past this?"

He told himself not to let her stinging words hurt or deter him. She was aching, grieving. Not thinking straight.

Or maybe her true feelings were just now coming out.

"Honestly," he began in a low voice. "I did want you to admit that you needed someone. And, yes, I wanted that someone to be me. I'm not asking you to deal with your father's death and our past all at once. I'm not a jerk, Tam, but I'm also not going to beg."

Once again, she stared and said nothing as he showed himself out. He'd let her think about that for a while. Pride and lies had gotten them in trouble before, he didn't make the same mistakes twice.

If she wanted to keep everything from here on out businesslike, then he would go along with her wishes. But he wouldn't make the process easy for her. Because he was finally coming to realize that maybe, just maybe, they did need each other in more than just the boardroom.

Rain poured down and Tamera willed her wipers to go faster. She had no clue where she was driving this morning, but she knew she couldn't go home. Not right now. She couldn't go into work, either. Not when her father's memories still lingered and hovered in every corner on every floor.

As her car passed over the bridge to Star Island, she realized what she was doing. She needed to do this. Now that her father's funeral had passed, Tamera knew life was too short to hold grudges. She'd forgiven her father, now she needed to forgive Cole.

With yesterday evening's funeral replaying over and over in her mind, Tamera knew today had to be a new beginning.

She pulled around the fountain in Cole's circular drive and killed her engine. Leaving her keys and her purse in her car, she hopped out. No need to take her things with her. What she came to say would only take a minute.

When she stepped from the car, rain pelted her skin, drenching her instantly. Her hair clung to her neck and shoulders.

But she just stood there. Everything about her life

played through her head. Her father holding her hand when her mother had passed away, her father teaching her to drive and dance. The moments when he'd taken time to show her his little secrets about the company she'd now inherited. The moment when the pallbearers settled her father's casket onto the platform at the cemetery.

The flowers and card from The Marcum Agency. Cole.

"Tamera."

Tamera turned her head toward Cole's voice. He stood in his doorway wearing nothing but a pair of running shorts.

And in the second he saw her face, he must've known. Even though they'd severed their connection from years ago, he still knew her heart and her vulnerabilities. He came out into the rain and pulled her into his embrace.

That was all it took. She wrapped her arms around his bare waist and clung to him, wishing she could draw strength from him. But all that happened was the meltdown that had been a long time coming.

No matter what had happened with Cole, she still had feelings for him. He was the only man she'd ever loved and she needed him right now. She needed that shoulder to cry on and she didn't care if he thought her weak. At this moment, she was.

"I'm sorry."

She'd been hearing those simple words so much over the past few days, but for some reason, coming from Cole's mouth, she believed him.

He kissed the top of her head and eased her back to study her drenched face. "Come in out of the rain."

Her eyes darted to his moist lips as the rain continued

to beat down on them. Desire like she'd never known coursed through her, fighting against the hurt and emptiness she'd been feeling for far too long.

Maybe she needed him more than she thought. She eased up on her toes to angle her mouth toward his.

"No," he said over the downpour. "That is not what you need."

"That's exactly what I need, Cole."

She framed his face with her hands and drew his lips down to hers. He didn't resist.

Cole's arms came around her, lifting her up off the driveway and flush against his taut, wet body. Her moment of control over this situation, if she ever really had it, was long gone and in Cole's hands. Which was fine with her.

She didn't want to think, didn't want to worry about anything but taking the comfort Cole had to offer. Didn't want to think about the actions and the events that led her straight to his door. Nor did she want to consider the reality that she was weak, vulnerable and Cole was the only rock in this storm she could cling to.

When he turned to carry her into the house, Tamera wrapped her legs around his waist, her arms around his neck. Toying with the wet hair at the nape of his neck, she kissed along his strong jaw. God, she'd missed him.

With a swift kick, he had the door closed and her pinned against it. But he kept his touch soft, light, as if he were afraid of breaking her. She couldn't break anymore than she already had.

"Don't be gentle with me," she demanded against his lips.

"I'm giving what you need." His husky tone and

warm breath excited her even more. "Whether you know it or not."

"I need you. Only you."

He peeled the wet straps down her arms, she tugged free of them as he pulled the garment below her breasts. She arched her back as he slid a hand behind her to unfasten her strapless bra and toss it without a care to the tile floor.

Reaching beneath the short hem of her sundress, he pulled at her bikini panties until they slid silently to the floor, leaving her bare for him.

His mouth ran from her neck down to the slope of her breasts. Tamera clutched his wet, messy hair with her fingers.

"Wait," she panted. "Condom."

"Relax. I've got you protected. Always."

The meaning behind his words was so much more than here and now, but she couldn't think about it, didn't want to get false hope.

Cole pulled her away from the door, took her hand and guided her up the wide, sweeping staircase. But Tamera didn't want to follow. She bypassed him in a mad dash toward his bedroom.

As soon as she crossed the threshold, she shimmied out of the dress, allowing it to fall to the tiled floor of his master suite with a wet slap. Cole's eyes raked over her bare body, the muscle in his jaw clenching as he crossed to the bedside table and pulled out a condom.

Tamera walked up behind him, kissed her way across his taut shoulders before falling back onto the bed in a provocative position. She raised slightly up onto her elbows, quirking a brow at him.

Cole tossed the condom onto her stomach. "Cover me."

Once he was ready, she guided him into her.

How could she ever think the two of them was a mistake? How had she not seen that she cared about this man more than she wanted to admit?

Cole captured her mouth once again as her body started rising toward its peak. She wrapped her legs around him once again and climaxed just before him.

Their bodies shuddered together as Cole placed a tender kiss to her lips. He lay on her body, chest to chest afterward, his fast, heavy breathing tickling the side of her neck.

"I didn't know where else to go," she murmured, afraid of the words and what they meant.

"I'm glad you came here." He lifted up, rolled to the side and rested his head on his hand. "I'm also sorry you're hurting."

Tamera didn't want to diminish the afterglow of their lovemaking, but she had to face reality. She had to tell him what was in her heart, and hopefully salvage the best part of the relationship they'd had and rebuild a life from there.

"I actually came to just tell you that I forgive you."

His eyes widened. "Really?"

She turned to her side to face him. "I can't live holding grudges and with Dad's passing, I know that life is too short to stay mad. Besides, being on friendly terms with you has its benefits."

His eyes roamed down the dip in her waist and over the swell of her hip. "Yes, it does."

He pushed her onto her back once again and showed her just how beneficial their friendship could be.

"I don't think I can handle this."

Tamera hadn't wanted to admit that to herself, much less aloud. But her fears were out in the open, in Cole's darkened bedroom. His roman shades had dropped at the click of a switch just after they'd made love in the glow of the sunset. But resting was something Tamera knew wouldn't happen for a long, long time.

Cole rolled from his back to his side. "This as in us?"

Tamera kept her eyes averted to the ceiling. She didn't want to face him, not when she was voicing her waking nightmare.

"Running the company without the guidance of my father."

Cole's gentle fingers cupped her chin and turned her head, forcing her to look him in the eye. "Then sell it."

"What?"

"Don't stress yourself," he told her. "If you feel like this is something that isn't right for you, then get out."

"But I love what I do."

Sell her father's legacy? Something he'd worked so hard for? How heartless would that be to consider selling his empire not a full week after his funeral?

"I know you love it," Cole told her, a hint of a smile playing around his mouth. "Come work for me."

Tamera jerked up in bed, the sheet falling to pool at her waist. "Work for you? I can't do that."

Cole sat up beside her. "Why not? We make a great team."

She'd already shown him her vulnerable side. Might as well lay it all on the line.

"Working for you isn't such a great idea, Cole." She gathered her courage from deep within as she clutched the sheet to her breasts. "Let's say I do sell my father's company and come to work for The Marcum Agency.

What happens if we don't get along? You know how we butt heads."

"We'll be fine. I argue all the time with Zach and Kayla. It's just part of powerful people working together, but the outcome is amazing when our clients' praise is heard worldwide."

He didn't get it.

"Let me put it this way," she said, holding his gaze. "What happens when you decide you don't want to be with me anymore?"

"Who says that will happen?"

She lifted a shoulder. "Happened before."

Cole closed the gap between them. "Not by my choice."

Tamera closed her eyes, not wanting to pull her father into this.

"I'm not going to discuss blame," he said as if he could read her mind. "But the reason I didn't tell you all those years ago was because I didn't want to come between you and your father and I knew his actions would drive a wedge between you."

She opened her eyes. "I didn't want to lose you, either, Cole. Didn't you know I would've done anything to be with you? That's what hurts the most is that you didn't believe in what we had enough to come to me. Obviously our relationship wasn't built on the trust and honesty I'd depended on."

"Maybe it wasn't," he agreed. "I know I loved you then, but that point in time doesn't even compare to what I'm feeling now."

Tamera turned away, scared to look into his eyes and see what she'd longed to see from him for so long. Love, commitment.

"I just don't know if my heart can take that chance

again, Cole," she whispered, wrapping her arms around her waist. "I want to. More than anything I want to be what you need, because you're certainly what I need. But not at the risk of being broken again."

Cole's hand covered her shoulder. He turned her to face him, and she found herself looking up into his dark eyes. Eyes that held so much hope, the same hope that she knew was reflected in her own stare.

"I was a fool." He ran a fingertip down her cheek. "I won't be a fool twice, Tamera. I love you. Marry me. Let me have a lifetime to make it up to you. Let me show you how special you are to me, how much I need you in my life. I can't function without you. I've tried. The monotony from day to day was meaningless. I need you to fill that void that was left so long ago. Say you'll marry me."

She'd heard those words from his mouth before, but now, the proposal meant so much more. Now they mended every crack, every wound of her broken heart.

"You'll always be honest with me?" she asked.

"Always."

Tamera wrapped her arms around Cole's neck. "Yes, I'll marry you."

"Victor was right," he whispered in her ear.

"About?"

He urged her back into bed. "We make a great team."

Epilogue

"When you do something, you don't do halfway," Zach said, pulling a beer from Cole's office refrigerator.

Kayla poured champagne, passed out the glasses to Cole and Tamera. "They always worked well together. Now it's just carried on into their business."

"Speaking of that, what are you going to do, Tamera?"

Tamera looked to Cole's twin and smiled. "You haven't mentioned this?"

Cole nuzzled her neck. "I've been preoccupied completing a design and keeping a certain woman happy."

"Someone better tell us something," Zach piped in. "Kayla and I are getting uncomfortable in here."

Cole straightened, addressing his siblings. "We'd like to merge the firms together since we're merging the families."

Tamera held her breath, awaiting the reaction of two-thirds of The Marcum Agency's approval.

"We'd definitely monopolize the architectural world of Miami," Zach stated, rubbing a hand over his stubbled jaw. "I think it's a great business move. Kayla?"

Kayla beamed. "I vote yes."

Cole grinned, winking at Tamera. "Told you it wouldn't be a problem. We're still simple people who know when we see a good thing."

Zach raised his beer. "To mergers."

Champagne flutes clinked together in the air. "To mergers," they all agreed.

"May the next part of this project be as exciting as the design."

Tamera laughed. "Zach, you'll make the next stage exciting no matter what the circumstances are."

"Don't make it too exciting," Cole countered. "We don't want our wedding in a few months overshadowed by anything."

"Trouble," Zach said, "is like women. It just follows me."

Cole simply shook his head, laughed and kissed Tamera. "He's on his own. I have more important things to attend to."

* * * * *

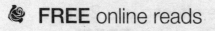

MILLS & BOON
Book Club
2 Free Books!

Get your free books now at
www.millsandboon.co.uk/freebookoffer

Or fill in the form below and post it back to us

THE MILLS & BOON® BOOK CLUB™—HERE'S HOW IT WORKS: Accepting your free books places you under no obligation to buy anything. You may keep the books and return the despatch note marked 'Cancel'. If we do not hear from you, about a month later we'll send you 4 brand-new stories from the Desire™ 2-in-1 series priced at £5.30* each. There is no extra charge for post and packaging. You may cancel at any time, otherwise we will send you 4 stories a month which you may purchase or return to us—the choice is yours. *Terms and prices subject to change without notice. Offer valid in UK only. Applicants must be 18 or over. Offer expires 28th February 2012. **For full terms and conditions, please go to www.millsandboon.co.uk/termsandconditions**

Mrs/Miss/Ms/Mr (please circle)

First Name

Surname

Address

Postcode

E-mail

Send this completed page to: Mills & Boon Book Club, Free Book Offer, FREEPOST NAT 10298, Richmond, Surrey, TW9 1BR

Find out more at
www.millsandboon.co.uk/freebookoffer

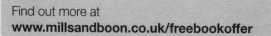
Visit us Online

0611/D1ZEE